CRAIG MARTELLE

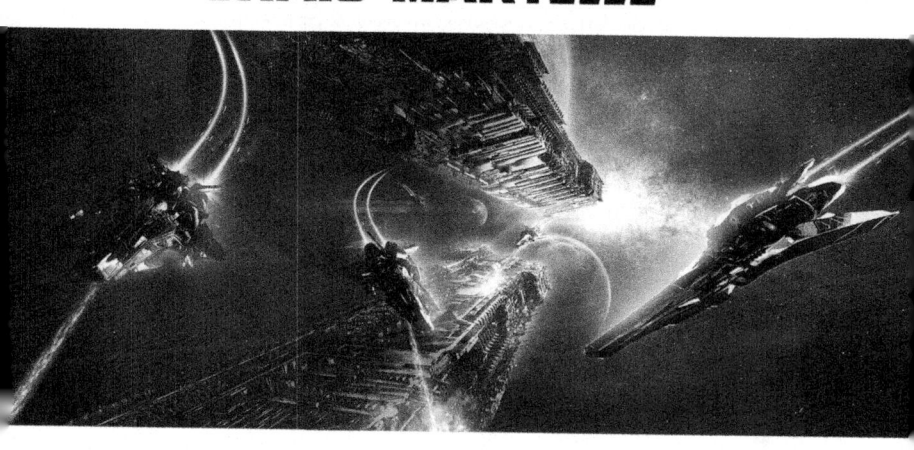

STARSHIP LOST

FALLACY

aethonbooks.com

FALLACY
©2024 CRAIG MARTELLE

This book is protected under the copyright laws of the United States of America. No part of this publication may be reproduced, stored in a retrieval system, or transmitted, in any form or by any means, without the prior permission in writing of the publisher, nor be otherwise circulated in any form of binding or cover other than that in which it is published and without a similar condition including this condition being imposed on the subsequent purchaser. Any reproduction or unauthorized use of the material or artwork contained herein is prohibited without the express written permission of the authors.

Aethon Books supports the right to free expression and the value of copyright. The purpose of copyright is to encourage writers and artists to produce the creative works that enrich our culture.

The scanning, uploading, and distribution of this book without permission is a theft of the author's intellectual property. If you would like to use material from the book (other than for review purposes), please contact editor@aethonbooks.com. Thank you for your support of the author's rights.

Aethon Books
www.aethonbooks.com

Print and eBook design and formatting by Josh Hayes. Artwork provided by Vivid Covers.

Published by Aethon Books LLC.

Aethon Books is not responsible for websites (or their content) that are not owned by the publisher.

This book is a work of fiction. Names, characters, places, and incidents are the product of the author's imagination or are used fictitiously. Any resemblance to actual events, locales, or persons, living or dead is coincidental.

All rights reserved.

ALSO IN STARSHIP LOST

Starship Lost

The Return

Primacy

Confrontation

Fallacy

Engagement

Check out the entire series here! (Tap or scan)

SOCIAL MEDIA

Craig Martelle Social
Website & Newsletter:
https://www.craigmartelle.com

Facebook:
**https://www.facebook.com/
AuthorCraigMartelle/**

Always to my wife, who loves me even though I work every day writing stories.

STARSHIP LOST TEAM

Beta Readers and Proofreaders - with my deepest gratitude!
James Caplan
Kelly O'Donnell
John Ashmore
Rita Whinfield

Get ***The Human Experiment*** for free when you join my newsletter. There's a zoo, but the humans are the ones being studied.
https://craigmartelle.com

PREVIOUSLY FROM STARSHIP LOST

The nature of a person can be changed, but it takes work.

Deena waved as the latest group of customers left. "What do you think, Boss?"

"I think it's nice to have customers back. Word of mouth travels fast. A hot babe working the tables."

"I'd like to think it's a person who embraces cleanliness and doesn't put up with any garbage. And I'm also nice to look at, but if any of them touch me, I'm going to pound them into next week."

"Where'd you learn to fight?"

Deena had her answers prepared. "When you look like me but don't like being touched, you learn to protect yourself. I've had good teachers." Thinking of Max and Crip made her smile.

"We could use another employee. We're swamped," the boss stated.

"Did I hear you say you were looking for help?" a young soldier asked.

"We don't take military who are moonlighting. You might get assigned to a different gate or sent somewhere on short notice. Too unreliable to schedule."

"No." The man waved his hands. "My wife could use a job, and I would never recommend a place like this except for you." He nodded to Deena. "The men respect you and keep their hands to themselves. If you can help my wife, I'm sure she'd be a great employee. She's smart and beautiful. I trust her, but I don't trust them."

Soldiers filled half the tables in the restaurant.

"Of course we'll take good care of her. You have my word." Deena saw the opportunity to ask questions about the base and the military within without looking like she was collecting intelligence. "She's hired. Do the paperwork, Boss man."

"Wait a minute! This is my place. There has to be an interview, and I say whether she's hired or not."

"Send her by as soon as possible. I'll teach her the ropes while Boss man decides to hire her. She can start first thing tomorrow."

"I don't know why I'm agreeing to this, sight unseen. Fine. Send her. We'll see if she can hold her own carrying trays and putting the plates in front of customers."

"If what's-his-dumbass in the kitchen says 'fresh meat' again, I'll pound him into next week. You might want to warn him or better yet, hire someone who's not a repulsive derelict."

"If we hire two more, I'll do the cooking. You can run the

seating operation. I got into this business because I cook well. I make good-tasting meals. We've lost that with a simplified menu that even he can cook."

"We'll find you another," Deena promised. "You, get the word out on base. Looking for another wife who will be taken care of. And you..." She looked at the boss. "Ask your wife to come in. I'd like to meet her. I bet she'll be willing to work the counter, check people in and out, when she finds the place is clean and the staff is friendly." Deena flicked his apron. "Can you wash that?"

"It's clean!" he shot back. "Those are stains that won't come out."

"Then buy a new one." Deena clapped the young soldier on the shoulder. "Send your wife to us. We'll do the rest."

Deena served up the next order and cleared dishes from the last order. She deposited all of it directly into the automatic dishwasher.

She wasn't hating her undercover assignment. There was a banal normalcy that came with a job. She had already pocketed enough money to rent a real apartment but thought it better to stay over the restaurant. She didn't need comfort as much as she needed friends and proximity. She watched the comings and goings of the soldiers, but that wasn't telling her what she wanted to learn.

She needed to know particulars about the refueling station at the spaceport. She needed to know when the Malibor would deploy to the forest to harass the Borwyn. She wanted to know if they had missiles, where they stored their munitions, and where the space fleet headquarters was located. It was all vital information that the Borwyn could use.

Being in a hurry wouldn't get her what she wanted, but having a friend who owed her and had a soldier as a husband would.

She looked forward to getting help cleaning the restaurant. They almost had it completely cleaned, top to bottom with an inventory of what needed to be replaced, like the tables and chairs. Despite the boss's claims that they added charm, Deena suggested that they needed to go. She planned to replace the chairs four at a time, buying them with her own money if she had to. Her cash payments weren't the only money that was skimmed. The boss maintained enough to keep the auditors happy, but not so much that he paid what he really owed.

Deena didn't care about any of that, but what was important to her was not falling under the scrutiny of the government. Keep the customers happy with good food at a good price and pay the government their share.

"Don't skim too much, Boss man."

"Hey! Them's fighting words," he replied.

"We don't need any government officials stopping by to check your records. They'll find me and that will highlight me to my abusive stepfather. I can't have that."

He nodded. "I get it. I'll keep my nose clean. Just when I started to turn a profit."

"You'll be fine. We'll keep growing the clientele. When are you going to fire what's-his-face?" She jerked a thumb over her shoulder.

"Need two more good employees. Three like you and this place will be filled from the moment we open until we close."

"Working it, Boss man. Soon. And we'll dominate the restaurant business in this part of town. Your neighbors will be envious."

"That'll be the day." He put the help wanted sign he'd been holding back under the counter. "But, I can see it. You're making a difference, Deena. Pretty soon, I might even be able to take a day off."

"I tell you what, the day before the first workday of the week has low clientele. You're barely breaking even. I suggest you close on that day. Let all of us take some time off. I can work six days a week. But seven? I can use a day off."

She needed to see some things for herself and couldn't do that outside of the restaurant's hours because she'd look suspicious walking around at night or too early in the morning. No. She was better conducting in-person reconnaissance during normal hours with the usual crowds where she could blend in.

It was going according to plan. With the impending new employee, Deena had her way into the inner workings of the base without having to cozy up to any of the customers. That idea nauseated her. She wouldn't go that route no matter how much information she needed. They'd done without intelligence collection before. It had been looking like they would have to again until the young soldier had interrupted.

The battle is joined, she thought.

Jaq Hunter and the battle commander had built a tactical engagement plan that resulted in the destruction of the five gunships and the capture of the cruiser that had been used as a carrier for the smaller vessels.

Chrysalis is racing to remove power plants from the Malibor ship to reenergize the ion drives. The ship was heavily damaged, and the crew continues to make repairs. *Cornucopia* is flying in tandem, ready to resupply as needed, but spare parts are growing sparser with the massive repairs needed.

On Septimus, Crip, Max, and the expanded combat team continue to train with the western Borwyn military for the next major battle with the Malibor. It could be in the city of Malipride, where Max's wife, Deena, is under cover with a hidden radio to report opportunities.

From the inside, she can help open the way for the combat team to attack vulnerable and vital military assets. In the end, the battle will be fought for control of the entire planet.

How many Malibor will have to die? Will the Borwyn survive? So many questions. So little time.

CHAPTER 1

It always seems impossible until it's done.

Captain Jaqueline "Jaq" Hunter scowled at the sight before her. The engineers were cutting bulkheads to get the oversized power plant off the Malibor cruiser. It wasn't going well. Despite the zero-gee, the ship groaned and creaked with the loss of its structural integrity.

Captain Brad Yelchin, her deputy now that Crip Castle was leading the combat team on Septimus proper, had already put everyone into spacesuits rather than attempt to get environmental systems online. Both heat and air were at a premium in outer space.

Crew numbers were down due to losses from continuous combat and also from splitting their forces. They crewed multiple ships, had a robust force on Septimus, and had a limited number of functioning spacesuits.

Jaq grumbled from where she watched. She wore one of

the suits and used a mobility pack, but only after she ensured that it wasn't needed by the working crew. The totality of effort focused on cutting the cruiser apart to create a gap to move the room-sized power plants out. The ship had been built around the plants and the engines. They were never intended to be removed.

The Borwyn were taking what they needed. Other teams were removing the electrical systems that *Chrysalis* might need.

Jaq had not initially embraced the idea of becoming a space pirate, but they weren't taking anything that hadn't been used against them first. Maybe they were just the spoils of war, but in the Malibor's mind, they'd won the war decades earlier. Even though this was war, Jaq wasn't willing to compromise the morality of the Borwyn position. She wanted the Borwyn to be worthy of winning this war, fifty years in the making.

She had every intention of winning. They had dominated every engagement, getting damaged in the process, but only one ship flew away at the end. The others were no more than expanding clouds of space debris. Memories of the crew performing in the face of overwhelming odds gave her pause to appreciate them under the watchful eye of a benevolent Septiman. She hadn't been religious when they renewed the war, but she was now.

They had no business surviving engagement after engagement, but they did. Jaq had heard that there were no atheists in combat. She understood what that meant. When all else failed, belief in a higher power gave them impetus to continue.

A voice crackled over the short-range suit radio. "We're making the final cuts now. The power plant has been disconnected," Brad said.

"As soon as the plant moves into space, we'll roll the ship to align Cargo Bay Four. The crew is clearing it now. It'll be ready by the time you're ready."

"I'll let you know." The channel closed.

Jaq decided that she was more of a hindrance than a help and returned to *Chrysalis*. She put the suit on the rack to recharge, docked the mobility pack, and headed two levels up.

When she arrived, she found the corridor almost completely filled with cases and boxes. She squeezed through to find Teo with two engineers cutting a harness through an open bulkhead.

"Captain," Teo said by way of greeting. She returned to her work.

Jaq recognized the backup trunk lines. The primary followed the central shaft. There were three backups equidistant from the central shaft in case of catastrophic damage to one side of the ship.

With the Malibor power plants squeezed into this space, the trunk would become a unidirectional line to the power storage bank. It would be vulnerable to a lucky hit from the enemy.

"How many battles remain?" Jaq wondered. They only had to hold the ship together for one more fight.

And then the next.

The Malibor would keep fighting because they'd been lying to their people for decades about the horror that would come with a Borwyn victory over the Malibor, but their own civil wars had gutted them as a fighting force. Five civil wars in fifty years.

Jaq snorted. "You people can't be trusted to govern yourselves."

"I'm sorry," Teo said over her shoulder. "What was that?"

"Just talking to myself because I needed some expert advice. For the record, I'm not very good at giving myself advice."

"You're in the right place. We'll give you advice as long as you don't promise to follow it unless it's good. If it's bad, we'll deny ever saying anything," Teo said without missing a beat.

The engineering team was making a hundred connections to a de-powered system. It was a mountain of work but didn't require detailed focus as they watched over each other.

"The Malibor are incapable of governing themselves."

"Well, duh," Teo replied with uncharacteristic brevity.

"My thought exactly." The captain clapped the chief engineer on the shoulder. "They're almost finished cutting the ship apart to get the plants out. It won't be long."

"We'll be ready. We'll work up until we need to depressurize the bay, then we'll tie them in. Check the reactor fuel, which I expect to be minimal, but we recovered the fissile material from our own plants. If we get them rebuilt and back online, we'll need a new source of fuel."

"We'll take it from the shipyard that's soon to be in our hands."

"Ooh!" Teo stopped working and faced the captain. "What's the next evolution in this war? You have something in mind."

"Thinking out loud. I need to talk with your dad and Alby."

Teo gestured for the captain to come close. She whispered, "Are you my mom now?" And laughed until tears floated free in the zero-gee.

"Are there no secrets aboard this ship?" Jaq asked as she backed away. "Get back to work, you upstart! You might find yourself cleaning blackwater systems next."

"Yes, Mom." Teo continued to chuckle.

Jaq smiled thinking about bringing Brad into her quarters and her sleeping cube. It worked for them both. Morale—especially her own—was critical if they wanted to win the war. The crew sensed her mood and feelings. She had to be all things to all of them.

After *Chrysalis* restarted the war, they'd dispensed with military protocols because they became unnecessary. They were one family working toward a common goal. The Borwyn would return to Septimus to live out their lives in peace in the sunshine of their world.

Deena wiped the last table of the evening. A young woman flopped into a chair nearby.

"That was some day, huh?" Deena asked. She was the mentor for the new employee, helping her navigate the hard life of a bar's waitress.

Lanni thumbed through the paper credits filling her apron. "I made more today than I have in the past month watching other people's kids. A lot more." She smiled tiredly.

"Time to wrap up. Put the chairs on the tables, and I'll sweep and mop. You go home. Get some time with your husband."

"He's not home. He was sent to the western wall. They're going to take a patrol out. I don't like it."

Deena's ears perked up. "How often does he leave you alone?"

"This will be the first time. He said the officers talked about an increase in activity. The Borwyn need to be put in their place." She pounded her small fist on the table.

Deena wanted to educate her on the Borwyn, but that wasn't her mission. She kneeled next to the young woman and hugged her. "It'll be okay if they don't try to do too much. A single patrol won't get overly ambitious."

"The last patrol never returned. I know one of the wives. She's still inconsolable. And…" She stopped herself from saying more.

"It's okay. It stays between us," Deena lied. Ending the war would benefit all the wives.

"They brought in barbarians from Fristen as shock troops."

Deena nodded. She knew all of that, including exactly what had happened to the last patrol. If the new patrol went too deep into the forest, they'd suffer the same fate. Deena would be making a call as soon as Lanni left.

"Go on home. I'll take care of the chairs and the floor." She pulled the young woman to her feet and directed her toward the front door. She followed her out, waving as the other woman walked away.

Deena locked the door when she came back inside, threw the chairs on the table, and ran a mop over the floor without bothering to sweep. She raced upstairs. The first thing she did was to make sure no one was up there. Both her boss and customers had gotten creative. She guaranteed her own safety first.

She barred the bathroom door and dug the radio out of the overhead. Deena turned on the shower to create white noise in the background. She set up the transmitter and sent the first series of numbers to establish contact.

She sent once a minute for seven minutes before she received a reply. She asked to go to voice because she didn't have codes to cover what she wanted.

The approval was a long time coming.

"Infiltration squad en route. Same as last. Interdict and prevent entry to forest."

"Roger," came the operator's voice in reply.

She clicked the numbers to sign off. She quickly wrapped the device and hid it in the overhead away from prying eyes. She threw her clothes in the chair and jumped into the steam of the shower. Her heart raced, and she gasped for a full breath.

What if she was discovered?

She would experience the worst violence that half of her heritage could bring. They needed to be stopped, and it was worth the risk right up until it wasn't. After a rudely long shower, she dressed in clean clothes she had stored in the bathroom locker. She tossed her work clothes in the hamper next to the washing machine.

Deena slowly walked down the stairs, listening for someone outside, like an enforcer strike team. She peeked out the front door and through the windows. Normal evening traffic flowed up and down the street, many heading to the bus stop to catch a ride home after a late evening at work.

She couldn't force herself to relax. It would be days before she'd calm from the effort. No more voice calls. It was too much stress. It was encrypted but rudimentarily. Was it enough? Would they find the signal and triangulate it?

Deena poured herself a beer from the bar. Drinks were a guilty pleasure that they didn't have on board *Chrysalis*. The Borwyn didn't waste resources. Sugar was a rare commodity, so they didn't use their sugar beets to make alcohol. The beer tasted good and hit the spot.

She took a deep breath and glanced toward the door to find a man in uniform standing there staring at her.

She stared back, the whites of her eyes showing.

He motioned with his thumb toward his mouth, his little finger in the air.

He wanted a drink.

"We're closed."

"Come on, baby. I'll buy you a beer and one for me, too. It's like free money!"

She jerked her thumb at him. "Move along, baby. I'm not opening that door because we're CLOSED!"

Deena turned out the lights and carried her beer upstairs. The insistent knocking ended after a few minutes, and peace returned to her life. She found that being angry was easier to deal with than wondering if a strike team was coming after her.

Maybe they would, but the more time that passed from her transmission, the less chance they would confirm her location.

She flipped her middle finger in the direction of the military facility. "The battle is joined," she whispered.

CHAPTER 2

With the new day comes new strength and new thoughts.

Lieutenant Commander Eleanor Todd shook Crip awake. "We've received a message from Deena."

"I'll get Max," Crip said when he sat up. He hadn't been asleep for more than an hour and was having a hard time getting the cobwebs out of his brain. They'd been training hard. He'd collapsed into his bunk after dinner and immediately fallen asleep. "Max, stop being lazy. They've heard from Deena." He kicked the cot next to his.

Max snuffled and raised his head, but his eyes were still closed. "Deena?"

"Yeah. They've heard from her. We need to see what it was all about. Come on." Crip slipped his trousers on while seated and then stood. He shrugged on his shirt. He smacked Max across his bare midriff because he was moving too slowly.

"Ow," Max mumbled. He dressed quickly enough, and

the two headed for the command bunker. They went the wrong way first. This was the fourth camp they'd been to in the past three weeks. They moved often to keep the Malibor from zeroing in on them.

Eleanor and Commander Glen Owain each held a cup of coffee to hand to the combat team leaders.

After a sip, Glen read back the message.

Crip stopped him. "She sent that in clear voice?"

"Surprised us, too," Glen replied.

"Squad en route. Deny entry to the forest, or something to that effect. Why does she want the same squad as last time to be kept out of the forest? What isn't she saying?" Crip growled his annoyance at having nothing but questions. "More soldiers from Fristen? Why can't we let them get into the forest? We could ambush them and wipe them out if we drew them in. But she doesn't want that. Why?"

Glen shrugged. "I'd rather destroy them. Pretty soon, they'll stop sending squads if they never return. Or they won't get anyone to take the assignment. That'll have the effect on morale that we want to see. I vote to conduct business as usual. We draw them into a kill-zone and waste them."

"Wait a minute," Max said. "Deena wouldn't have broken protocol if it wasn't important. She knows something we don't. I say we do our best to repel the squad before they get to the forest. That means we better get on our horses and get going if we're going to beat them to the border."

"I agree with Max," Crip added.

"They have a point." Eleanor nodded slowly. "As much as I'd like to kill unsuspecting Malibor, I say we do as she asks. Let's spook them before they get into the woods, chase them back to the city."

"Then that's what we'll do," Glen replied. He hadn't been married to the ambush idea. He wanted to see what the others thought. "Better saddle the horses. We'll head out tonight. Three squads heavy, two kilometers apart. Crip and Max, you'll have two of the squads. Bring your bows. The silent attack will strike the most fear into their hearts because we've never hit them with arrows before, and the bark of your pulse rifles will be new, too. I'd be surprised if they didn't turn tail and run."

"We won't count on that, but we'll get them turned around. If they don't leave, then they'll die. We're not going to play games with them," Crip confirmed.

"Then we're agreed. Get your people up. We push in fifteen."

"You're coming?" Crip asked.

"Damn straight. Eleanor will stay here. I want to see what made it worth a voice message. What's special about this inbound patrol?"

"Maybe she panicked thinking we wouldn't be ready for them," Crip suggested, but he didn't sound convinced.

Max vigorously shook his head. "She wouldn't lose her mind about that. She knows we're ready to deal with a Malibor squad. We have the numbers and the better position. We know the woods. No. This has to be something else, but I can't fathom what it might be."

"Get your stuff. We're leaving," Crip said. He nodded to Glen. "Let's see what this is all about."

"Ease it out," Brad called from where he clung to the outer hull of the Malibor cruiser. *Before this ship comes apart and kills us all,* he thought.

The black metal of the power plant appeared in the massive gap cut into the side of the ship. Crew in spacesuits appeared to ease it through the opening.

"Make sure you don't get between the plant and the hull!" Brad nearly shouted over the radio.

The crew drew back and eased the plant out. Brad used his mobility pack to get in front of the power plant, which was easily three times his height. He activated the pack to slow it down. Once it was out, it started to tumble.

"A little help," he called, adjusting to activate the jets and stop the spin. "Easy does it," he counseled himself.

With the crew lining up across the power plant, the situation worsened. Each tried to fix the spin. They worked at cross-purposes.

"Everyone, stop what you're doing. Magnetically attach your boots to this monstrosity." As the plant drifted toward *Chrysalis*, Brad made a radio call. "Jaq, better move the ship in case we don't get this thing under control. We don't want to crash our new toy."

"What's going on out there?" Jaq demanded.

Brad didn't have time to explain. He aimed counter to the rotation and activated his mobility pack. He powered down before the spinning stopped, counting on momentum to end the spin. He was on the wrong side.

"Who has their back to *Chrysalis*?" Brad asked.

"I do." It was Carlow. He'd been there from the beginning to make sure they got the power plant out. He activated his pneumatic jets, and the power plant slowed. Not that the power plant had been going too fast, it hadn't been, but Brad had wanted the movement to be under their complete control. Even with slowing the plant, they were still one miscue away from it spinning out of control.

"I'll handle the movement. Break, break. *Chrysalis*, align the cargo bay with the power plant, please. We're coming in whether you're ready or not. If you miss the window, the lot of us could end up in deep space."

"Slow it down and we'll meet you there. We have your vector mapped. Slow to one meter per second," Jaq directed.

Brad's mobility pack didn't show speed.

"*Chrysalis*, you'll have to give me speed updates. I seem to be lacking the correct gauges."

"Roger," a new voice replied. It was Chief Ping, the sensor chief. "Two meters per second, present speed."

Brad touched his jets. The unit started to roll. He angled himself and touched them again.

"Sorry about that. Angle changed."

"Noted," Slade Ping replied. "Speed is point-nine meters per. Hold it steady. Ship is aligning."

Brad risked a glance over his shoulder to where the stars were blocked by the massive cruiser. It angled to receive the first plant. Brad thought the closing speed was too much, even at less than a meter per second.

The opening seemed too small, until they closed within a few body-lengths. Then it seemed just right.

"Get out of there, Brad. We'll take it from here," Jaq said.

Brad wanted to move away, but he didn't think he could clear out in time.

Chrysalis used thrusters to match the power plant's speed. It seemed to hang in the limbo of space. Halfway into the cargo bay.

Brad let go. He activated the magnetic clamps on his boots, hoping they would pull him toward the deck. He was too far away. He angled the pneumatic jets toward the overhead and touched the controls.

That was all he needed. Once he hit the deck, he stepped out of the way.

Two suited engineers hooked chains from manual come-alongs to the unit. They started ratcheting the levers and moved the power plant into a location with welded guides. It only took two minutes to get it into place.

Phillips appeared. The ship's master welder made quick work of securing the plant.

Brad hung out, secured to the deck, watching the evolution. He had no doubt that Teo had put everything in order to ease the transition of the unit from the Malibor cruiser to *Chrysalis*. She had taken the measurements on her one trip to the enemy ship before disappearing.

The crew that had accompanied the power plant found themselves together in the cargo bay.

Brad activated his radio. "One is done. Let's grab that second one and get it over here. Let's make sure we don't impart spin on the next unit. Ideas? Because the way I did it didn't work."

"Put three on the outer side," Carlow suggested. "Push the unit out using only magnetic boots. Stop it at the outer hull breach. Align and give it one final manual push. Half a meter a second is probably a good speed. We're not in a rush to crash that thing."

"We're too close to take any extra risks. One on each corner pushing and three on the hull-breach end to control it using the mobility packs once it's clear of the ship. Hang on and follow it out. Thanks, Carlow." The team doubled up to cross the short distance to the Malibor cruiser.

Once inside, they released the temporary clamps holding the power plant in place and eased it toward the opening.

A groan sounded through the ship so loud that it vibrated their bodies and shook their very souls.

"We better hurry," Brad said unnecessarily. "Plan is out the airlock. Push!"

The unit started to move toward the exit, which seemed to shrink and expand. Skid plates had been temporarily affixed to the front to protect the unit if it made contact with the hull.

Brad clung to the front, watching in helpless horror as the Malibor cruiser's hull started to twist.

He hadn't thought it was under stress from external forces, but it had to be. They must have started traversing a gravitic wave, something a fully powered ship would skip through with barely a bump, but for a ship with a compromised hull structure, it was too much.

The ship was coming apart.

"Attach your boots and activate your packs. Full power. Aim toward space."

"Attaching boots," Carlow confirmed from behind the unit.

Brad hadn't been talking to the pushers, but it made sense. They needed to get off the ship, too.

"Now!" Brad shouted over the radio, not wasting time with a countdown. The three punched their mobility packs, and the plant slowly picked up speed.

The sound of rending metal fought through the void of space and shrieked into their helmets.

Brad held his button down and willed the unit to pull faster.

The Malibor cruiser keened its death cry as the ship split on the seam they'd created to build a gap for the power plant. The cruiser started to spin. The skids scraped along a deck plate and over bulkheads until it hit the outer hull. The skids were ripped off in that final moment before the spin threw the power plant free and into space, carrying seven stalwart souls.

"Hang on," Brad said, trying to project calm in his voice. They were free of the cruiser, but the prow was spinning toward them.

Chrysalis loomed above, but the Borwyn weapons were offline because of a lack of power. *Chrysalis* used thrusters to clear the arc through which the Malibor cruiser would pass.

"Run the mobility packs to zero. Full burn," Brad encouraged. They were left with no choice.

The power plant picked up speed, but it wasn't going to be enough.

CHAPTER 3

Quality is not an act; it is a habit.

Deena slept fitfully. Every noise from the active area outside the bar sounded like an enforcer coming to arrest her.

She questioned making the call as she did. She had strict protocols for extremely short transmissions. Digits only according to a memorized code. Why had she done it?

Lanni's husband was a member of the infiltration squad. If he was killed, then Deena would lose her access to base goings-on. Was future intelligence worth the risk of exposing herself?

She could find a new source.

The reason was that she liked Lanni. She liked the other people she worked with. Except the cook, but she accepted his fear of her as an acceptable compromise.

She wasn't returning to being a Malibor. She had no desire to live under decrepit leaders ready to sacrifice those who worked for them with every change in the wind. But she recognized there were good people who weren't her enemy. That would be the greatest challenge if the combat team infiltrated the city to sabotage military facilities.

It would create chaos. It also might rally the people against a common enemy. The Borwyn.

Deena was forced to rethink their whole plan.

She dressed and went downstairs, happy to find nothing out of place and no police presence outside, waiting for her to make an appearance.

Deena helped herself to the kitchen, removing cheese and sausage to make herself a sandwich on a loaf of yesterday's bread. She poured juice from the fruit of the ranji tree. It perked her up.

But so would the coffee that the boss stocked. She made a pot at half the strength he preferred and poured a cup the instant the brew was finished.

She returned upstairs to sit on the bed in her small room. Deena needed to think.

If the western Borwyn repelled the infiltration squad before they made it into the forest, Lanni's husband could still be killed.

But if the Malibor made it into the woods, they certainly would all be killed, every single one of them. At least this way, she gave Lanni's husband a chance to survive.

Deena leaned forward to hold her head in her hands. She could only see the worst. Had she said nothing, maybe they would have gone unnoticed. But since she warned the Borwyn, the confrontation was guaranteed.

What would Max do?

The right thing. She convinced herself that Max would

know what concerned her even though it didn't make sense that he would. He didn't know she was working in a bar. That she was enjoying both beer and coffee and ranji juice, delicacies that the Borwyn were denied.

A wave of guilt washed over her. She threw her head back and cried out in anguish.

The sound of an insistent knock stopped her descent into the darkness of her mind. She stood and straightened her clothes. Being found out was a better fate than wondering.

She walked with measured step down the stairs to find the boss hammering on the door.

Deena opened it. "Can I help you?" she quipped while blocking the entrance.

"Forgot my key. Damn, woman! What took you so long? I was beginning to think you left me high and dry."

Deena scoffed. "What? And leave free coffee behind?"

"Hey! That costs a pretty pfennig. You need to pay for that."

The relief that it had been the boss and not the police slammed into her despite the quips and light-hearted banter. She dropped into a chair.

"You okay? You ain't pregnant, are you?"

The thought took Deena aback. She felt fine. No nausea, no cramps, nothing that suggested she was with child. "I'm pretty sure I'm not," she finally answered. "I didn't sleep well last night. There was a creeper hanging around outside after closing trying to get me to let him to drink with me."

"You're drinking after hours, too?"

"Boss. *Creeper*. Come on, focus."

"You're drinking me into the poorhouse!" He threw his

hands up and stomped around the counter, where he put on a clean apron. Deena made sure he had at least one clean apron to wear at the start of the day.

"Open the cash drawer," Deena said calmly while leaning over the counter.

"Maybe you're not drinking me into the poorhouse, but I'm taking it out of your tips!"

"You'll do no such thing," Deena replied. She held out her palm since he'd never paid her the night before. "Yesterday's cash. Don't be a day behind, Boss man. You'll suffer mightily. We've tripled revenue since I started working here without a commensurate increase in costs. I think you're doing just fine."

A tap at the door drew her attention. She waved them away until the individual held up a badge.

She whispered to the boss, "Hide the cash." She blocked the view as he stuffed a wad down his pants.

Deena waved to the officer and opened the door. She wasn't able to talk because her heart had leapt into her throat, where it beat a staccato.

"Officer," the boss called. "What can I do for you? A little breakfast? Not our usual fare, but we can accommodate our partners who keep us safe."

"I've seen a huge increase in business here. What are you doing?" he asked pointedly, ignoring Deena. "Are you running prostitutes?"

"Running what? Hookers? Ladies of the night? Mattress bags? No. None of the above." The boss laughed uproariously. It wasn't forced. "No. I hired two new employees who have cleaned this place up. The boys come for a clean place to eat good food, with a little eye candy on the side. Nothing more than that, Officer."

The Malibor official strolled around. "I still wouldn't eat here," he mumbled, running his finger along the underside of the service counter. It came back covered in grease drips. "I should shut you down."

"That's my fault," Deena interrupted, immediately diving for the cleaning supplies. With cleansers in hand, she turned to making the underside of the counter as clean as the topside. She glared at the boss like she often did when she found a new source of filth.

He shrugged.

The officer continued his walk around the bar. He found his way to the stairs and headed up. Deena wanted to go with him, but the boss held her back. "You don't have anything up there, do you?"

"No. I keep my cash on me, just like you."

"Smells like a woman, up here," the officer called down the steps. "You know you can't stay here. You're not licensed for residency. That'll be a fine."

He moseyed down the stairs sporting an evil grin.

"I'm sure we can come to some sort of arrangement," the officer continued.

Deena's anger started to boil. She tore her eyes from the man and went to the kitchen, where she dug out the morning's delivery of vegetables. Prep would take her excess energy and turn it into something positive. She couldn't kill the government official, as much as she wanted to, but she could slice and chop the vegetables with great zeal.

The officer and boss talked while Deena started slicing and chopping. Her vigor drew their attention.

"Take it easy back there!" the boss called through the pass-through window.

"Sorry, not sorry. Prepping for the day, Boss man. Gotta have those vegetables tiny and ready to cook," she yelled back.

The door to the kitchen opened, and the officer walked in. "Have I upset you in some way?"

She snorted but tempered her answer. "I wasn't trying to get away with anything. I'll get a place and move out, today hopefully."

"I have an extra bed at my place," he offered with a smile that sent a shiver through her whole body.

She shook her head. "I don't think so. There's a lady who works here. I'll stay in their extra room until I can find my own place. I appreciate your selfless offer, though." She held his look, but hers was one of disdain and potential violence.

He thought better of pushing her. "Take care not to violate the law again. Next time, I won't be so lenient."

She swung her blade with such strength that it stuck in the cutting board. She wrenched it out and slammed it in again.

He took the hint and left the kitchen. He settled his extortion with the boss and departed.

After he was out of view, Deena rejoined the boss out front. "What did it cost you?"

"Yesterday's revenue. All of it, even what I stuffed in my pants." He rolled over his belt so Deena could see that there was nothing there. The bulge of cash had been obvious.

"I guess only Lanni gets paid."

The boss started to shake his head, but Deena grabbed his arm. "She gets paid. Take it out of mine if you have to."

"There's none. He took it all."

"He took yesterday's. There have been a lot of good days. Save for a rainy day. Well, today, it rained. Don't make me beat it out of you, and next time he comes in to shake you down, we take him to the kitchen, kill him, and bury him under the floorboards."

He laughed until he realized she wasn't kidding.

"I don't think we can kill him," he said nervously.

"Of course we can. He's a bully, a typical government scumbag. A man in charge who has no business having power. He's also weak. I'll kill him. You watch my back, and then we move his body out of the city when we get a chance. I'll break his neck so there won't be any blood. It'll be fine. Next time, bow to him, but lead him to the kitchen. We'll do him in there."

"What if there are people around?"

"He doesn't want any witnesses. What he's doing is more illegal than me staying upstairs. That's an administrative fine. He's a thief. That would get him added to a press gang if anyone above him was honest, but I doubt they are."

The boss nodded. "We'll do it your way. Give him a few days, but if no one is here after hours, then he might not see the opportunity to stop by."

"We can always hope, but as I heard from someone I respect, hope is a lousy plan. We'll be ready. Keep the rolling pin where I can get to it." Deena went back into the kitchen and continued the day's prep work. She no longer worried about her transmission being discovered. She worried about her personal disdain for the people she'd learned to hate. It wasn't because she'd joined the Borwyn's side in the war, but because they had shown her how decent people acted. Her heart skipped a beat in the instant as she missed Max. Her husband was out there, in the safety of the Borwyn camp because he was among friends.

I need more friends, ones I can count on when the war comes to town. She counted the boss and Lanni among her small circle. She needed to grow that number. *Let the insurrection begin.*

CHAPTER 4

Do the difficult things while they are easy and do the great things while they are small. A journey of a thousand miles must begin with a single step.

Jaq stabbed her finger at the screen. "The Malibor ship is coming apart," she reiterated following Brad's call. "Move us clear. Recall anyone left on board."

Mary and Ferd angled the ship away and used thrusters to ease it out of the failing vessel's reach.

"Engineering team departed after the first power plant was seated. Ship is clear except for the power team," Alby reported.

"Wait!" Jaq shouted. *Chrysalis* was already moving away. "Slade, is that ship going to hit our people?"

"Confirmed. It will hit them and the power plant. If they evacuate right now, their mobility packs will move them clear."

"Brad, evacuate the plant. Get yourselves clear as quickly as you can," Jaq transmitted. She clicked off her microphone. "And give up our new power plant?" Jaq shook her head. "Alby, what weapons are online?" The captain knew the answer but needed Alby to confirm.

"Defensive only. Chain guns and lasers."

"They won't do anything to that hulk. Mary, can you nudge us up against it?"

"What's the speed at the bow?" the navigator asked.

Slade was ready. "Five meters per second."

"Roger." Mary's fingers danced across her console, and the view on the screen shifted as *Chrysalis* corkscrewed through the space between the Malibor cruiser and the team still clinging to the power plant.

"Why are they still there?" Jaq wondered.

Chrysalis eased into the space and initially matched the speed of the hulk's prow.

"Brace for impact," Mary said.

Ferd tapped a rhythm on his screen as he incrementally slowed the ship's movement.

Jaq closed her eyes as the live feed of the Malibor cruiser filled the main screen. Ferd increased his pace until it reached a frenetic level. The bump was barely noticeable until the ship jerked when the thrusters ran to full power. The energy gauge had already dropped to forty-one percent and ticked down to forty.

"Buying the team time," Slade said. "Speed through the arc has decreased to three meters per second. Two meters."

"Brad, get that power plant out of there. This thing is

going to eject debris with the additional strain on the superstructure."

"We're working it. We had full confidence in *Chrysalis*. Taking it on the shortest route to space. Pick us up soon, honey. We're about out of air."

"How long until they clear the impact area?" Jaq asked, ignoring Brad's quip.

Slade replied, "One minute, probably less. At two meters per, they'll clear well before the ship's prow reaches them."

"Disengage and move clear. Prepare to receive the second power plant. Line us up and match the speed of the team."

"Roger," Mary and Ferd replied together.

"Cruiser is breaking apart," Slade stated. "Ejecting debris."

"Mary, come into the power plant from behind. Put the ship between that debris field and our people."

Mary nodded while correcting the course. Ferd tapped the thrusters to orient the ship, putting Cargo Bay Three facing away from the Malibor vessel. *Chrysalis* moved into position, covering the team's backsides.

"Thanks for that, Jaq. It was getting ugly out here," Brad radioed. "This is going to be interesting. We'll have to turn the unit around before you can wrap us in your cruisery embrace."

"Get it done and secure the outer doors. Let's get those plants installed and working for us instead of against us. Good work, Brad, you and the whole team. We can get back in the fight. It'll be nice to tell Crip and his folks that they're not alone."

They arrived at the boundary as dawn's light dusted the open fields before them. Crip climbed down from the saddle, wincing and standing gingerly.

"I hate riding a horse."

"Did you want to run that?" Glen asked as he slipped to the ground and patted the brown steed's rump. Handlers gathered the horses and guided them back into the woods. "We'll be walking home. They need those horses back at camp. Resupply. It seems to be what I live for."

Crip forced a laugh. "I get you. The troops wouldn't live very long without food and water. Someone has to make sure they're fed, clothed, armed, and housed."

"At least the troops pull their shifts running supplies. They all know this company runs on food. Horses are the deliverance, otherwise the soldiers would be humping the packs all over the western forest. No one wants that."

Crip looked out over the plain. He didn't see any movement, but in the limited light, a line of enemy soldiers would be easy to miss.

Glen took out his binoculars and scanned the horizon beyond where Malipride's tallest buildings rose. "I don't see anything. Makes me wonder if they got here before us."

"That would be a problem," Crip agreed.

"I'll deploy half our people in search of any sign that an enemy force has penetrated the forest. The other half will hunker down and watch. Three kilometers each way from this point, which is the closest to the city."

Glen gathered the squad leaders and designated who would search for sign of a Malibor intrusion.

"Rules of engagement?" Max asked.

"Locate and report back. If they're here, we need to hunt them down, but I don't want them eliminated. I want them captured."

Crip raised his eyebrows in surprise. "That will be expensive. We could lose people."

"If it's kill or be killed, then kill them. I don't want to lose any of our people, but I think we can create the conditions where they'd rather surrender. Head out, three klicks north and three south. Make it happen. Report by nightfall if not sooner."

The soldiers deployed in pairs, scattering deeper into the forest in search of any sign that someone had passed through. They quickly disappeared into the shadows and underbrush.

Max, Crip, and Glen looked at each other. "Crip north and Max south?" Glen offered.

Crip looked around at his combat team and their girlfriends and wives who were also soldiers. He shook his head. "What do you say we stay in the center and your people take north and south?"

"My people will be gone until nightfall," Glen countered.

"We'll send four to the farthest watch points in both directions," Crip said. He looked to Max for advice.

Max pointed at a small group. "Hammer, Anvil, Ava, and Mia. You four head south three klicks and establish an observation point. Watch the fields from cover. You'll be relieved by nightfall."

He looked over the remaining members of the group.

"I'll go north with Danny Johns and the Finleys."

"I thought you'd stay here," Crip countered.

"You don't need all three of us. You and Commander Owain can hold the line without me, can't you? Do you need a hug?"

Glen snorted and started laughing. "Upstarts one and all. Being raised in space makes you weird. Head out. Let's get eyes on the transit area sooner rather than later."

"We'll be there by the time the sun is above the city," Max replied.

The four hurried into the woods.

"Teams of two, make yourselves invisible and then one on, one off. Two-hour shifts. Get some sleep," Crip ordered.

"I feel okay," Glen said.

"I'm in pain from that damn horse. It'll take a while to calm the fires burning through my thighs."

Glen laughed again. "You guys. If this wasn't a fight to the death, I'd have a good belly-shaker about all this. Why aren't you guys more serious?"

"We've been at war our whole lives. We've lived in tight quarters aboard a ship our whole lives." Crip held his arms wide and looked into the branches above. "This is paradise to us. We're loving life. This is how we show it. If the Malibor show up, we'll fight them with every fiber of our being, but we refuse to be miserable while we're waiting for the bad guys."

"I like your attitude." Glen curled up on the ground and drew a thin blanket over himself. "I'll take you up on your offer to get some sleep. Wake me in two hours."

"Sleep fast, buddy. It'll be your watch before you know it."

"That's a nighttime lullaby for the mentally ill. Now go away." Glen closed his eyes and ten seconds later, his breathing had become slow and regular. Falling asleep like only a soldier who lived his life in a perpetual state of near-exhaustion could.

Crip picked up Glen's binoculars and scanned the area in front of them, working to memorize every bit of it so it would be easier to tell if something changed.

"Lanni, I have a favor to ask." Deena waited for the young woman's nod to continue. "Can I stay with you while I find my own place? The morality police found me living here and bilked boss man out of yesterday's receipts to let it go."

"We have the baby's room, but while my husband is gone, the baby can stay with me."

"Who watches your baby when you're working?"

"My mother," Lanni replied. The age-old story. Parents raise their grandkids while the first generation works to survive.

Deena nodded and wrapped an arm around the young mother's shoulders. She sounded guilty when her family was only doing what they had to do. A junior-ranked soldier. The pay was minimal and not enough to support a family without making too many sacrifices.

If her husband was killed trying to infiltrate the Borwyn position, she'd be in far worse shape. The Malibor didn't pay for "incompetent" soldiers who were killed in battle. Their reasoning was that the soldiers should have taken their jobs more seriously, been better at soldiering. The Borwyn were backward, little more than wild animals living off the land. The Malibor thought dying at their hands was comparable to getting killed by an average sewer rat.

Maybe she had warned her friends in time.

"When will you hear from your husband?" Deena pressed.

Lanni shrugged one shoulder and put on her apron. "We better get to work. Don't want the boss mad at us."

"He's always mad. He'll get over it."

"He's not when you're around. He respects you. As I do," Lanni admitted. "The cook, he fears you because you punch him when he's out of line. I think he's in love with you, too."

Deena laughed. "I don't doubt that. Next time he's stupid, I might have to kick him in the choice bits."

Lanni laughed but quickly sobered. She put the first chair on the floor, starting the daily ritual to open the bar and restaurant.

They went about their business and were finished fifteen minutes before it was time to open the door for customers, and the first group was already waiting. The cook came in the back door. "Who cut up these vegetables? They should be smaller."

"Don't make me come back there," Deena shouted through the window.

He grumbled until she went away, then threw a big chunk of carrot. It flew past her and bounced off the front window.

"You break that, you pay for it!" the boss bellowed from the back. He'd been checking the inventory to put in his order for the next week.

"All ready to open the doors, Boss man!" Deena called toward the kitchen. She took Lanni by the shoulders. "I can't tell you how much I appreciate the short stay in your spare room. I'll pay, of course. I won't eat any of your food. I'll be as low maintenance as anyone can be until I find my own place."

Deena waited for the boss to come out front. As soon as he did, she ambushed him.

"I'll need time off to go house hunting. I need to find a place. Lanni's spare bedroom is *not* a long-term solution."

He groaned and threw up his hands as if he'd been told he lost his business to tax collectors. "What am I going to do?"

"You'll work, just like you used to, but you'll have help. Lanni is up to speed." Deena threw a harsh glare in the boss's direction.

"How old are you?" the boss shot back. "You're like talking to my mother."

"Twenty."

"By Ratman's hell, woman. Go give grief to someone else. No wonder your step-father threw you out."

Deena's glare turned to ice as she stayed in character. "Don't go there. I'll leave and not come back."

"And I'll leave, too." Lanni stood as tall as she was capable of.

"Fine, fine. Take a couple hours after the rush. And good

luck. May the apartment gods smile on you so you can get back to work without giving me grief."

"Then I'll need time to buy furniture, household stuff."

"You can have my extras," the boss offered. "I'll deliver it myself. Well, not me, but some boys I know."

Deena was skeptical. She didn't want any boys the boss knew sniffing around her or her place. "You know what? I'll make do unless your wife comes along to oversee the delivery. A woman living alone. I don't want anyone to get any ideas. I've sworn off men, for the time being."

"We'll all come. Why not?" he replied. "It's about time to open the door. Let's get to work. No more talk about anything other than food or booze!"

"We'll do our best but no guarantees, huggy muffin," Deena said.

"I feel like you've been raised wrong and that it's my fault." The boss smiled and shook his head. "Here's to a good day." He saluted them with a glass of water and then threw it back. He dropped the empty into the automatic dishwasher as the first customers rolled through the door. Deena and Lanni greeted them warmly and showed them to their seats. In two minutes, the restaurant was filled. Shouted orders filled the air along with the smell of home cooking with a slather of extra grease.

It was everything growing boys needed to weather a full day of soldiering. The talk at the tables revolved around the infiltration squad and the follow-up exploitation. The units were forming. They would all be deployed soon enough.

Deena delivered an order. "You won't be gracing us with

your presence? Why would anyone do that to us?" she asked pleasantly.

"It's hush-hush," a soldier replied behind his hand in a loud whisper. "They've seen a ship on the Iliatrix Plateau. We'll be going in to take it out and wipe out anyone who came off it. Afterward, you'll be able to call me Gary-sa. Maybe this will end the Borwyn plague."

"I hope we get you back quickly, if you have to go at all. I like peace myself. It's nicer to live, don't you think?"

"It'll be nice to live without the Borwyn parasites looming over our fields, polluting the pristine woodlands. Those scum breed like rabbits. Do you know what they do in those woods?" The soldier shook his head.

Deena didn't get angry. They were victims of propaganda, just like she'd been until she learned the truth.

"The forest is their home. If someone broke into your home, how would you take it? As far as I know, they haven't left the woods to take a dump on our house."

"Spicy words. Are you a sympathizer?" the solder asked pointedly.

"A sympathizer? How would you come to that conclusion? Did you miss the part where I'll miss you guys if you stop coming in?"

"You'll miss our money!" another soldier suggested.

"Of course. Girl's gotta pay her bills." She waved and returned to the kitchen window for the next bunch of orders. Cook was on a roll, getting the meals ready in record time.

Deena glanced through to tell him thanks, but the boss was in there too, slinging burgers and frying tubers.

She saved her appreciation. The operation worked better with two people working each side of the window.

More importantly, she'd learned another tidbit. The restaurant was a lucrative source of information if she didn't blow her cover.

Could she undo years of programming or should she simply stay undercover? It wasn't an easy question. They would have to win the hearts and minds of the populace if they were to ease the transition.

She was getting ahead of herself. They needed to win first, and that meant she needed far more detailed information regarding the weapons that could affect a large-scale aerial attack. Imagine seeing *Chrysalis* coming in over the city. That would scare the Malibor out of their minds.

Would it destroy their will to fight?

She dropped off the food and whipped by the bar to pull four beers. She brought them to the table with the information givers. "Here you go, boys. On me. Good luck clearing the decks."

"Decks? You sound like fleet," the first soldier scoffed.

"I dated a spacer for a short while, but he had his eyes on the stars and not me, so good riddance."

This earned her a bunch of catcalls, but that was expected. She needed them to forget her call for peace.

How easily they were distracted. She smiled while inwardly shuddering at her loss of focus. Milk them for information.

Deena's role wasn't to change their minds about anything. She only needed to gather information that would help the Borwyn win the war.

She also needed to find a place to stay. She hadn't gotten a lot of sleep the previous night. Maybe she'd delay looking for a new place for at least a day. She'd be better with a clear mind.

"Hey, Boss man. I'll start looking for a place tomorrow. We're a little busy, and I'm way tired. I hope you don't mind if I work instead of taking time off."

"I'll have to make it work." He gestured for her to get back to it. He wasn't big on showing emotion, especially positive ones, but he was pleased. His body language showed that he was relaxed.

Deena was far from relaxed. The Malibor had discovered *Matador*, the gunship that the Borwyn had captured, and they were going after it. She needed to make another call, but for this one, she wouldn't use voice. That had scared her too much.

She'd have to find a new hiding spot for the unit. Maybe she'd keep it at the restaurant. It wouldn't do to put Lanni at risk after what Deena had done to save Lanni's husband. Maybe save. She wouldn't find out how it went until the patrol returned, if they returned.

The not knowing would drive her crazy. She reported and that was it. She wouldn't hear back unless it was to give her instructions. It was like screaming into the void of space and counting on Septiman to answer your prayers.

Septiman. The Malibor were faithless. It kept them self-centered, away from working for the greater good. They didn't need a deity, but they needed leaders who embraced better for all, like ending the war against the Borwyn, but they had their chance. *Chrysalis* was systematically destroying every Malibor combat vessel in the Armanor system.

At least she hoped they were. Another void of information. What was happening in space? The soldiers seemed to have no idea. She needed to get inside the officers' mess and listen to their complaints. She wouldn't get there if she showed any favoritism toward the Borwyn. Deena needed to do better.

CHAPTER 5

Keep your eyes on the stars and your feet on the ground.

Brad pulled his helmet off to expose sweat-matted hair. He sucked a massive amount of air into his lungs. He'd been breathing shallow for too long in an effort to extend his air supply.

Jaq waited for him to gather his wits.

"That was close. That ship was a piece of garbage. No wonder they didn't have any weapons on it, that would have stressed it enough to break it in half. As it is, all it took was us compromising the structural integrity to send it over the edge into being nothing more than scrap metal. When will we know if they work?"

"That's a good question. We don't have any checklists for a startup and operations process so Teo is building one on the fly. Also, we don't know how they work."

Brad dragged his fingers through his hair. "I'm sure Teo is

working on it. Nothing like decrypting a puzzle to keep her busy."

"I've asked Bec to take a look, too. We need them up and running as soon as possible."

"They came off a pile of garbage. They may be well past their useful service life," Brad countered.

Jaq shrugged. "Even so, they're better than what we have. We still have plenty of fuel that we took from *Hornet*, and that was Malibor fuel so it should work in these plants. I'd like to think that was the only thing holding them back."

"Reaction chamber. As they get older, they get increasingly poor at maintaining the reaction. The reactions become less and less efficient over time until the reaction can no longer take place," Brad replied

"You sound like you're spending too much time with your daughter," Jaq said. "And still, a bad reaction is better than no reaction. They were working, so they'll work again. If we need to replace reflective plating inside the reaction chamber, then that's what we'll do. It's easier than rebuilding a plant from scratch."

"Let's see what Teo is doing," Brad offered. He took one step before he realized he was still in his spacesuit. He didn't remember the last time he was out of the suit.

"How about you take a shower, get something to eat, and grab a few hours of sleep first? Don't make me give you an order."

"Would I follow it if you did?" Brad countered.

"What would you tell someone in your condition, Captain?" Jaq smiled. She knew the answer.

"You're right, of course." Brad knew the right answer, too.

He trooped down the corridor on his way to turn in his suit for cleaning and recharging.

Air and heat had been restored in the cargo bay. The engineering team was working in their normal uniforms and not spacesuits. It would help expedite the process.

At least that's what Jaq hoped. She released her boots and pulled herself down the mid-rail toward the former cargo bay, now the power plant space.

Inside, she found a dozen people checking connections and stringing cable. It was little more than controlled chaos. Teo floated from one person to the next, giving orders along with encouragement. She carried a clipboard that she annotated after each interaction.

Jaq waited until Teo had a moment.

"I'm sure I'm the last person you want to talk to," Jaq started.

Teo raised a hand to stop her. "Actually, he's the last one I want to talk to." She nodded toward Bec, who worked on the first power plant by himself. He looked to be rewiring a panel on the side of the unit.

"What's he done?"

"Just the usual. Nothing we do is adequate and he's better off doing it by himself rather than waste time training the rest of us failures of evolution."

A laugh burst from her before Jaq could stifle it. "It's been a long time since he used that slight. Maybe he's the one failing to evolve." Jaq gripped Teo's arm. "I'll talk with him, as painful as it will be, but how's this plant coming? Are these nasty things going to be able to generate power?"

Teo smiled. "Out of all the pain and anguish, the answer

is yes. They will generate power almost as well as our original plants. The bad news is that we've already had to cannibalize some parts, which means those old generators are now completely useless. We'll recover their metal for scrap or something. Oh. There's more good news. We have all the fissile material at hand—what was left in these, the stuff Bec found on *Butterfly*, and what was in ours. We have a healthy reserve, so we can juice the system as hard as we need to, whatever it will take."

"Coolant?"

"Using the cold of space. When the plants are up and running, we'll open the outer doors. Sometimes the easiest solution is the right one. The other plants didn't have access to space. Admittedly, it makes them more vulnerable during a Malibor attack, but we'll have to deal with that. How many more engagements do you think we'll have?"

"That's the lifetime achievement award if I had that answer. At least one? More if we win that fight. I know it's not a very good answer, but the condition of that Malibor cruiser suggests they are out of operational cruisers. They have two in the shipyard getting repaired or upgraded. They have that new behemoth of a ship being built, but I don't think it'll be ready before we can take it out on a flyby. Maybe two? The board is nearly clear of combatants. There are only a couple of us still flying, as much as this ship shouldn't be. But it must."

"I know." Teo was tired, every bit as much as her father.

"What do you say you take twelve hours off? Everyone except Bec because we don't need to give him orders that he won't follow. We're not in a big rush, and tired people make mistakes. We can afford the time more than we can afford a catastrophic mistake."

Teo smiled slightly and called her team to her. They carried their tools as if the interruption would be brief and they'd be sent back to work.

"The captain has something she wants to say," Teo said and took a step away.

Jaq threw her hands up. "Teo asked to give all of you twelve hours off to get food, sleep, more food, and then come back with a fresh mind. Teo is right. Take the time off. Secure your tools and gear so nothing accidentally impacts this Malibor piece of garbage. We don't want to break what we've rightfully ripped from the guts of that ugly ship."

"Normal people would say stolen," Teo clarified. "Secure your gear. See you in twelve."

The crew cheered on their way to pack their tools and instruments into zero-gee storage netting. They secured the panels and wiring leading into and out of the unit. Teo made sure the main power cable was disconnected.

Jaq waited until after Teo departed. That left her and Bec alone. He'd glanced at the crew as they made their way out.

"Thank you," he told her when she approached. She raised her eyebrows. "For clearing out the noise so I can work in peace. You can go, too. I'll have this up before they get back."

"No risks, Bec. You can wait. Because once this is running, you'll need to open the cargo bay doors to cool the unit."

"I'll want to test it with no one around. I'll shut it down before it gets hot."

She wanted to tell him to make sure that he did, that he didn't get a runaway cascade failure. She settled for the only thing that wouldn't lead to an argument. "Thanks, Bec." Then she left.

The day passed uneventfully. The soldiers watched, slept, and watched some more. The midday sun shone faintly through a heavy cloud cover. Rain would complicate things but not make them impossible.

Rain during the night would make finding the Malibor difficult.

The two-soldier patrols returned without finding any sign of an infiltration squad passing. They sent word back to the company headquarters, with the troops taking the horses, that they had not made contact with the Malibor.

Lightning sparked across the distant sky.

Rain was coming, and that was the curse of every soldier in the field, but it was also a blessing. The flash of light showed a line of people moving across the field, maybe a kilometer away from the center of the Borwyn's position. They disappeared with the return of the darkness.

"Here they come," Crip said softly. The ambient noise was sufficient to cover normal conversations. "Estimate fifteen minutes before they arrive. They didn't appear to be moving quickly."

"Why were they walking in the open?" Glen asked.

"That's a high risk and low reward strategy." Glen rubbed his face, brushing the stubble that had built up over the past two days.

"We can hit them with volley fire with the next lightning bolt. They won't even realize its weapons fire until their people go down."

"Your people can hit them from this range?" Glen had seen the weapons fire at a shorter range. He'd been impressed then with their accuracy and the seemingly instantaneous impact after firing. The high velocity of the obdurium projectiles meant they would hit a target well before the target heard the crack of the shot leaving the barrel.

"I suggest we wait until they're half a klick away, and then we pour all the fire we have into them."

"Nothing from the bows?" Glen asked.

"If we let them get that close, they'll be able to shoot back. At five hundred meters, their return fire will be ineffective. We own this battlefield, Glen, thanks to Deena's warning."

"Concur. Plan approved. I'll pass the word. You fire first and that will be their sign. It'll be your estimate of five hundred meters. I'll send runners up and down the line."

Glen moved out of their observation point and into the woods. He returned a minute later. "Notifications are going. It's your show, Crip."

"What about the clean up afterward? Are we going out there once we've shut them down?"

"Do you want to find out what got Deena so spun up about this group?"

Crip nodded. "That I would, and we can only do that by interrogating the prisoners."

"Call ceasefire after we've killed half of them?" Glen offered.

"Five hundred meters. Half their squad will be dead. Their backs will be against the wall, and we'll have to cross open ground. I think we might have to let this opportunity pass. I don't want to risk any of my people. We'll wait for them to pull out and then check the bodies, if they leave any behind. Deena's message sounded like she didn't want to see them enter the forest. Maybe they're headed for the mountain."

"That's the plan. We hit them until they run," Glen confirmed.

"That's the plan." Crip eased into a prone firing position. He dug small pits in the ground for his elbows. He braced himself and waited. It wouldn't be long.

Lightning flashed with increasing anger.

It became darker, even though Armanor hung low in the sky. Its light was blocked by the darkening clouds. The last vestiges of sky disappeared under the onslaught.

Lightning crashed, showing an empty field.

"Where'd they go?" Crip scanned the field with wide eyes, blinded to the darkness because of the flashes. In between the lightning, he could see nothing.

"There was a cut to the right of where we saw them. Maybe they dove in to get off the skyline. I wonder what took them so long to decide to stay out of sight." Glen watched with both eyes open, afraid to blink so he wouldn't miss anything.

"They were five hundred meters away. They probably thought they were safe from fire."

A flash of light hit close. "There." Crip pointed. "In the cut. Their heads are exposed. We'll wait until they get closer. They'll lose cover about a hundred meters out."

He kept his pulse rifle trained on the spot where they would emerge while he kept both eyes open and looked over the barrel.

"I'll let them know down the line," Glen said. He was gone an instant later, leaving a thunderclap in his wake.

Ten seconds, then thirty, then a minute passed. Not a single bolt of lightning showed the field before them.

An electric flash right on top of them made his hair stand on end. The squad in the open, barely fifty meters away. Crip pulled the trigger, quicker than he wanted but he was zeroed in on the soldier with the beard. A mercenary from Fristen.

Deena's words came back to him. *Same squad as last time.*

Pulse rifles barked to Crip's right where the squad was danger close. Lightning flashed in rapid succession. The combat team filled the air with volley after volley.

The next flash showed the Malibor infiltration squad in chaos. The survivors were running, backs turned to the forest. Bodies littered the open field before the cut.

"Cease fire!" Crip bellowed. "First fireteam, forward. Second fireteam, prepare to move."

Glen waved two of his soldiers forward. He ran five steps and dropped to the ground. The two ran past him, zigzagging until they also dropped. Then Glen ran. The three conducted a bounding overwatch until they reached the bodies.

The rain pounded down, heavy and in waves.

The combat group's first fireteam, a new organizational structure that Crip and Max had adopted, did the same as Glen and his people. They had trained together, and the bounding overwatch was a standard tactic. It made sense. Minimize exposure while maximizing counterfire.

But no one fired at them. The infiltration squad had been dealt a heavy blow. Two-thirds of their members were down.

Glen waved the first fireteam forward into the cut to establish a blocking position. They aimed their weapons in the direction where the Malibor disappeared.

Crip made his way forward and counted the enemy soldiers as he checked each. "Eight down, two still alive, but they're in bad shape." He waved to the third fireteam. "Emergency medical. Keep these two alive."

The wounds from pulse rifle impacts were ugly. One soldier was missing an arm. The other, a leg. They applied tourniquets while the rain washed the blood into growing puddles.

The lightning stopped, and visibility dropped to near zero.

"Recover to the forest," Glen called. "First fireteam, bring up the rear."

They carried the injured to the woods and camped out under a tree that provided a minimum amount of shelter. The trauma of the injuries had sent them into shock. Both soldiers were clammy and unconscious. Their hearts beat too rapidly.

"Build a carry-drag. Use shirts from the dead."

They forced an antibiotic and pain reliever into their veins using a syringe more crudely made than what they had on *Chrysalis*. The dead were stripped of their weapons and possessions before they were left behind.

The Borwyn soldiers pulled back to the forest until only the first fireteam remained. That fireteam consisted of two men with pulse rifles and two women with bows. Each couple took turns backing up until they were into the woods. Once there, the soldiers who hadn't gone into the open provided cover until the injured were secured to two saplings held together with uniform blouses. Belts held them in place as two soldiers took each pole and headed deeper into the trees.

The torrent pounded the forest, sending leaves and small branches cascading down around their heads. They hunched down as they walked, trying to keep as little water as possible running down their backs.

"We need to put some distance between that ambush and us. Just in case the survivors have a radio," Glen told Crip.

Max appeared. "Headcount. Make sure we have everyone," Crip ordered. Max nodded and disappeared back into the rain.

Crip wondered how he saw anything, but the group had bunched up because of the visibility. They moved almost as a mob and not a tactical formation. Visibility was barely two meters.

Max returned after a minute. "All soldiers present. What'd you see? I never got a look at them."

"Squad of twelve, exactly like Deena said. We killed six,

four ran like rats, and two lost limbs. We've got them up front, hauling them back to camp. I'm happy not to be on the wrong end of a pulse rifle."

"They can do some damage. Any of our people injured?" Max asked.

Crip shook his head. "I don't think they fired a single shot. Looks like you and the Malibor have something in common."

"That's not even remotely funny, Castle-sa."

"For the record, I don't like killing them. I wish they'd surrender so we can talk. Judging by how they ran, their stomachs weren't in a straight-up fight. Both the soldiers with beards were killed, so no more Fristen mercenaries, not until next time, anyway."

Max walked in silence.

Crip knew what he was thinking about. "We still don't know why Deena called us about this group. Maybe she saw them as more of a threat, but according to Glen, these teams are fairly common. The Borwyn usually engage them directly when they find them."

"Then we need those two to recover enough to tell us what was special about that squad. They'll realize pretty quickly that they're out of the fight. Maybe that'll make them more cooperative."

"We'll see. It'll be nice to get out of this rain, but the camp is probably a two-day hike. We're going to be squishy for a while."

"You know what they say, my friend. It's not that it sucks, but how can we make it suck more." Max clapped Crip on the back of his pack. "I'll get everyone to change their power packs, just in case we run across any more Malibor."

Max eased away from the center of the formation and went from soldier to soldier. The women looked more comfortable than the men. Their deerskin clothing was more water resistant than the combat team's uniforms. They didn't carry as much weight since they didn't have body armor or pulse rifles with spare cartridges and power packs. That was a solid fifteen kilograms' difference.

They looked unperturbed, mirthful even. The men walked in silence and misery.

CHAPTER 6

Septiman tells us from an asteroid belt of despair comes a single stone of hope.

The energy gauge ticked upward two percent at a time. Jaq studied the numbers in disbelief, leaning back against her chair. "I'll be down in Cargo Bay Four."

She didn't want to deliver a scathing tirade on Bec because it may not have been warranted. Jaq wanted to see for herself.

She flew down the corridors, taking advantage of zero-gee, then down the central shaft to the fourth deck where Cargo Bay Four was located. Extra cabling trailed from the corridor and through the shaft before snaking out to the engineering section where the ion drives were located.

Jaq felt better about it until she found Bec staring through the monitoring window at the Malibor power plant in the cargo bay. The red warning light flashed incessantly.

Excess radiation.

Jaq checked quickly to make sure no one was unprotected while inside, but it was empty.

"What's up?" Jaq said in her best conversational tone. "Looks like a little bit of sadness going on."

"Those Malibor power plants are piles of junk. We should probably eject them," Bec replied. He glanced at Jaq and started to float away.

She caught his arm.

"The space is flooded with radiation. How is the next crew supposed to work?"

"We'll open the outer door and the worst of the alpha and beta particles will find their way outside after bouncing off the thin lead shielding. You worry too much."

"Bec!" Jaq almost came unhinged but caught herself before she took a swing at him. It was something that wouldn't happen on a normal ship, but on *Chrysalis*, where the most combative were siblings, it was a way of managing. Whether it was healthy or not was irrelevant. It happened, and no one was going to control it without physically separating the crew throughout the ship—a solution that no one could implement or enforce.

"Yes?" Bec asked, waiting for what he would consider nonsense coming out of Jaq's mouth.

"Now the next crew will have to work in radiation equipment and the cold of the bay. It's not optimal. We have a lot of work to do on that second power plant."

Bec nodded. It wasn't his problem. He'd gotten his plant up and working in less time than it took the whole team to get the second one operational.

Jaq smiled. "Maybe you could get the other plant up and

running. You are experienced, more than anyone else, and you know the adage that you live by. It's easier for you to do it yourself. I agree. Get your suit on and get back in there."

Bec scowled his displeasure but didn't articulate it.

"I can't believe you flooded the compartment with radiation," Jaq continued.

"It wasn't intentional. It was the power plant! It's absolute garbage."

"And those garbage plants are going to get us back in the war so we can finish it. Then we can jettison them into space, declare victory, and descend to the surface of Septimus to stand under a benevolent Armanor sun."

"I see," Bec replied. "You're deluded. You don't really think you're ever going to set foot on Septimus, do you? Whether Septiman determined it or just our own bad luck, we're stuck in space. We were born here, we live here, and we're going to die here."

Jaq let go of Bec's arm. Her face wrinkled under the onslaught of Bec's negativity. "You should probably go."

He huffed and hawed but activated his boots so he could walk away instead of pulling himself down the corridor using the mid-rail.

Jaq was tough. She carried the burdens of the ship's crew on her shoulders, taking personal responsibility for everything that happened to them, good or bad. Much of it was at Septiman's mercy. The rest was their own shortcomings. Tears welled in her eyes, and she couldn't hold them back.

The truth was, she thought Bec was right. Refusing to admit it was part of the burden she carried. Give hope to others while denying it to herself.

Jaq's tears drifted into the air. She stared at the two power plants, not seeing either, no longer hearing the radiation alarm.

A hand rested on her shoulder. She turned to see Teo staring at her.

"What's wrong?" she asked, which wasn't the right question. "What happened?"

Jaq shook her head and sighed.

"It was Bec, wasn't it?" Teo didn't wait for an answer. She yelled down the corridor at the retreating figure, "Bec! I'm coming for you."

She vaulted into the air and pulled herself faster and faster down the corridor.

Bec turned in time for Teo to body-slam his chest. His boots were magnetically clamped to the deck, so he swayed from the impact but didn't fly down the corridor.

Teo grunted in pain, but she reached out and grabbed a handful of his collar to keep him from getting away. She pulled herself back to stand on the bulkhead. She reared back, hand curled into a fist.

"Wait!" Jaq called from behind her.

Teo snarled into Bec's face. "I want to punch you so bad."

"What'd I do? Tell Jaq the truth and she comes apart."

"Whose truth? Yours? You're such a jack-wagon. And what did you do to my power plant? The space is radioactive!"

"It was radioactive before, just not as glowingly," Bec replied.

"Is that humor?" Jaq said, eyes red from the last time she talked with Bec.

"I can fix it, Jaq. I was going to get a lead-lined suit. I'll be back."

They let him go.

"Teo," Jaq said softly. "You probably shouldn't beat him up every time he gets under your skin."

"He didn't get under my skin. He upset you, and I'm not going to put up with that."

Jaq hugged the smaller, younger woman. "That means a lot to me, but don't beat him up. Septiman knows he deserves it, but we need his inspiration. He'll come up with something that will save us, just like you will."

"What did he say?" Teo pressed.

"It doesn't matter. Help him to get that second power plant up and running. Now that he's done one, the second will go more smoothly. Figure out why it's irradiating that cargo bay, and maybe seal the breach?"

"I'll look into it." Teo took a step after Bec and stopped. "Can I knee him in the groin?"

"As tempting as it is to say 'yes,' I'm going to defer until such time as this war is won. Then you can do whatever you want."

"I'll hold you to that, Jaq. Let me get a suit on." Teo checked the time. "We have four hours until my team reports."

Jaq waved over her shoulder. She passed the cargo bay window on her way to the central shaft. The alarm was still sounding and the light was flashing, but the power plant gauges that showed on the small screen suggested the plant was running at seventy percent without any problems besides overheating.

Jaq accessed the comm unit on the bulkhead. "Alby, Jaq here. We have nominal power restored. Get the lights on, the computers up, and run environmental systems to one hundred percent. We don't have enough power to move yet. Let's get DC teams cleaning up any lingering issues. And let's bring *Cornucopia* alongside for a resupply."

"Good news all the way around, Jaq. I'll spread the word."

She smiled at the tone in his voice. Godbolt was on *Cornucopia*. Jaq vowed to find a replacement and keep the couple on the same ship. Unlike Crip and Taurus. They were in the same orbital plane but in two far different places.

"I am going to stand on a free Septimus," Jaq told the empty corridor. "As Septiman is my witness and in His honor, we will return in triumph."

Deena made contact and sent her message using the compressed feature of the unit. The radio was live for one to two seconds at a time, nothing more. She tucked the unit into the overhead and shoved it back as far as it would go, almost out of reach. She covered it with a dark cloth, making it even less visible. It would take someone knowing it was there to find it.

She put everything back in place, took a shower, and then walked out with her clothes in a bag. Lanni had taken her other meager possessions earlier.

Armed with written directions and her dirty clothes and

toiletries, she headed out the front door. She locked it after her and tucked the key safely in her pocket.

She headed down the street to find the individual from yesterday standing there.

"Hey, you wouldn't have a drink with me yesterday. How about today?"

"Still not happening," Deena replied. "If you'll excuse me."

"You're anti-military, aren't you? That's a crime around these parts." He moved back and forth to block the sidewalk.

There wasn't much traffic. Deena was ready to jump into the street. "What filthy lies just came out of your mouth? What kind of scumbag are you harassing a defenseless woman. I'm sure your commanding officer would love to hear why his soldier is walking with a permanent limp. They don't take kindly to soldiers getting beat up by a woman they attacked."

"Say what?" The man recoiled.

"That's how your lies sound. Now, get out of my way before you get hurt."

"You can't hurt me," he replied and moved closer until his body was nearly touching hers.

She shuffled half a step back and raised her arms. She looked at her bag and then let it drop from her hand. Her knee started upward before she looked back.

He was still watching her hand when her knee hit home. The man doubled over, reaching for Deena on his way down.

Deena danced out of his reach. She picked up her bag and threw it over her shoulder. She leaned down. "I told you to leave me alone."

"Bitch!" he cried out.

"Move along!" a voice ordered. "Clear the sidewalk." It was the officer who had extorted the boss the day prior.

"I'm heading for my new place, Officer," Deena said. "Now you understand my hesitation. It's dangerous out here for young women."

"I agree. We'll see if me and the bar can come to an arrangement." He hauled the injured soldier to his feet. "I'll take this one to the authorities. We'll see what they have to say."

"Thank you, Officer. I feel safer already." She waved and walked away with a measured pace, not looking to hurry and not looking to be caught lagging.

Once she was around the corner and out of sight, she hurried as if being followed. She opened the map Lanni had drawn on the back of a napkin. Right at the corner. Alley to the left. Third entrance. Climb the stairs to the top floor. Door on the left. Deena knocked softly.

The door opened and Lanni's smiling face greeted her. The two women hugged in the doorway.

"Ran into a little trouble. Some creeper intercepted me. He got himself jacked up for his troubles, and even better, the officer who made me leave the bar came to my rescue."

"What does that mean?"

"It showed him it was dangerous for a young woman to be alone, which is something he should have already known. But he said he'd see if he could come to an arrangement with the boss man. I'm sure that'll be too rich for our blood, but it wouldn't hurt to have an officer watching out for us. Keep your friends close and your enemies closer."

"He's the police. Is he the enemy?"

"I don't consider him a friend because I don't trust him. He took money from the boss. Is he enforcing the law or is he padding his pocket?"

Lanni replied, "I hadn't thought of it that way, even though that's what they do. I would expect no less from them."

"Still doesn't make it right."

Lanni motioned for Deena to follow her across a cluttered living room. The far side had a small room with a mattress on the floor and a dresser with a child's decorations on top.

"This is great. I could ask for no better, and thank you for helping me in a time of need. I'll start looking for my own place tomorrow," Deena promised. "Where's this little curtain climber you told me about?"

"Sleeping, but she'll be up soon." Lanni took Deena by the hands. "I'm glad you're here. It's lonely thinking about what my husband is doing out there. Did you see those clouds?"

"I wouldn't envy anyone outside in that mess. I'm sure your husband will be okay. They'll see that thunderstorm and just come home. It doesn't make any sense to try any field operation in that kind of weather, does it?"

"My husband told me the worse the weather, the better the chances at getting in unseen. I think they waited for the bad weather."

"Maybe we should share a drink? Just a little one," Deena offered. She had seen a couple bottles on the sideboard. "Are you saving this for anything special?"

"Today is a special day," Lanni replied softly. "Every day we're alive is a good day."

"I'll drink to that." Deena knew that the Borwyn would have been waiting for the infiltration squad. No matter the weather, it wasn't going to be a good day for Lanni's husband and everyone else on that team.

They drank in silence while the baby slept.

CHAPTER 7

A leader is best when people barely know he exists. When his work is done, his aim fulfilled, they will say: we did it ourselves.

The prisoners remained unconscious, which was best for the bumps their bodies endured.

Around midnight, Glen called a halt. They couldn't see their hands in front of their faces. They could have been walking in circles for all Glen knew. And some of the soldiers hadn't slept for nearly two days.

They huddled together to ensure they had no stragglers. They gave the prisoners more pain relievers and antibiotics while adding to the dressings over their stumps. They didn't dare remove any of the bandages for fear that they'd restart the bleeding and wouldn't be able to stop it a second time. Better for the doctor and nurses to handle that once they made it back to camp.

"Your pulse rifles do some serious damage," Glen whispered.

"You don't want to be on the wrong end of one," Crip replied.

Binfall and Charlotte eased in close to Crip. "Permission to establish a women's latrine," Binfall requested.

"Thirty feet and put up a rope to guide them from here to there. I don't want anyone getting lost in this muck."

"Two knots for women, one for men," Binfall said. "We'll take care of digging both slit trenches. Thank you, sir." Binfall and Charlotte stayed there, glancing back and forth between each other and Crip.

"Is there something else?" Crip asked, cringing as he awaited the expected response.

"We want to get married."

"When we get back to camp." Crip raised his hand to forestall further conversation. "It's too dark. You can't see each other to ensure you're serious about your vows."

"We wanted the privacy of out here," Binfall countered.

Crip sighed, exasperated. This wasn't what he wanted. He liked to maintain morale, but he wanted a situation where they weren't in the middle of a rainstorm on a pitch-black night. "Back at camp. We'll hike into the woods and we'll marry everyone who wants it."

"I only want to marry Charlotte," Binfall countered.

"That's not what I meant. Go dig your toilets and cool your jets. It's not happening tonight. We have prisoners who are in bad shape. We're going to sleep fast and then we're going to get moving. We need to get back to camp as soon as possible if we want any chance of these two surviving. Please,

I'm begging you. Don't be a distraction to the main purpose of why we're out here. You'll have your time, soon, I promise."

"Sorry, Crip. We'll wait."

Charlotte nodded from over Binfall's shoulder.

Crip leaned back and closed his eyes.

"I'll wake you when it's time for your watch," Max whispered and then tickled Crip's ear. "You should have married them. It would have taken one minute and meant the world to them."

"I don't want anyone's wedding to take one minute, Max. It's a lifetime commitment in Septiman's eyes. I want to show the ceremony some respect. Look at how you and Deena did it. The whole ship squeezed in to watch. It was a total party. I don't want to deny anyone the chance for that same celebration."

"You keep us grounded, Crip. I'll help with the toilets. Get some sleep. No one is sneaking up on us tonight. There isn't anyone left to sneak up on us."

A pulse rifle cracked from behind the group. "Everyone down," Crip roared as he scrambled toward the sound of the weapon.

Another shot helped Crip zero in on the location of the engagement. He hit the ground and crawled through mud and puddles.

He found Danny Johns aiming into the darkness. The second he arrived, Danny fired again.

"We're being followed," Danny said casually. "I think I cooked two of them, but there are two more. The rest of the Malibor squad. They're still out there."

"Hammer, Ava, Anvil, and Mia, with me. We'll conduct a

recce in that direction." He pointed using his whole arm. "Hammer and Ava, left flank. Anvil and Mia, right. We're not in a hurry to die, so take your time and cover each other."

"I'm coming with you," Danny Johns said. "I want to make sure I'm not seeing things. My eyes are old."

"I expect you hit what you aimed at, Danny. You take point because you know where they were."

"Roger." Danny crouched to move from tree to tree. Lightning would have been welcome to give them some visibility. As it was, the enemy could be behind the next tree or the one after that. The group moved slowly, embracing Crip's strategic guidance.

Don't be in a hurry to die.

It took five minutes to cover fifty meters, but they took no risks. When they reached the place Danny indicated, they found three bodies.

"You saw four?"

"Must have gotten two with one shot," Danny said, but he took the greatest care in checking the bodies to make sure it wasn't a trap. Crip covered him while Hammer and Anvil moved wide.

"We're looking for one soldier who is lost and alone. In the morning, we'll send our best trackers after him," Crip said. "Or maybe we could give him a chance to live."

Danny shook his head. He wasn't sure what Crip meant.

"It worked on Farslor, where I had a good conversation with Gregor. We left each other in peace." He stood and cupped his hands around his mouth. "Malibor soldier. We know you're out there, alone and afraid. You've been tracking us so you know we saved the lives of the two soldiers who survived the first battle. We don't kill for no reason. Just being Malibor isn't enough. Have you heard anything from fleet personnel lately? Have your ships and their crews been disappearing? Fleet personnel not returning from space? Sound familiar?"

Crip moved to the other side of the tree while Danny Johns removed personal effects and weapons from each Malibor soldier.

He cupped his hands around his mouth and bellowed, "We won't harm you if you surrender. There is no shame in it. If you return without your squad, how will your commander treat you? You know the answer. Come on in, hands up, weapons down."

Danny Johns shifted back and forth while staring into the darkness, willing his eyes to work better.

They'd never gotten the night vision they wanted. It was one step too far for the manufacturing section aboard *Chrysalis*. It would have come in handy.

"How long do we wait?" Danny asked.

"Tell me, did you hear anyone running away after you fired?" Crip wondered.

"No. I agree, there should have been splashing or something."

Crip looked into the tree above them, where a shadowy outline looked different from the others.

"Come on down, son. We're not going to hurt you," Crip said and slung his weapon. "Following us wasn't a winning strategy."

Danny aimed his weapon, but Crip caught the barrel and gently pushed it back down.

"This fight is over. You may get a shot at us and at this range, we probably wouldn't survive, but you won't either. Our people will turn this tree into kindling. You have something to live for, otherwise you would have already tried to shoot us. Come on. I'll give you a hand."

A heavy sigh preceded the scraping of equipment on bark.

He threw his legs off the branch and eased down until he was hanging with his feet nearly two meters off the ground. Crip guided them to his shoulders.

"Hang onto the tree as I ease you down." Crip bent at the knees until he could lean into the trunk. "Let go. The drop is less than a meter."

The soldier scraped his toes down the trunk on his way down. He hit the ground and stumbled. Crip looked into a too-young face.

"They're sending babies against us," Danny Johns said. "How old are you?"

The young Malibor puffed out his chest. "I'm twenty. How old are you?"

Crip snorted before laughing. "He got you there, Danny Johns. Danny was born right over there, in the city that used to be called Pridal. He spent a little time in space and now he's back."

"Should we be telling the enemy any of this?" Danny asked.

"His war is over, and if our strategy pays off, assuming *Chrysalis* can do what Jaq needs the ship to do, then this war will be over for everyone soon enough."

Crip never took his eyes off the enemy soldier.

Danny relieved him of a rifle that used propellants and bullets in brass-cased cartridges. "Old school."

"What's your name, son?" Crip asked.

"My name is Raftal Barman."

"Are you hungry, thirsty?"

The young man didn't reply.

Crip gestured to Danny. "Take him to the injured, keep a guard active on him but get him something to eat and drink. Give the rifles and ammunition to any of our soldiers who want to upgrade from a bow." Crip had taken to calling them soldiers instead of 'the women.' They were fighters, every bit as capable as their chosen partners.

Danny led the lad away. "Binfall and Charlotte," he called toward the camp. "Get back to digging those latrines. Hammer and Anvil, Mia and Ava, bring it in. This battle is over."

Glen was first into the camp. He shouted instructions and orders to gear up his company to receive injured and prisoners.

Eleanor ran across the small compound, waving as she passed on her way to get the surgical tent ready to receive.

The group enjoyed the late afternoon haze. The sun and clear skies helped turn the puddles into one hundred percent humidity. The soldiers who'd gone out to repel the Malibor infiltration team returned, soaked to the skin.

The makeshift stretchers were picked up, and the injured were hauled to medical for evaluation. Max followed them, leaving Crip to deal with the prisoner who wouldn't talk with anyone but Crip.

Eleanor turned Max over to the medical staff, where the individual missing the leg was covered and left outside. He'd died before they arrived. But the other was alive, and the frenzy of activity suggested the medical team believed they could save him.

Eleanor ran back to Crip, Glen, and the prisoner. Danny Johns hovered nearby.

"One dead and one alive," she reported.

"Two alive," Crip replied. "Meet Raftal. He'll be staying with us until the war is over."

"Not by choice," the young man said casually.

"He's got a great sense of humor, too. We'll make him responsible for rehabbing our other survivor, assuming our people can keep him alive."

Eleanor looked at the ground. "He's probably going to lose the rest of his forearm. He needs blood, and his type isn't common among the Borwyn."

"I'll donate," Raftal said.

From Crip's perspective, having the prisoner down five hundred milliliters of blood was a good thing. It would keep him from getting too precocious. "Take him to see if he's a match, and Raftal, thank you. We don't want any more Malibor to die."

The young soldier tipped his chin in reply. Eleanor led him away.

"Will he be a problem?" Max asked.

"I don't think so, not as long as we make him responsible for the injured soldier. He won't want to leave him behind if he wanted to escape. We need to keep an eye on him, but I think we can also work with him to see how we can win the hearts and minds of the Malibor. We don't have enough firepower to kill them all, so we need to kill only the ones who leave us no choice. For the others, we need to give them a better option than a future civil war under their current leadership."

"How do you know they'll fight themselves again? It's been a long period of peace, if I get the latest in Malibor politics correct."

"Not six months ago, they were headed to Sairvor to start another fight with the inhabitants because they thought those Malibor were killing their ships. No, this regime is weak and afraid. They'll lash out at anyone, most especially their own people. I don't get the Malibor."

"They are all about power. Those with it don't share. That doesn't allow for any compromise," Glen added.

Crip kicked at the ground. "We had to grow up on a ship with too many competing opinions. We didn't have the luxury of beating someone into submission and holding them hostage. Everyone needed to carry their own weight. Like Bec. He hates everyone. I can't imagine what things would look like if he was in charge." Crip stared into the distance. The rigors of the past two days were catching up with him. "I wonder how they're doing. I miss Taurus."

Max gripped Crip's upper arm. "I miss Deena. We're two men risking everything while our better halves risk all that they are in the hopes that one day, we'll be able to establish a new normal where we get to live in peace."

"Why don't you lovebirds get some sleep before you tip

over into philosophical poetry? I don't want to find you sitting in a tree, half-naked, contemplating your navels."

"There's a lot to be said about a contemplated navel, don't you think, Max?" Crip said as the two took a slow first step toward their quarters, a mat in a big room shared with everyone else from the combat team.

"We have some weddings to perform as my boys are getting restless and so are my girls. I wish I had something more profound, but I'm exhausted. When we're upright again, we'll conduct the ceremonies according to what the couples want. Probably a private clearing not far from camp, but far enough to make them think they aren't at war, if only for a day."

"You should try not to talk to anyone else until you've gotten some rest," Glen advised. "I'll be racking, too. It'll be nice to be dry, well, at least as dry as one can get in this soup." He raised his head toward the shimmer in the sky and shook his head at the humidity.

"What day is it?" Crip asked over his shoulder. "Do you know when we can next contact the ship?"

"A couple days," Glen replied.

Crip knew that he'd sleep most of the time away, and it would be here before he knew it. He looked forward to sending reports of marriages, successes, and kind words to loved ones. War didn't have to be bad all the time, just at the worst of times.

CHAPTER 8

You alone make the choice to live well and in Septiman's good graces.

Jaq climbed into the captain's seat and sulked, although she wanted to think she looked contemplative.

Alby climbed out of his position and pulled himself across the command deck. He hovered in front of Jaq's seat until she acknowledged him. "Got something on your mind, Battle Commander?"

He smiled. "I like that title. I hope I'm doing it justice. We've been beat up badly since I moved into that chair. Maybe you should pick someone else, like Taurus."

"Let me guess. You want to take over *Cornucopia* with Godbolt as your second or you're willing to be her second."

"That's part of it, but I feel like I've failed the ship, the crew, and most of all, you."

Jaq climbed out of her seat so she could push him away. "Stop that. We've won our fights. They've grown more and more challenging, and that's why we've gotten hurt, but we're close to getting back up to speed." She nodded toward the front screen showing the energy gauge already at sixty-five percent, despite all ship systems being active.

Jaq continued, "Look at the extent of the Malibor losses. We've done more than anyone could have ever asked of this old girl. Yet, we still stand. We have survived to fight another day while the Malibor forces dwindle. What do you recommend next, Battle Commander?"

"You tell me the target, and I'll develop the attack plan that we can work together to refine." Warmth washed over Alby to erase the niggling self-doubt that had crept into his psyche. The entire crew had been involved for weeks in fixing the ship. It was all he heard and all he saw while trying to get something, anything, online.

A smattering of defensive weapons had been available, but if they'd been attacked, a single gunship would have been able to destroy the cruiser. It would have been the end of their war, no matter how hard Alby worked or how much the crew performed damage control. There was no combat if the ship wasn't capable of firing its weapons.

"I appreciate that, Captain. I'll get right on it. It's good to be back at the helm of determining our own course."

"It is, isn't it?" Jaq agreed.

Alby returned to his position, calling Taurus and Gil Dizmar to him. He laid out the enemy's order of battle and reiterated their goal. They looked over a map of the system with the current locations of the planets. Septimus was moving away from Farslor. Its shorter orbital arc was leaving Farslor in its wake.

"Eat my stardust," Alby proclaimed.

"What does that even mean?" Taurus wondered.

"The dust from a vehicle in front of you. It means you're in second place," Alby explained.

"When have you been in a ground vehicle?" Taurus pressed.

"We've seen the videos from the originals and the before time. I am well versed in aged videos," Alby claimed.

Taurus laughed. "According to Max and Crip, Larson is the biggest collector and restorer of those things. He has hundreds of them, supposedly."

"Hundreds! I'm eating his dust!"

"Do you have my battle plan yet?" Jaq called.

Alby raised his hands for calm and focus. "We're just working out the finer details, Captain. You'll have to give us a few minutes."

The radiation alert turned from flashing red to green.

Jaq climbed out of her chair. "I'm on my way to Cargo Bay Four," she announced and hurried off the bridge. She planned on stopping by her quarters to check on Brad. It was about time for him to get up. He'd gotten his four hours of sleep. It would have to do.

She found him still asleep.

"Get up. No time to be lazy. We'll be getting underway soon and could use all hands responding to any quirks in the ship since last time we flew."

"Lazy," Brad rasped. "I'm up with all the energy of a schoolboy." He reached an arm out of the sleeping cubicle. "Give us a kiss."

"I'll do no such thing. You've got a case of New Septimus

breath. And I need to get down to the new power plants. They are both up and running. Seems like the radiation has fallen below the alarm threshold. I wanted to see what that's all about. You should come, too."

"Let me brush my teeth. I'll be right there."

Jaq looked at her messed-up bed knowing that he wouldn't straighten it. She didn't say anything to him. She waved as she left. She stopped in the corridor and thought better of it all. She'd counseled many on their relationships and knew what she'd tell them.

She reentered her quarters.

"Forget something?" Brad said, now out of the sleeping cube and floating, buck naked.

Jaq pulled him close and kissed him, closed mouth. "Make that bed before you join me, and make sure you keep that—" She gestured from his head to his toes. "—in peak performing operation."

She left him with a smile on his face and, she hoped beyond hope, a desire to straighten the room.

Jaq hurried down the corridor and into the central shaft. She accelerated downward for a few decks before grabbing the rail to slow down. She turned into the fourth deck corridor. A single engineer stood at the window.

"How's it running?"

"Nominal. Seventy-five percent. Teo didn't want to push them beyond that, but even at seventy-five, they are outperforming our old power plants."

"What happened to the radiation?"

"Teo and Bec sealed the breach in the casing and then flooded the compartment with a cleanser mix superheated to vapor. Then they opened the outer door. It sucked out the cleanser and the radiating particles. It was crazy. It happened over the course of a couple minutes."

The doors remained open, and the power plants were on the low end of their optimal operating temperatures. They didn't need any coolant lines, just the power of space.

"I like the ingenuity." Jaq studied the systems through the window, but there wasn't anything to see. There weren't any moving parts. Everything operated internally. "When Brad shows up, send him to Engineering, please."

Jaq used the mid-rail to casually pull herself along. She checked the shaft to see if Brad was on his way, but he had not yet made it. Jaq headed down. She hit bottom and bounced up one deck to depart the shaft on the engineering deck. The hatch to Engineering was open because of the heavy cabling, the direct feed from the Malibor power plants.

Inside, she found Teo tethered to the bulkhead and floating free. She was sound asleep.

Jaq cruised by noiselessly to the space with the dead Borwyn plants. She found the chaos of the attempted rebuild. It was clear why Teo was so willing to embrace the Malibor technology. There was no hope for the Borwyn plants.

The cables hooked into the energy storage feeds had been cut free from the dead plants. There was a pigtail connector to a cable that tracked to the biggest cargo hold, where Brad's ship was still providing power. Jaq wondered if it worked with the Malibor plants or not. She'd ask Teo when she was awake.

Jaq hit the doorframe to the power plant space deftly,

with the palms of her hands, and pulled herself through without making a sound.

"Woohoo!" Brad cheered from the hatchway.

"What? Oh, hey, Jaq," Teo muttered.

"All the grace of a supernova," Jaq said before attaching her boots to the deck. "Good work, Teo. You and Bec both."

"Eight percent an hour, Captain. Four percent if we're running full power on the ion drives. We're better than we were before."

"Impressive, Teo," Brad said from across Engineering. "I expected no less. Are you hungry? Can I bring you something? Never mind. I'm bringing you food. You look skeletal. You have to keep the meat wagon tuned up. Don't become the next Bec."

Teo half-smiled while regarding her father. "Bec made it all possible in less time than I was able to do it with a whole team. I don't know what to say. He's a jerk, but he knows engineering."

"Use him as you need, Chief Engineer. Get some sleep. We'll get underway soon."

"We can go now," Teo suggested. "I'll double-check when the engines start cranking, and then I'll hit the rack."

Jaq shook her head. "I'd love to, but we don't know where we're going yet. As soon as we have the next battlefield designated, we'll add speed to that vector."

Teo yawned.

"Go back to sleep, honey," Brad said over his shoulder. "Sorry for waking you."

Jaq followed him out.

He met her in the corridor. She pulled up short thinking

he was up to something, but he only wanted to float an idea past her. "Are we going to hit the Malibor shipyard?"

Jaq nodded. "I think so. We need to eliminate their ability to project power. I'm tired of seeing Malibor ships coming after us."

"I bet they're tired of seeing us, too," Brad quipped.

"That is funny." Jaq laughed easily. "Things are looking up, Brad."

"I know. We're back in the game. We should probably stop by New Septimus and see if they have any missiles ready. We could use them. The E-mags are nice, but there's nothing like sending a missile up someone's backside."

"Let's see what Alby has come up with, and then we'll decide what we're capable of doing. I had forgotten about the missiles. I wonder if Alby has."

"I did tell you that we received another message from Deena, didn't I?" Eleanor said over breakfast.

Crip and Max both perked up. "You did not," Crip replied.

Eleanor grimaced. "Sorry about that. I forgot with all the excitement. She sent it in code and not open voice. She said they were coming after the gunship."

Max looked at Crip in alarm.

Eleanor continued, "Tram and Kelvis know. They're planning right now to take the gunship out."

Crip stepped back. "They're going to destroy the gunship?"

"No. Take it out as in fly it away," Eleanor clarified.

"Where? There's no fuel."

Eleanor smiled. "That's not exactly true. The leadership wasn't convinced you were for real, despite all the signs. They're old and skeptical. They've grown set in their ways. Risk has become an increasingly foreign concept."

Crip sighed. "It sounds like they've given up on the goal of restoring Borwyn rule on Septimus."

"We have Borwyn rule," Eleanor replied. "What we don't have is freedom."

"I selfishly want it all. We're at war with the Malibor. We need to win this war. The more we fight, like this infiltration squad, the more I don't want to keep killing these people. Look at that boy we brought in. They're sending children to fight their parents' war."

Max and Eleanor both saw the humor in Crip's claim.

"Aren't you the children who swore to fight your parents' war?"

Crip glanced at the sky and wondered what *Chrysalis* was doing, but only for a moment. "We vowed to end our parents' war and in doing so, reclaim our home planet. We're so close, I can taste it."

"That would be nice. Going out to a restaurant. Choosing food as opposed to eating whatever is put in front of you. Every day would be like that when we were on board *Cornucopia*." Max stared into the distance.

"You better eat something," Eleanor said. She'd intercepted them before they made it to the mess bunker.

"Ask Tram to join us, if you would be so kind," Crip requested in a pleasant voice.

"He's kind of busy. Evelyn and Sophia keep him and Kelvis hopping."

"Of course they do. Ask all four to join us, then. They all have a part to play in this war. Clarification on your previous statement. We can fuel the gunship somewhere?"

"Behind the mountain. There's a dump we were slowly building until the general abandoned the idea, but the stocks are still there since we had no way to get rid of them without destroying the land. That stuff is toxic."

"We will do our best to clear your stocks. You wouldn't happen to have any projectiles, would you? We need to load that ship up. Maybe a missile or two?"

"Afraid not on the missiles, but I'm sure we can manufacture a few projectiles on short notice. Repurposed metal that can withstand the friction of high-speed acceleration and flight."

Crip grinned. "The physics of the E-mags. That's sexy talk right there. I didn't expect you'd know such things, being a forest dweller."

Eleanor pushed him. "I was raised in the city, just like everyone else out here. We received a classical education before we chose to live austere lives to protect those who don't. We ensure their pampered butts remain pampered."

Her tone of voice had changed. There was animosity between the civilians and the military when the entire Borwyn race was only trying to survive.

It was the vision that Jaq had convinced everyone to embrace, no matter the cost. A free Septimus was the only answer. They could argue about philosophy and the direction of life once they guaranteed it for their descendants. Until then, everything had to be a compromise.

"It's on us, Eleanor. We fight the fight because we can. We trained for it. We believe in ourselves, and we know what needs to be done. We're going to win this war. Then those in the mountain can choose to live there or return to the city. Free choice. That's what we're fighting for."

Eleanor rested her hand on Crip's arm. Her eyes held his for a moment, then she nodded and walked away.

"She's got a thing for you, my man," Max said.

"She's a good soldier. You know that I miss Taurus. I can't wait for her to join us on the ground. This *is* worth fighting for."

"I agree. I'm glad we came down here, and it's okay if I never go back to *Chrysalis*," Max replied. "I don't hate the ship, but I do love the sky. I love gravity, and I like eating meat. I know, that makes me a barbarian, but I'm going to embrace it."

Crip laughed. "You're not the only one. I'm glad we heard from Deena again. That's good news in and of itself."

"Makes me wonder how she's getting the information," Max said darkly.

"She'll tell you when we see her. This information is important. It allows us to stay one step ahead of the Malibor. We're going to instill a failure mindset until they give up. No one from the fleet returns. No one who goes into the forest returns. Until they hear footsteps creeping up on them in the night. Fear is our most effective weapon. Call it asymmetrical warfare. In space, *Chrysalis* is a better ship, faster and more powerful. Down here, it's our wits."

They entered the mess bunker and got in line.

"I'd like to think our pulse rifles give us an advantage." Max clapped Crip on the back.

"There's that, but we only have eleven of them. It's hard to overwhelm the Malibor with so few. They have far greater numbers, despite their only sending a dozen at a time against the western Borwyn." Crip sniffed the air. "I love the smell of a hearty camp breakfast."

They filled their plates with ham, eggs, and beans. They took the first two seats they could find.

As usual, the soldiers filled the bunker for the short breakfast time. No one was willing to miss a meal.

Tram, Kelvis, and their crew appeared, but there weren't six seats together.

"I guess we're done eating," Crip said.

Max looked at Crip as if he'd lost his mind. His mouth was stuffed to capacity and he had trouble chewing. He shook his head and spoke with his hand in front of his mouth to catch any bits that might fly out. "They can wait."

The group hovered around the table until the soldiers sitting there decided it was better to leave. They cleared the four seats. They waved as they left.

Max swallowed hard. "Problem solved."

"We're taking the ship to a hidey-hole!" Tram announced in a heavy whisper.

"So I hear. What kind of security are you taking with you?"

"None. We'll get there before the Malibor, and we'll be away before they know it," Tram explained.

"I'll make sure Glen sends someone to guide you. Can't

have you walking around the woods lost. When you get to New Pridal, make sure you rearm the gunship's projectiles. You won't get any missiles, but you can make do with loading the cannon. That'll give us some punch for when we attack the spaceport."

"Are we still doing that?" Tram asked.

What struck Crip like getting slapped with a cold, wet towel was that Tram was serious. He was the former battle commander.

"Of course. Why wouldn't we?"

"We haven't heard from *Chrysalis* in a while. That last battle took them away. I hope they're okay, but we have to plan for our future, you know?"

"Our window to contact *Chrysalis* is tonight. They said they needed a month. That wasn't quite a month ago. We'll see what kind of progress they've made, but we will never count them out, not Jaq Hunter." He stared so hard at Tram that he nearly burned holes through his brain.

"Sorry, man. It's hard to have faith when there's a void of information."

"You don't need to fill it with surrender. When Glen's people can take you, save that gunship. It gives us a significant advantage over the Malibor. We haven't heard from Deena about any craft on the ground at the spaceport, but I bet we're going to find that there aren't any combat craft. They are out of gas, unlike us, who are going to get a refuel." Crip nudged Max at his joke.

Tram raised his hands to cut off a further butt-chewing. He'd made a mistake thinking they could bury their heads.

The war was very much alive.

"Go on, see Eleanor and Glen, and get yourselves to *Matador*. Then save that ship. Get it ready to go into battle. We need you, Tram."

"We're going with them," Evelyn stated unequivocally. "We'll make sure they stay out of trouble."

"We couldn't manage that in decades on board *Chrysalis*. How are you going to do it?"

"Do it. Good choice of words. Leave it to us. Ready to fight? That'll depend on those who can resupply the ship. We need fuel and ammunition." Evelyn spoke with authority. She'd been paying attention as Tram and Kelvis rambled on about the ship. "By the way, we're all going to get married, too. I think the weddings are on for today? This afternoon."

The four stood, nodded, and walked out.

Max pursed his lips and contemplated the conversation. "I think Evelyn is in charge of that group."

"Clearly," Crip agreed. He frowned. "A group wedding. Joy. I can think of better ways to spend our time, but I have to admit that the combat team seems happy. And if Evelyn is going to watch Tram and Kelvis, then that frees us up to focus on more important issues."

"We better find our people and get this thing rolling."

"The gunship?" Crip asked.

"Ha! I wish. The wedding, Crip. Our people deserve us doing that right. You care about them, don't you?" Max put him on the spot to make a point.

"You know I do," Crip said softly.

"This is important to them, Crip. Give them their time."

Crip nodded. "I'm sorry to give the impression that I didn't have their best interests at heart. I just want everyone to focus on the fight." Before Max could say anything, Crip raised his hand. "I know, I know. We're in between fights. This is our well-earned downtime. We should enjoy it, which means they should enjoy it while you and I worry about the next phase of the war."

"Something like that. I suggest you finish your breakfast. You need to keep up your strength." Max took a huge bite comprised of everything that remained on his plate.

Crip's had gotten cold, but he ate it anyway. He'd missed a couple meals over the past thirty-six hours. It tasted good, filled his belly in the right way, and he didn't have to cook it or clean up afterward. "Yes, Mom."

CHAPTER 9

To the mind that is still, the whole universe surrenders.

After the ceremony that Glen and Eleanor attended as the reps from the western Borwyn, only Crip, Danzig, Danny Johns, and Fantasia remained unmarried. They had cheered, shaken hands, and hugged.

"You should give it a try," Max suggested.

Crip looked to the sky. "Someday. Taurus fought me off all those years. It took near-death experiences for her to settle for me."

"The captain gave you your chance when Deena and I got married, but you didn't take it."

"I was afraid of chasing her away again. Ours is a fragile relationship." Crip looked at the ground before he realized he was casting a dark cloud. "But rewarding!"

Eleanor grunted. "It shouldn't be that much work. I'm going to check on the prisoners." She made to walk off, but Crip stopped her.

"I'll come with you. I want to talk with Raftal and... What's the other one's name?"

"He's still unconscious. The doc thinks he should come out of it soon. Raftal gave him a unit of blood. We used one of our limited units of plasma, too. Then a lot of saline."

"Which means we had better not get anyone injured where they need extra help. I should get all my people lined up to donate blood," Crip offered.

"I'm surprised the doc hadn't already hit you up. I'm sure he can get your people set up today, at least the ones who won't be going to your stolen gunship."

Crip laughed. "We won it in a card game, fair and square." He hadn't known what a card game was until he joined the western Borwyn. They had too many games of chance to wile away the time.

The medical bunker was little more than an indent of one to two meters in the hard ground, covered by a dark-green, heavy canvas tent held down by a series of tent pegs in the ground that sloped away to prevent rain from getting in while allowing the breeze to help keep it cool.

Crip appreciated the engineering aspects that he had no idea were necessary since his life's experience was exclusive to one spaceship.

Inside the structure, they found a guard watching over Raftal, who sat in a chair next to the other Malibor soldier's bed.

"How is he?" Crip asked.

"He's been stirring. They removed the tube from his throat. That was gross."

"But it kept him alive when he couldn't breathe for himself. Losing a limb is tough," Eleanor said.

"It's tougher if you're the one who lost it." Raftal remained seated. He hadn't risen to meet the ranking officers.

Crip noted the behavior. Maybe it was a lack of military discipline or it was related to the trained hatred the Malibor had for the Borwyn.

"What's his name?" Crip asked.

"It's Moran. He's my age. We were added to the infiltration squad in the week prior." He scowled at himself for sharing information unbidden.

"What am I supposed to do with that revelation?" Crip asked. "You've told us no military secrets, nothing we can exploit. And you already believe me when I say I don't want to keep killing Malibor. If you can think of something that can help us end this war without fighting another battle, I'm all ears."

The one-armed patient stirred, but he was secured to the cot. His eyes fluttered open and he tried to make sense of what he could see.

"Moran," Raftal said with a smile. "It's good to see you with us. I didn't want to go through this alone."

"Go through..." His eyes closed while he took bigger and bigger breaths. When his eyes opened again, they were clearer yet still glossy.

The Borwyn doctor squeezed in and checked his pupils and vital signs. "The good news is that you don't have a fever. That means no infection. I think you're going to be just fine."

"You're Borwyn," the young man said.

"I'm a doctor, and between this good man here and my medical team, we saved your life."

The soldier noticed Crip and Eleanor. He tried to get up, but his one arm was strapped down. The remaining bit of his upper armed moved and swung around while Moran reached for Raftal. "Where's my arm?" A look of horror flashed across his face.

"It was a casualty of this war. At least you're alive," Crip suggested.

"One arm? How am I supposed to hold my baby?" he demanded angrily.

"A lot better than if you were dead. A one-armed father is better than none, a lot better," Crip said more loudly than he intended.

Moran ground his teeth together and glared at everyone who looked at him, including Raftal.

"It'll take time," Eleanor said. She felt for the soldier. His job was done and until he accepted his limitations, he had no prospects. "Change is the only constant."

The soldier didn't reply. He had to wallow in self-pity for a while before they could coax him out of that pit.

"Raftal, we'll leave you to talk with him. It could be a lot worse. You two are the only ones who survived the infiltration team's attempt to get into the forest. The others' bodies are littering the ground." Crip turned and walked away.

Crip understood but didn't. He wanted some appreciation for saving the young man's life, but it was too soon. They had to allow the man his anger.

Crip stopped once he was outside the bunker.

Eleanor lifted his chin. "What did you expect?"

"Happier to be alive, but I understand. He received more bad news than he could handle. He lost an arm and he's a prisoner. He's a survivor of a failed mission. That won't hold him in good stead with his people." Crip dug his toe into the mud. "I know he'll come around. Do you have anyone with one arm to help him acclimate?"

Eleanor shook her head. "Afraid not. Not out here, and there's no way we're taking him to the city."

"I didn't think so, but I had to ask. We'll make do. Raftal will have to become a soldier of Septiman if Moran is going to come through this with his mind intact." Crip clasped his hands behind his back and strolled slowly, deep in thought. "I'll let you go. I have to think about a message to *Chrysalis*. That message gets sent this afternoon."

Eleanor watched him walk away.

Crip gave the radio equipment a final glance. Larson made a few last-second adjustments before giving the thumbs-up. Crip had already drafted the message and had it coded for burst transmission.

Jaq: All is proceeding. Deena infiltration complete and intel flowing. Have not tasked her yet, but that will be soon. We need a recce of the spaceport before we can attack with any precision or purpose. We have captured two Malibor from the last infiltration team and killed ten. With insight into Malibor movements, they have lost all advantage. We are not yet ready to go on the offensive, but Matador *can be refueled and rearmed. Just need a few more days. Are able to integrate with your plans anytime after that. Tell Taurus I miss her. Also, Danzig, Danny Johns, and I are the only members of the team who traveled to the planet who remain unmarried. Please confirm receipt. Crip.*

Max and Larson thought it worked.

Crip wasn't sure, even after it was sent.

"Now we wait."

They kept the radio receiver active. It took three minutes to get a reply from *Starbound* that it had received the message and would pass it on.

Crip crossed his arms and tapped his foot. The longer he waited, the more the stories he told himself regarding the extensive damage to *Chrysalis* worsened. They had been hurt badly and were heading toward deep space the last he'd heard.

"Relax. It's like you expect them to be waiting with bated breath, ready to respond to a message from the team on the ground. They're probably too busy with their hot showers and Malibor food packs."

"Those things were good," Crip admitted.

"You ate Malibor food?" Glen asked.

"We did. It's the one thing they do very well, better than the Borwyn. Their field rations make Septimus go 'round."

"I would have never guessed," Glen replied.

A messaged blipped into the queue. Larson opened it. "It's from *Chrysalis*." He grinned at Crip, who leaned in to read over Larson's shoulder.

Chrysalis is repaired and back in the fight. On our way to Sairvor first, then Septimus where the Malibor shipyard will be destroyed. We will cripple their ability to counterattack.

Then we will assume orbit over Septimus to begin a strategic bombardment of the planet while delivering terms for a Malibor surrender. If need be, we'll coordinate for a diversionary attack. Most of all, we need a list of strategic targets. We can guess, but we prefer not to. Give us that list, and you'll get us that much closer to ending this war. Taurus says 'me, too.'

Crip nodded. The stories he'd told himself had been diametrically opposed to reality. They had made the repairs and were flying free once more.

"*Chrysalis* is back in the fight!" Crip called to the sky, shaking his fist in triumph.

Eleanor appeared. "Why all the shouting?"

"*Chrysalis* is on its way. Repairs are complete. Big fight coming to remove the last of the Malibor fleet. Eliminating the Malibor's ability to project power beyond Septimus will be the defining point in this war, right after the fateful day we left Hunter's moon on the trip to the inner planets. This will be a day that becomes a holiday, a memory celebrated each year, where freedom is the greatest prize of all." Crip couldn't wipe the smile from his face.

Max was equally taken. He hadn't admitted it, but he also had been concerned that *Chrysalis* couldn't be repaired and was permanently out of the fight. He was happy to be proven wrong.

"Shoot straight, you space-happy fools!" Max yelled at the sky.

"Good thing we're not on tactical watch, otherwise the enemy would already be drawing a bead on you two." Eleanor crossed her arms and made a face.

"Not if we draw a bead first. We need to prepare a message for Deena next time she makes contact. We have to get a message to her. We have to have those targets. She has the grid memorized, so she only needs to give us the coordinates."

Crip dictated the short message to be sent to Deena, but Larson wouldn't be the one sending it. That would be the western Borwyn radio crew, and they would get it to her.

Max volunteered. He'd take any chance he could to be closer to Deena, even if it was only carrying a message. Max hurried away with the scrap of paper.

Larson tapped the keys for a quick acknowledgement.

Crip stared at the radio even though he knew an answer, if there was one, wouldn't come for several minutes.

"How about that rainstorm?" he said.

"Your small talk sucks," Eleanor replied.

Larson laughed. "Sorry, your sir-nesses. I wasn't listening in."

"How's married life treating you, Larson?" Crip asked.

"I'd say wonderfully, but I seem to be on duty while the rest of the team is taking care of business, if you know what I mean."

"I fear that I do know. We'll be done here and you can be on your way. Is that Pistoria?"

Larson waved her over. A young woman, tall and lithe. "I didn't want to interfere."

Crip shook his head. "We're one team, in this fight together. You're always welcome. Learn what Larson knows so you can back him up in case he becomes incapacitated."

She frowned. "I don't think I can. We don't have anything for me to use to learn."

"She has a point," Larson added. "We can do comm equipment, but we don't have anything else. I have so many videos in my pocket right now. It is completely ridiculous, but there's no place to watch them to gain the sum total of the universe's knowledge."

Pistoria caressed Larson's shoulders.

"Is that what they are? I thought they were entertainment. Don't pull a fast one, Larson. We're not getting a computer out here to watch videos."

"Was that my sordid plan?" Larson smiled. It was not a guilty expression. Crip clapped him on the shoulder.

A short communique from *Starbound* registered. *Roger, out.*

"That's it, Commander," Larson reported.

"Shut it down, stow the gear, and enjoy your all-too-brief honeymoon," Crip said.

Larson and Pistoria broke down the equipment, secured it in the carry-bag, and took it to the sleeping bunker. They reappeared without the gear a few moments later and headed for the woods to find a private spot. They carried a blanket and single pillow.

"I can't believe you allowed the distraction of relationships in your combat team," Eleanor said.

"I can't believe you guys don't. I think it makes us stronger, even with the inevitable spats and miscues and the over-protective nature of our boys. They need something to live for, not just die for. They need something to bring out their ferocity when in a fight. On a cold and mostly dead planet, we saw what it was like with just us, the combat team facing a determined enemy."

"Farslor?"

Crip nodded. "We lost two people on that deployment, our first time facing the Malibor, but these weren't the Malibor we were brought up to fear. These were little more than cave dwellers with ugly bows and arrows wearing heavy furs. I wonder if Jaq tossed my fur out the airlock. She threatened to because it wasn't exactly the best smelling. Maybe Taurus threw away all my stuff and replaced it with hers."

"If she cared about you, she wouldn't have done that. Maybe she cleaned it to remove the stench. That's how you welcome your lover home."

Crip didn't want a contest between Taurus and Eleanor. He was on the spot, but he had a war to fight. If they played their part, then it would shorten the war. *Chrysalis* in orbit bombing the Malibor military and government installations.

"That will be glorious!" he blurted.

"Having a clean fur?"

Crip blinked as Eleanor's comment brought him back to the moment. "*Chrysalis* giving Malipride the big hairy what-for. A taste of real war is coming. I bet we're going to find that the citizens who have grown fat, dumb, and happy in the city will have no stomach for it. We'll sue for peace, on our terms. If the Malibor have one whit of intelligence, they'll take our terms."

The night bugs clicked, whistled, and chirped in the twilight at the end of a Septimus day. The first star shown through the darkening blue.

"I haven't known the Malibor to be smart when it came to

their ego. They'll try to rally the populace to put a strong defense or some such nonsense." Eleanor stepped back. "I'm going to pack it in, I have an early watch. But if anyone approaches the camp, they'll step on your lovebirds who are scattered to the high reaches."

"We can call it the yowl alert. All sexed up and nowhere to go. Newlyweds. They better get it out of their system quickly because we're going to war." He gritted his teeth and squinted into the growing night.

"You and your fixation on the war," Eleanor quipped. "What will you do when it's over?"

"Enjoy being alive. Enjoy this." Crip waved his hands to take in the trees and the sky. "Without having to be armed, with a woman on my arm."

"Will she come down here?" Eleanor wondered. "Have you asked her?"

Crip pursed his lips. "Have a good evening, Eleanor. Sleep well. I'll see you in the morning. You're making me think more than I planned, and it's giving me a headache."

Eleanor waggled her eyebrows and half-smiled before waving and heading off.

Crip hadn't asked. They never had much time to talk about everything and nothing. Self-doubt crept into his thoughts. He'd always assumed they had the same desires. Descending into the one-sided depth of despair helped no one. He could only guess how Taurus would answer. She had finally chosen him after years of deliberation.

"I'm a good catch," Crip told the departing twilight. He laughed. "I'm spewing nonsense. We have a war to fight. Everything else is a waste of time and energy."

"But it's not," Max said from the shadows.

"How long have you been there?"

"Long enough. Do you want some advice?"

"I bet you're going to give it to me regardless of whether I say yes or no." Crip waited impatiently.

"Eleanor is angling for the post-war world, one where you're in it. Stay alive until then so you can make the best choice."

Crip wanted to argue, but he was too close. He couldn't see the forest for the trees. "I'll focus on the war and make all of you miserable because of it."

"I don't doubt that. If I had any of that Malibor money, I'd bet that Taurus doesn't come down here. She's a ship girl."

"I fear you're right. All I can do is be who I am, which is going to have to be good enough."

"That's the right attitude. How about you get some sleep. Don't dwell on what's out of your control, and that is most definitely the emotions of your women."

"Woman, as in singular," Crip shot back.

Max laughed and laughed. He clapped Crip on the back hard enough to stagger him. "Not from where I'm standing. What are we going to do about the team? I think we need to give them one more day off. Let them enjoy time with their spouses."

"Their spouses are also members of the team," Crip replied. "I concur. Give them an extra day. We don't need anything tomorrow. All we can do is keep trying to make contact with Deena."

Max grimaced before composing himself. "I'd like to find out more. She's alone in the heart of the enemy's power.

Everything she does for us puts her at risk. I'm worried, Crip."

Crip instantly felt bad. His problems were trivial compared to the demons Deena was fighting.

"I'm sorry. We'll check on her when we make contact. We'll ask her for a one-to-five evaluation—risk, threat, and personal health. Five is great, one is bad. It'll give us some feeling, but the question is, do we want to ask? If she tells us she's at high risk but healthy, what do we do?"

"Tell her to get out," Max replied without hesitation.

"We need her where she is doing what she's doing. For all Borwyn. Like you said, it's not as easy as it sounds."

"I don't think I said that." Max's mood turned dark. His eyebrows plunged toward a deep scowl. With troubled thoughts following him like a storm cloud, he went straight to the sleeping quarters, where Crip knew neither of them would get much sleep.

A day off would be a welcome distraction. Play cards, maybe even a little sportsball, to take Crip's and Max's minds off their worries. They knew worrying solved nothing, but logic and emotion had taken separate paths long ago when they realized how much they cared about their people and their lives outside of a rebuilt ship and a crew raised to fight a war.

CHAPTER 10

Anticipate the difficult by managing the easy.

Jaq made one last check of the command deck. Every seat was filled.

She had to stretch to see Dolly in her seat. The thirteen-year-old seemed to be wasting away. Jaq glared at Donal. He had dark bags under his eyes, too. She wondered what they'd been working on that took their waking hours along with their sleep periods. She'd find out later.

"Give me ship-wide," she requested.

Amie Jacobs, the original who filled the comm officer position, nodded and pointed.

"All hands, this is your captain. We are leaving Farslor's shadow and going to Sairvor to check in with New Septimus. We'll add crew as needed and, hopefully, missiles. Then we're accelerating past Armanor on a high-speed run to Septimus. We're going to destroy every weapons platform, gunship, and cruiser we can find. This is a search-and-destroy mission. At the end of it, we will be the last active warship in the system. We will settle for nothing less. Be prepared for extreme maneuvers, starting as soon as all department heads report green. We'll accelerate at all-ahead standard, three gees. Everyone into your seats. Let's get back into this war."

Jaq waited until the departments reported and the lights were green. The only red on the board was for munitions. They had no missiles. That wasn't a surprise. They would make do without. They'd destroy the rest of the Malibor using their E-mags, unless New Septimus had something for them, but Jaq doubted it.

"Course locked in," Mary announced.

"Ready to accelerate." Ferd looked over his shoulder at Jaq, waiting for the final order.

She climbed into her seat and pointed at her thrust control officer. "It's been too long, Ferd. Kick it."

The engines slowly pushed Chrysalis through half a gee, then one. The ion drives continued to push the ship to three gees, where the acceleration settled.

"Engines are nominal. Teo reports no issues," Brad said. "Energy reserves are at one hundred percent."

"At three gees, how quickly will we use stored energy?" Jaq asked. With the grossly oversized Malibor power plants, they added energy faster than before. She needed to get the calculations firmly in her mind so she didn't overextend the ship, or worse, underuse their capabilities and leave them more vulnerable than necessary.

"Standby," Brad requested. He whispered into his seat's comm unit, back and forth with the chief engineer. "Two percent an hour."

"It used to be three," Jaq replied. "Nice work, Teo. Helm, bring us up to a million KPH."

"One hour at five gees followed by one hour at three gees will put us just over a million," Ferd replied.

"Roger," Jaq confirmed. "I then recommend a constant acceleration of one-point-two gees, with a comparable decel curve. What is the time to target?"

"Calculating a one-point-two-gee burn for thirty hours, before inverting the ship and decelerating for thirty hours at one-point-two gees, then three-gee decel for an hour, and a five-gee deceleration for the final hour. Is that acceptable?"

"Sixty-four hours to New Septimus, sixty of which we will have apparent gravity. I feel like we should throw a party, but we have a lot of bulkheads to install emergency overrides on. Brad, let Teo know that's the priority during accel and decel at one-point-two gees. Break out the wheels to move the gear around."

"I'll pass it on. The good news is that when we arrive at New Septimus, we should still have about ninety-five percent power in reserve. Maybe more," Brad replied.

Jaq would have given him the thumbs-up, but three gees weighed heavily on her arms because they had been too long at zero-gee and she hadn't worked out like she should have. A little mattress PT with Brad, but that didn't keep her mobility muscles strong.

"I like arriving and still having all our power at our command. Kudos to you and your team and Teo, Bec, and their teams. We have more than a chance. We have a good chance. Engineers are our key to winning this war."

"I might add our damage control teams are also a huge

contributor to keeping this ship and its crew alive. The medical team. Poor old Doc Teller is going to work himself into an early grave."

Jaq laughed. "He's already the oldest person on this ship," Jaq said with a measured pace, taking a breath between every three words as the five gees seemed heavier than usual. "Early grave. Is this acceleration right? It doesn't feel like five gees. My eyeballs are getting squashed into my brain."

"Recalculating," Ferd said.

Slade Ping shouted from his position in the sensor section. "We're double normal. I'm showing ten gees."

"Holy father of Septiman," Brad grunted.

"Standby," Ferd cut back the thrust until it showed two-and-a-half gees on his instrument panel. The crew waited, breathing easier with each passing moment. "How about now?"

"Five gees," Slade replied.

Jaq relaxed. "Thank Septiman it wasn't me. I thought I'd grown weak."

"Me, too. How long since the last time we were under acceleration? Three weeks? That's not enough to grow flaccid."

Jaq shook her head. "I'm not sure that's the right word."

The bridge crew snickered, as much in relief as at Brad.

Jaq could feel him smiling behind her, but at five gees, she couldn't turn and give him her captain's side-eye. She settled for giving him an earful later.

"Donal, was that you? Did you mess up our instrumentation?" she called.

"Might have been, ma'am. I'll take a look as soon as I'm able," Donal Fleming replied.

"Adjust accordingly, Ferd, Mary," Jaq stated. She let the gel embrace her and take the pressure off. She didn't realize how tight her muscles had been from both fighting the high gees as well as the concern about the ship. *Chrysalis* had been damaged, the worst Jaq could ever remember, but then, she had selective memories of her home, her parents, and the other originals.

She focused on her breathing while trying to relax.

Next stop in less than three days was New Septimus. The moon orbiting Sairvor, Septimus's twin planet.

"You haven't heard anything?" Deena asked, not as incredulous as she tried to sound. She expected the infiltration had been captured. She'd contact the western Borwyn and find out. She needed to know.

Lanni was coming unhinged. She didn't answer Deena's question, only sobbed uncontrollably.

"I know people inside the headquarters. I'll ask what they know." Deena knew that she'd have to keep up appearances because she didn't know anyone on the inside. She'd get better information than anything the Malibor had. Deena knew she'd have to contact the officer who'd had his eye on her since that fateful day when he rousted the boss and extorted a day's worth of revenue. He'd left them alone after that, as far as she knew. Maybe he hadn't.

"Please ask. Find out what happened to my husband."

Lanni degenerated into an inconsolable mess.

"Stay here. I'll take care of all the customers," Deena told her.

"No. I need to work," Lanni blubbered.

Deena pushed her back into the chair at the rear of the kitchen. "Once you get yourself straightened up, you can join me. Until then, I got it."

Deena took the latest orders with her and bumped through the door into the overfull restaurant. She swept through the crowd to deliver the plates, take a new order, and clean a table, carrying a too-tall stack of dishes to the automatic washer.

The boss served up drink after drink. The delay in seating was good for business. Drinks earned the profit, like he always said.

All the while, Deena glanced furtively out the window, trying to catch a glimpse of the officer. She had a feeling he was close, even though she hadn't seen him in a while.

She bet the increase in traffic was partly his doing to build a bigger cut for himself.

Deena stopped by the bar and pulled the boss aside. "Is that officer still shaking you down?"

"It's actually not much, and for what it's worth, you can move back in, if you want. Even with his cut, yours and Lanni's pay, we're making more than ever before. There's something to surrounding yourself with good people."

Deena wanted to punch him for not telling her about the room earlier, but she wasn't sure she could leave Lanni to herself. Not while she was trying to figure out what had happened to her husband.

But if she moved back to the bar, she would have unrestricted access to the radio. It would broaden the window where she could communicate with her team. Maybe she could even talk with Max.

She didn't have to convince herself. Deena was happier here than having to walk to Lanni's apartment. The bar was secure with locking doors between the outside and her, plus she'd already planned ways to defend the upstairs from intruders. She had "weapons" pre-staged.

"I'll move back in soonest, although Lanni shouldn't be alone. I'll talk with her mother. She'll need to keep her company until her husband returns."

The boss shook his head. He didn't care about Lanni's husband. Military took risks. The spouses had to accept that, no matter how young they were or if they had a family. The military paid the survivors for those lost during the war.

Didn't they?

No one was sure. Losses were few nowadays since the Malibor weren't executing a full campaign. They only recently ramped up their efforts. No one except Deena knew why.

The Borwyn had returned and were destroying the Malibor fleet. The Malibor on Septimus thought it had been their brethren on Sairvor. They sent an invasion force to suppress the uprising. They found *Chrysalis* waiting, and none of those Malibor returned home. Over a thousand dead. All the ships were destroyed except for the one renamed *Cornucopia*, but its crew had died in a subsequent Malibor attack.

Deena wished she could listen to the conversations at the

big table where the Malibor leadership argued about the war, deployed troops, and detailed the building of warships. Were they panicking? Deena hoped so.

The crowd slowed and then drifted away in the early afternoon, giving Deena a respite. Lanni hadn't joined her. When Deena went into the kitchen, she found the chair empty. Deena looked to the cook for an answer.

"She left an hour ago." He nodded toward the back door. His pupils were big, seemingly immune to the rigors of light.

"Are you stoned?"

"Not as far as you know. Please don't hit me!" He cowered.

Deena shook her head and returned out front to tell the boss she was leaving to get her stuff.

"Did you even look for another place?" he asked.

She shook her head. "They all wanted one year in advance or things I wasn't willing to do to get the place. There are a lot of scumbags out there, Boss man. I'm glad you're not one of them."

He didn't react. He waved her away. "Try to be back before the dinner rush."

"Shouldn't take more than an hour." With her hood up and head down, she hurried out and bolted across the street. She waited a block before looking behind her to see if she was followed, but she didn't find anyone being coy.

Deena continued to the apartment, running up the stairs to the third floor. She found the door unlocked. She crouched as she entered, but found Lannie, her mother, and the baby together on the couch.

"The boss said I was cleared to move back in to the spare

bedroom at the bar," Deena said after a few moments of standing there uncomfortably.

Lannie nodded.

Deena took a knee next to Lanni's mother. "I think you should stay here until we can find out what happened to Moran. I hope to have news soon."

"How would you find out before her?" Lanni's mother snapped.

"The military is never forthcoming with information, not via official channels. I have other contacts within the headquarters who I'll ply, not with favors but with the thought of future favors. I'm not prostituting myself for anyone, understand that, but I have ways of getting information from men in high places."

She meant the Borwyn men, Crip and Max. She had no intention of giving an impression that favors could be had to any of the Malibor. She'd talk with the officer, but in the most antiseptic way.

If she could find him.

She gathered her sparse things, which had grown during her short stay with Lanni. Gifts and shopping. Their day off was dangerous in an odd way.

Hefting the bag over her shoulder, Deena headed for the door.

"I'll let you know as soon as I hear something," Deena promised. She left before they could lament further. Deena wanted Lanni to snap out of it rather than sink into a dark hole, but she didn't know what to do.

Deena reached the bottom of the stairs, where she found the officer waiting for her.

"So, that's where you stayed. Are you going somewhere?"

"Moving back in to my cupboard. Do I have you to thank for that?" Deena stayed beyond arm's reach. She didn't want to get too close.

"In a way. You have your boss to thank for that. He's covering your fee."

Deena's blood turned to ice. He was making no secret of his scheme. There was no fee for staying in the bar. Why should anyone have to pay rent to stay in the place they own?

But they did. All of them. They paid a cut to the government or to some official who shielded them from the government.

"What guarantee do we have that someone else won't come knocking with their hand out?"

He feigned distress. "Do you think I'd do that to you?"

"No. I think your replacement would do that to us. Don't they move you guys around to keep you from shaking too many people down, denying the higher-ups their cut?"

He lunged for her and snarled, "You won't ever say those words again. Do you hear me?"

"I'm sorry." Deena shrugged out of his hand with as much anger as he'd shown. "What words? Shakedown, taking a cut? What are the right words that I can tell an administrator?"

"You'll never get that chance. Who would believe a bar maid? They'll think you're a prostitute and that you're hooking out of the bar. I think you're doing that. I'll include that in the next visit. I'm off at seven. I'll see you then."

"You'll get as much as anyone else, which is nothing. I don't hook. Anyone makes a grab for me, they'll get their fingers broken. That includes you. Don't try to touch me. We'll go to the administrators together and discuss why you got your fingers broken, black eyes, and a split lip."

"Threats? I should probably take you in right now before you can dig yourself a deeper hole. I'll see you tonight." He backed away with a lurid grin.

Deena shivered with the thought that she'd have to see him again. The next time, there would be a fight she couldn't cover up.

Or could she? She'd already told the boss. He could stay late and hide. Together...

She tried to put that thought out of her mind, but abject violence seemed to be her only solution. She needed to hear Max's voice for him to reassure her that it was worth the risk. That they'd come for her.

Of course Max would come for her, even though it would cost him his life.

The walk back was longer than it should have been. Her bag was heavy, but the dark cloud of the officer and the missing husband weighed much greater. She made it into the restaurant before the next round of customers showed up.

Deena appreciated the relief she felt once inside. It had become a safe place.

The boss appeared out of the back. "Good. You're back."

"I ran into your friend," she said in a low voice. She motioned for him to follow her up the stairs.

After she dumped her bag on the small bed, she faced him. The boss stood with his arms crossed, expecting a tirade.

"We're probably going to have to kill him," she said matter-of-factly.

"I figured you'd say something like that. Maybe you can just give him what he wants."

"We'll never be done with him. He only wants power over us. The more we give him, the more he'll take, until everything we are, everything we have is taken from us. And then he'll do it to somebody else. It stops now."

"I'd like to argue with you, but he's already increased his percentage, and I use the term loosely. He knows exactly how many people come here and just takes what he can while leaving us enough to order the next day's food. I'm in. What's our plan?"

Deena deflated. "I thought you'd argue more."

"You're a bad influence. I should probably not be contemplating murder, but the whole system is ganked. I just want to provide good food and drink to hungry and thirsty people. No one gets sick in my restaurant. And they come back time after time. I deserve to be paid for that. I deserve to be able to pay you and Lanni and what's-his-face, our cook, a fair wage for making this place what it is. I won't let this guy take that away from us. Not him or the next guy either. They can get in a nice, orderly line and kiss my ass."

Deena laughed. She slapped him on the arm. "We have some work to do before we can close up and end our day strong. The hardest part will be making sure he didn't bring someone to provide oversight to keep us from doing what we're about to do."

"Then we take them out, too. Do you have a weapon?"

"We have a kitchen full of them. And it seems, we have a new sausage grinder, too. Why would you have bought that?"

The boss shrugged. "Maybe I expected this."

CHAPTER 11

An evil man will burn his empire to the ground to rule over the ashes rather than let someone else have it.

Deena closed and locked the door, like she always did. She finished mopping the floor and put the mop away.

The light tap on the door signaled the arrival of her expected visitor. She hung her apron up and walked to the front.

She crossed her arms and glared at the man. He tapped again and pointed toward the handle.

Deena moved closer and mouthed the words, "Not here." She hooked her finger and waved to the side. "Go around back."

She watched him intently to see if he looked for someone else, but he ducked his head going through the light from the streetlamp and dipped around the corner.

Deena hurried into the kitchen. She nodded, and the boss

unlocked the door and stepped back. Deena crossed her arms and leaned against the counter.

The officer slowly opened the door, then flung it wide.

"Really?" Deena deadpanned. "Come on, let's get this over with."

"Don't be in a hurry. Maybe you can make me a sandwich first. Yes. I'd like a sandwich." He stood taller as he stepped through the door and shut it behind him.

The scrape of a foot alerted him. He turned and caught the boss before he could hammer him in the head with a meat mallet.

Deena vaulted across a counter, hit the floor, and jumped to deliver a knee strike into the middle of the man's back. Her momentum carried both of them into the boss. All three went down.

A flurry of hands played out between the two men while Deena stuffed her arm under the officer's throat and pulled it with her other hand into her body while straddling the writhing bodies.

The officer pulled at Deena's smaller arms, but that left the boss to punch him in the face. The boss was a big man, well out of shape but with ham hocks for fists. The second blow drove the officer unconscious. Deena continued to add pressure until she was sure he was no longer breathing. She waddled backward, dragging the officer off the boss.

"That went about as well as could be expected," Deena said. She checked his pulse. He didn't have one.

"Pull the curtains," the boss said.

Deena yanked the shade over the serving window. When she turned back, the boss had the officer in his arms and lumbered toward the prep counter. He unceremoniously dropped the body and turned on the water to feed the trough around the cutting table.

"We're not going to feed that to anyone, are we?" Deena asked.

"Nah. It'll go in the back of the freezer with an old date. In case we get inspected by someone legitimate, the government will watch us throw it away. And if they aren't legitimate, we'll serve it to them when they want food. By the way, you were clinically efficient back there. How'd you learn that stuff, and how can you be so matter-of-fact about it?"

"Come on now, big guy. Don't ask questions where you don't want to know the answers."

"I wouldn't have asked if I didn't want to know the answer, but fair enough. What if you're a plant from the government to root out corruption? To maintain your cover, you put them out of your misery until the next one comes along."

"Don't think too hard about it. You might hurt yourself." She stepped away from the processing table, where the boss was nonplussed in his work. "I'll keep a watch out." She left the kitchen, turned off the lights in the dining area, and watched outside for anyone loitering or looking.

The high-pitched whine from sausage grinder signaled the next step in removing evidence of the intruder.

"I told you not to cross me," Deena mumbled.

"One-point-two gees standard acceleration," Ferd confirmed.

"Course is green. No obstructions. No identifiable gravity waves," Mary added.

Jaq was out of her seat and standing before they finished their reports. "Slade?"

"Space is clear," the sensor chief reported.

Donal didn't wait to be called. "Dolly and I are digging in. We'll have that little acceleration glitch fixed before you can say 'bundle up, it's cold in here'."

Jaq contemplated the original for a moment. She wouldn't let him get under her skin. He winked at her.

She looked at the deck, shaking her head at the absurdity of the originals.

Brad shrugged.

They'd seen their world taken over. They'd lived fifty years as outcasts and renegades, hiding from the greater enemy.

Now, they saw hope that the loss could be undone, and it freed their souls.

She leaned close to Brad and whispered, "Flaccid?"

"I couldn't remember the right word. 'Limp' seemed beneath me. How was I supposed to know they knew what it meant?"

"Because they're a well-educated crew with too much time on their hands!" Jaq fired back. She glanced around the bridge to find everyone watching her. "He meant to say lose body strength, not after three weeks."

"Sure," Alby replied. "Permission to join the engineering teams working on the emergency bulkheads."

Jaq nodded toward the corridor.

Alby acknowledged and casually walked off the bridge.

Taurus moved into the battle commander's position to continue cycling the weapons systems and ensure their functionality and responsiveness. "Weapons are nominal. Powering down E-mags. Idling defensive systems."

"Roger." Jaq leaned against her chair while Brad stood nearby. Both reveled in the apparent gravity of the steady acceleration. "Keep your eye on the bridge. I'm going to Engineering."

Brad threw his hands up. "My progeny," he started. "I'll go with you." He beamed his best smile.

"Taurus, you have the bridge," Jaq said in a quick recovery. They headed for the corridor and found themselves waiting for the elevator that was in high demand as crewmembers transited up and down. No free flight for the next sixty hours.

"We better check on the landers while we're down there, too. We'll need one to get to New Septimus."

"We can take my ship," Brad offered.

"But if we're to bring any cargo back, we'll need more lift capacity."

"We have three fully functional landers."

"I thought we had six remaining." Jaq's eyebrows knit in confusion.

"We had to help ourselves to give us three functional remote landers to use as space bombs."

"Is that what we called them?" Jaq shook her head. The originals took very little seriously and nothing too seriously. Jaq didn't know when to clamp down. They had farther to go before they could relax, but she didn't want to stifle their morale and let it go.

"I may have to fight Donal," Brad said casually.

"What for?"

"Your affections." Brad tipped his head back and looked down his nose at her.

"I will airlock both of you and anyone else who wants to fight over my affections!"

Someone cleared their throat. The elevator had arrived and the doors stood open.

Jaq smiled. "They're lunatics," she said as she boarded.

No one was willing to argue the point, least of all Brad. The elevator stopped at nearly every deck on the way to the aft end of the ship. People got off. People got on. It took much longer than when the ship was at zero-gee.

When they finally reached the engineering level, they were the last ones off. Brad continued to chuckle.

"You think that's funny, don't you?" Jaq quipped.

"She's the master of the ship as well as the obvious," Brad replied.

Jaq wasn't ready to lighten up, but she was close.

They found Teo tinkering with a side panel.

"Status!" Brad bellowed.

"Operational, with more where that came from. And keep your voice down. These instruments are finely calibrated."

"What does my voice have to do with your instruments?" Brad wondered.

"You bug me when you yell, and I'm using the instruments. The associative property teaches us that the instruments will then not be used optimally."

Brad raised his hands in surrender.

"Good work with those power plants. You and Bec," Jaq said. "You came through again. Saved us again. And set us up to survive the next attack, too. At this point, survivability is our main issue."

"Then we'd fly to the farthest reaches of the system and not engage the Malibor at all," Brad countered. "I suggest our main issue remains defeating the Malibor."

Jaq punched him in the arm but lightly. With the apparent gravity, he didn't sway from the blow. He remained firmly on the deck.

"I agree," Teo replied. "We're doing our best to make sure *Chrysalis* keeps flying with full maneuverability. The only limitation is to turn Cargo Bay Four away from an attack. The outer doors are open. Any projectiles would cause a great deal of damage, possibly leading to an explosion of the nuclear variety. In the black-and-white world of good and bad, that would be very bad."

"I hear you," Jaq said. "The plan is to engage nose on, provide the smallest target possible while hitting them with everything we have."

Teo waved and returned to her work.

Jaq and Brad left Engineering and took the ladder down to the lowest level, where the landers were located.

"A couple landers still have explosives on board."

"We have unstable bombs on the ship?" Jaq looked at Brad.

He shook his head. "They're not unstable, but the landers are unusable unless we need to drop a bomb in someone's way. I recommend we keep the two in reserve, ready to deliver the goods. The other one that's down was cannibalized for parts. Six total landers in their launch tubes, five flyable, three usable for cargo or passengers."

The numbers aligned with what she had previously thought. They'd lost landers, having started with ten.

"Will we survive the attrition?" Jaq asked.

"We're in good shape," Brad answered. "We have a lot of volunteers on New Septimus. We're going to have to turn some away. We'll get to pick and choose, make sure we have the best of the best on board."

"I hope the best of the best includes missiles," Jaq said hopefully. They crawled through the three operational landers that would be used for cargo and personnel. They found no issues that caused them any concern.

"I told you we were in good shape."

"Let's check on those emergency bulkheads. You take port side and I'll take starboard."

Brad nodded and headed outboard. The ship was cylindrical, which meant port and starboard were relative directions, but they had been labeled on the bulkheads at one point. Most of the designations were still visible, but many had been scraped off with the structural repairs following the damage received during Malibor strikes. Too many weld repairs.

Only two sections had been damaged that affected the main structure, and those had been ratcheted back together and then welded, complete with an overlaying strap. It had held together well enough, and that was verified after every engagement. The first stop of the damage control team was to the fifth deck to ensure the repair wasn't coming undone.

The pedestrian work of upgrading the emergency bulkheads would go slowly. There were too many to get them all. They'd selected certain decks with the most people, which meant the highest risk of losing them if a bulkhead slammed into place and stayed there. They prepositioned supplies to use to block leaks throughout the outer sections. *Cornucopia* provided them with extra metal supplies that they didn't have access to before.

Jaq visited two work sites where crew were installing a manual release on both sides of an emergency bulkhead. She didn't want to interrupt and settled for thanking them for doing the work.

She returned to the bridge without telling Brad, only to find him already there.

"I was going to be in their way," he admitted.

Jaq replied, "Me, too. They're doing what they're supposed to be doing and don't need us looming over their shoulders."

"Hit the gym?" Brad suggested.

"You go. I'll see you in two hours and then I'll take my turn. I have some things I want to check first."

Brad didn't argue. He wanted to get some high-gee work in. New Septimus was only seventy percent Septimus normal. One-point-two was a challenge and made him feel young again. He didn't like zero-gee. That made him feel helpless.

Jaq was the opposite.

"Weapons loadout, Taurus. How long can we sustain fire and how long can we maintain a max rate?" Jaq asked from where she stood near the front screen. She studied every number on the status displays, digging deeper than just the colors.

Brad eased off the bridge. He knew the numbers, too, but she was two steps ahead, calculating usage rates to the millisecond. She tolerated no surprises. The fight was coming, and Jaq was going to be ready.

CHAPTER 12

The aim of the wise is not to secure pleasure, but to avoid pain.

The boss had turned the body into five-pound packs of meat that included ground-up gristle and bone. The rest of the cleanings had been burned in the oven, scraped out, and reburned. It had taken three hours to do the work and clean up the kitchen, getting it ready for the next day.

The boss left after a simple good-bye. Deena locked up after him.

She was exhausted but had a call to make.

Deena locked herself in the bathroom and used a wire from the lower half of the curtain, meant to hold it down. She fished into the darkness of the overhead until she hooked her hidden package. She dragged it to the edge and brought it down. It was quick work to bring it online.

She sent the code to request voice.

It was five minutes before it was approved. She keyed the

microphone. "Request status of infil squad." She keyed off after the quick words.

Max's voice answered her. "Two captured, ten killed. Are you okay?"

"I'm fine. In a good place. What are the names of the prisoners?"

There was another delay.

"Raftal and Moran."

The wave of relief threatened to overwhelm her. She needed to share the news with Lanni, but it would have to wait. She wasn't going out at this time of night.

"Request recce. Standby to copy," Max continued.

"Alpha one, three, and four. Bravo three and five. Charlie six through ten. Need info soonest."

Deena had memorized a grid of potential targets. The spaceport, two different sets of targets, and the headquarters for space operations. She knew what that meant. More relief. It meant that the gunship would be refueled and rearmed. The combat team was going to develop an attack profile to deliver the greatest damage to the Malibor, maybe even eliminate their ability to conduct operations in space. That meant *Chrysalis* was coming.

She pumped her fist. The officer was gone. Lanni's husband was alive. And the Borwyn were on their way, not only to take over Septimus but to free the Malibor from their own corrupt leadership.

"One week, no longer," she transmitted. "I love you. Out."

She bundled the radio up and stuffed it back in the overhead. She took a quick shower, then snuck downstairs to look out the front windows, keeping to the shadows so no one would see her. She sat on the steps and watched the minimal activity in front of the restaurant. She held her hand out and watched it shake.

Deena tiptoed down the stairs and went behind the bar, where she poured herself a shot from the boss's private whisky stash. It burned on the way down, but if she ever needed a drink, it was now. She poured herself a second drink and sipped at that from her seat on the floor behind the bar. She looked up to see a box attached under an inside shelf. It had a lock that she easily picked with two metal slivers.

Inside, she found a blaster with two packs of reloads. Why hadn't the boss had this as a backup? It would have given her peace of mind in the fight with the officer, who had been unarmed. That had come as a surprise. He was clean with a simple identification card, a badge, and no money.

The last part made the boss angry since he had hoped to recover some of the money he'd handed over. He settled for realizing he wouldn't be handing over any more to the man.

Deena took the blaster and reloads, then thought better of it. She wiped down the weapon and put it back, locking it up. She knew where it was if she needed it. It was better that she not be found with it. Eventually, someone would realize the scumbag officer was missing. Whether they looked for him or not, that was the question. Deena guessed not, figuring he had no friends in his outfit. They'd accept that he was gone and promote someone into his billet.

It would be a shame to die with no friends. That wasn't Deena's problem. She smiled at the thought of the quality of her Borwyn friends. She peeked over the top of the bar. Still nothing. She let out a long, slow breath and then crept around the bar and back up the stairs. The whiskey continued to burn inside her. Deena embraced the feeling as she locked herself inside her closet-sized bedroom.

Max stared at the radio. He wore his uniform bottom and his jacket without a shirt underneath. He'd been called out of his rack when Deena's signal arrived. Max could do nothing but think about the cryptic message.

"Why did she want to know the names of the survivors?" Max asked aloud.

"I can't fathom," Crip said as he approached. "It's good to hear that she called. Did you give her the recce package?"

"All of it, yes," Max confirmed. "She said she'll have the info in a week."

"That's good. Why are you looking so glum?"

"Why did she want the survivor's names?"

"Maybe the person who told her about the squad coming knew them and had a personal interest," Crip guessed.

"But she can't share what we told her, can she? Wouldn't that expose her as a Borwyn spy?"

Crip tried to be nonchalant, but it wouldn't work with Max. "Yeah. It's high-risk. She must have her reasons, and there's no doubt they're good reasons. You trust her, don't you?"

"I do. Sometimes it's hard with her in harm's way. She's risking herself for all of us." Max sighed before he brightened a little. "The Malibor don't have a chance when we know they're coming."

"Good intel, my man. Never underestimate the power of good intel." Crip pulled Max to his feet. "Come on, back to the rack with you. Tomorrow's a new day. Don't tell yourself any ugly stories. Deena's a hero. Never doubt that."

Max smiled weakly. "It's hard being apart. Can't we win this war already and be done with it?"

Crip laughed. "If it were only that easy, I'd be all in."

The group moved quickly, counting on the horses to carry them and all their equipment. Tram, Kelvis, Evelyn, and Sophia had their own horses while their escorts drove them like a baggage train. The gunship crew rode in the middle of the line, not free to let their horses run. It was better that way. None of the crew were experienced riders. At least they knew their limitations.

"We'll be there before dawn," Corporal Tenaris advised.

They rode for another hour before the corporal called a halt.

"Good. I could use a break," Tram complained. He rubbed his backside, as did the others with their own.

Kelvis spat. "I'm too old for this. To think I'm going to have to climb back on that old nag pains me deeper than you can imagine."

"We're here," Tenaris told them, pointing at the ship's silhouette through the canopy of branches and leaves.

"Hey!" Tram cheered softly. He lowered his voice further. "Are we alone?"

"As far as we could tell. We saw no one," Tenaris replied.

Tram wasn't going to second-guess the professionals. "We thank you for the ride. We'll take our things and get the ship out of here. I wouldn't be right here when we launch. There may be a little debris from the engine exhaust."

"We'll be out of this area by the time you fly out of here, don't worry. But we'll be watching to make sure there aren't any Malibor saboteurs or snipers in the area."

Tram glanced wildly around. "You think there might be a Malibor sniper?"

"It's what I would do if I couldn't get into the ship. It'd be easy to pick you guys off one by one as you climb the ladder. But don't think about that. I'm probably wrong. Don't sweat it, spaceman."

"What?" Tram looked to Kelvis for support.

Evelyn threw her hands up. "You have to toughen up, Tram. Let's go. It's cold out here."

They gathered their things. With great trepidation, Tram took a halting step.

"You're killing me, Tram. I could grow old before we get there." Kelvis was already old, but he moved in front of the group and hurried up the slope before them. Evelyn elbowed him on her way past while Sophia grabbed his arm.

"I don't want to die, either. There's too much life ahead of us."

"Thank you," Tram told his wife. "But they're right. We have to show courage. If we're successful, we free all the Borwyn."

"Exactly," Kelvis called over his shoulder. His courage turned into caution when he reached the plateau. He crouched and zigzagged toward the ship.

Tram ran straight for the ship, counting on speed to foil any interlopers. He reached the craft and scurried up the ladder, slapping his hand on the access panel and praying to Septiman that the outer hatch would open quickly. He tensed so much while waiting for it that when it popped open, he had a hard time prying his fingers off the ladder to reach over the threshold and climb inside.

He rolled inside and lie there, panting as if he'd fought a great battle, which he had, but it was with his own courage. He smiled and relaxed.

Sophia appeared in the hatch and climbed inside. She stood there, taking a moment to refamiliarize herself with the ship. They'd flown the ship from the east to the west, but they'd been piled in like firewood.

Tram pulled her away from the opening. "Let's get the power on and get this beast ready to fly." He led the way inside, across the corridor to the command center. He felt his way into the captain's seat. With a couple taps of the keys, the lights came on. The outer hatch thunked shut, and Kelvis and Evelyn appeared.

"On my way to Engineering," Kelvis stated and headed down the ladder. Evelyn followed him.

"Running through the power-up sequence," Tram said. He followed the checklist they'd created. They took ten minutes to get through the list.

The system hummed with the promise of more power. "Prepare to take off. Belt yourselves in." Tram tapped the controls. He input the coordinates of the landing pad behind the mountain where the extra fuel was stored. He'd fly a low and fast route to avoid detection by the Malibor. The only problem was that flight profile burned more fuel, a precious commodity.

The system showed green.

"We're out of here!"

The ship climbed slowly at first, but it quickly picked up speed. It rotated horizontal and screamed over the treetops.

Tram stared at the fuel usage.

It was burning down too quickly. He thought they'd had enough but was starting to doubt his earlier estimate. Over halfway to the destination and they'd burned over half their remaining fuel. The power plant would run out of energy before the ship ran out of distance it needed to fly.

Tram changed the flight profile. He angled the ship upward, lofting it toward the target landing grid.

It reached an apex of three thousand meters before he throttled back the engines. The ship glided over the top and immediately started to descend.

"This thing glides like a rock," Tram groused. "I hope it has more juice after it hits zero."

"That makes no sense," Kelvis called cheerily from the engine room.

"At least one of us is happy about it," Tram grumbled. "Thanks for not making me feel like a coward."

"That's my job, but I don't want you to feel so brave that you take unnecessary risks. I know how men can be when they're trying to impress their woman."

Tram wanted to reply, but he needed to concentrate. It

was going to be close. He tapped the throttle to add energy, which increased lift. He added a little, dropped a little, then added a little.

The ship rose and fell with each cycling.

The gunship raced around the mountain. Tram kept it close to the slope to shorten the distance they had to fly. He cut through a rockslide area, but they were flying fast, and the gunship's maneuverability was limited.

He added energy. The gauge dropped toward zero.

"Come on!" Tram shouted at the controls. "Hang on!"

The landing pad came into view, but it wasn't concrete. It was little more than a square carved out of the surrounding trees and rocks. Tram tapped the attitude control thruster to spin the ship around. It dropped with the loss of the little lift it did have.

Tram waited.

The ship accelerated toward the ground.

He tapped the engines to bring up the power all the way. The fuel gauge dropped to zero. The engines howled for one more second before cutting out.

The ship oriented itself using thrusters as it hit the ground. The benefit of a landing pad that wasn't solid was that it had a little give. It was all *Matador* needed to settle.

Tram held his breath, waiting for the ship to come apart or fall over, but it did neither. It stayed right where it was, firmly planted in the soil.

"How are you doing down there?" Tram called.

"I'm not sure my butthole will ever unpucker from that landing," Kelvis replied.

"He's fine," Evelyn translated. "We're fine."

"Sophia?" Tram asked with a smile.

She looked shocked but aware. "Yes, no more flights on *Matador*," she managed to say.

The systems cycled down, leaving the emergency lighting on. "Time to leave. Grab your trash." Tram hauled his bag to his shoulder and guided Sophia to the airlock. They opened the outer hatch and climbed out, crawled down the ladder, and happily stood on the ground.

Kelvis secured the outer hatch after himself. He followed Evelyn. They hugged like an old, married couple, dispensing with the extracurriculars while Tram and Sophia did plenty of grabbing.

"Stay where you are," a voice ordered from the trees.

"You should have been expecting us," Tram shouted back. "Who else is going to crash land a stolen Malibor gunship?"

Two soldiers moved out of the brush, weapons raised and aimed.

Tram raised his hands obediently. The others followed his lead. "Please don't shoot. We're newlyweds."

The soldiers approaching them laughed. "There are a lot of reasons why we would shoot you, and that's probably number one on the list." The two shouldered their weapons.

"I'm G'Kar and this is Londo. You're right. We've been expecting you, but with less of a flourish. Did you damage the ship?"

Tram put his hands down. "What do you mean did I damage the ship?" Tram glared at the man and pointed at the sky. "That was the best flying I've ever done!"

Sophia hugged his arm.

He looked at her. "It was," he added.

She smiled at him, but it didn't make him feel better.

Evelyn stepped forward. "It was an incredible job to get us here in one piece. I'm Evelyn, Sophia, Tram's the pilot, and Kelvis is the engineer. We brought the ship to refuel and rearm, to have it ready when the next phase of the mission to retake Septimus in underway. This ship is going to punch a hole in their ability to fight back."

"Retake Septimus from the Malibor? We didn't hear anything about that, only that the Borwyn had returned from hiding in space."

Tram smiled when he tried to put himself into the shoes of these two soldiers out here with limited information and no hope.

"*Chrysalis* was heavily damaged. It took fifty years to get it operational in a way that it could return. I was born on that ship and lived my whole life out there." He pointed straight up without looking. The soldiers followed his finger toward the stars. "Kelvis escaped from the space station and has been living in a secret location called New Septimus. Our partners are from the eastern Borwyn. We crossed through there on the way here. *Chrysalis* was heavily damaged once again in the current fight against the Malibor, but they've come through it in weeks, not decades. Have you heard that the Malibor fleet is almost completely destroyed?"

"That seems like a stretch. If that were the case, why are we still out here, living inside a mountain?"

"Because the Malibor have the numbers. They live in Pridal, which they now call Malipride."

"We know that," Londo said. "But why are they still here if you've destroyed their fleet?"

Tram looked at Evelyn, who shrugged at the defiance of logic.

"Because they can't escape the planet. We're not going to kick them off the planet. We don't have the numbers for that. We're only going to show them that their fight with the Borwyn is over and that they're no longer in charge. The Malibor military will be wiped from existence. That's where this baby comes in." Tram pointed at the ship.

"We have fuel," G'Kar stated. "We better get you inside to meet with the council of elders."

G'Kar showed them the way. He opened the armored outer door from which no light escaped. The yellowish pale from within barely gave them enough light to see by.

Tram held his hand out in front of him as he stepped cautiously through a series of twists and turns. Small windows looked into the space from both sides of the cave tunnel, while other openings in the roof suggested the defense was multi-faceted. The entrance would fill with something toxic and shut down before the Malibor could exploit the opening.

They reached the end of the defensive part of the tunnel, where they ran into a window cut through the rock. A clerk was waiting there.

"We've been expecting you," the young woman said. "Please follow me."

She walked down a widening and brightening corridor. The rock walls had been covered with plaster and painted, making it look like the interior of a building or even a ship without the rivets.

Far ahead, the corridor let out into a space where buildings and open areas dominated. The glimpse they had promised something extensive. Tram pointed it out to the others, who moved beside him to lean around their guide for a better look.

She motioned toward a doorway. "In here, please."

Tram mumbled his disappointment. Their escort looked down her nose at him. "You'll get a complete tour later, but it's getting late. We don't want to keep the council up any longer than necessary. They are *elders*, after all."

"I've known so few old people—actually, almost none," Tram said. "My parents died when I was young, just like most of our parents, because of what they suffered between when the ship was broken and when the reactor leaks were repaired. They paid that price with their lives. It took some longer than others, but in the end, they all paid."

It was the escort's turn to apologize. "I'm sorry. It's easy to see things through our eyes and not yours. This way. I'll wait and take you to the city when you're finished."

"That's very kind," Evelyn interjected and gave the young woman a hug. The four entered the office area while their escort remained in the corridor.

An older woman met them. "I was told you were coming. You should have been here sooner."

Tram started to protest, but Evelyn stopped him and shook her head.

He nodded in understanding. Sometimes it was better

not to fight momentum when gentle nudges over time would eventually change the course.

They walked into the next chamber, where they found three white-haired and wrinkle-skinned individuals. One of them had their eyes closed and appeared to be asleep. The new escort announced the gunship crew's arrival. She went behind the table to wake the sleeping elder, who protested the late hour.

"Welcome to New Pridal. We hear you've brought us a prize?" the man wearing the uniform at the head of the table said.

"In the war against the Malibor, we captured this ship and resurrected it from cold storage where we found it in orbit around Farslor."

"It must be destroyed at once!" The sleeping woman half came out of her seat with her energetic declaration. She flopped back down, spent.

"We have discussed your gunship at great length, and we have voted that we will not destroy the gunship. Your Commander Castle has been persuasive about the ability of the spacefaring Borwyn to return us to power. You are they, are you not?" the old man at the head of the table asked.

Tram bowed. "We appreciate the time you give us and will keep it brief. Yes. We are the Borwyn from space. We have returned to reclaim Septimus as our home. We have destroyed the majority of the Malibor fleet. The last remaining ships are barely spaceworthy. Captain Jaqueline Hunter and *Chrysalis* will finish them in due course. The last and most significant part in this war is destroying the enemy's will to fight. That's where the gunship comes in. If we can remove the decision makers in the city they call Malipride, then we will be in a position to sue for peace. They will have no choice but to acquiesce."

"No choice?" the third member of the council scoffed. "The Malibor always have a choice. They'll fight each other if no other enemy appears. By fighting them, we give them a target to unite against. I say we use the gunship for defensive purposes and only if the Malibor appear near New Pridal."

The old man spoke, "In this, we remain undecided. We will allow the refueling of the gunship. We will need you to fly it for us, of course, in whatever way we determine it will be used. I think that's all for now." He looked to his compatriots on the council. They pushed away from the table without further acknowledgement. They each had a walker to help them move.

"Excuse me," Kelvis said loudly enough to draw their attention away from leaving. "I was born on the Borwyn space station, seventy-three years ago. I am of your generation, and I'm embarrassed by how complacent you've become. I, too, had grown weary and given up until these good people arrived with the greatest warship the Armanor system has ever seen. I joined their crew as an engineer as quickly as I could. I've seen the captain, thirty years my junior, stand up to the Malibor aggression and shove it down their throats. You don't understand at all. We're not joining you. You're joining us."

The escort moved between the table and Tram's party. "There's the door. Please take care in closing it quietly on your way out. I believe Janeece is waiting for you in the outer corridor."

The elders hesitated for a few moments, but they ended up turning their backs and fleeing the chamber as quickly as their old legs would propel them.

Tram wanted to argue. He had no intention of handing *Matador* to the council, but he needed it refueled and just as importantly, he needed projectiles for the railguns. He'd ask their escort when they were outside. Tram was glad Kelvis had stood up to the council.

Evelyn watched Tram closely, while Sophia was silent between the two. She was much younger and wasn't sure what was best to do.

Once in the corridor, Evelyn put a finger to her lips.

Kelvis ignored her. "I apologize for everyone my age who comes across as old and decrepit."

"You did great, my friend. We'll do what we need to do," Tram promised.

"You've addressed the council?" Janeece asked.

"It was short and sweet. They looked like they were late for bed and acted just as grumpy."

Janeece looked around before speaking quietly. "They probably won't remember that you appeared before them." She snickered softly.

"They make the decisions for New Pridal?" Tram wondered.

She shook her head. "There are elected officials who make the decisions when it comes to New Pridal, but the oldsters are still in charge of our defense."

Tram didn't understand and had no need to argue with Janeece about it. She seemed unamused by their role, but they kept them engaged in a certain way. Their authority was derived from the healthy souls who carried out their orders. Tram kicked himself for thinking about overruling the council.

That was something the Malibor would do. He'd have to let Jaq know that she might not have support from the locals. That would be the worst case, but under no circumstances would he hand over *Matador* to the council of elders.

CHAPTER 13

Removing toxic people is the first step in fixing the world.

Deena couldn't sleep. When morning came, she was a sunken-eyed wreck. She took a long shower, hoping the hot water would lessen the tension that turned her neck and shoulders into a solid plank. By the time she turned the water off, she was a well-steamed, rigid wreck.

She took deep breaths to drive oxygen to her sore, tired muscles.

What bothered her but shouldn't have was how she'd killed the officer. She felt remorse because she hadn't killed anyone with her bare hands before. *But I'm a soldier,* she told herself. *A former fleet officer.*

It wasn't a convincing argument.

She dressed and headed downstairs, where she fixed herself a large cup of coffee. The street outside showed the usual activity, people going about their business, oblivious to what had happened the previous night less than a stone's throw away.

"Is it that simple?" she asked the emptiness around her. The hot coffee went down well, like a soothing elixir. Deena hugged the cup with both hands. She worked through it and then made a second cup. "It's history. Bury those memories and take them to my grave."

She'd talk with Max about it when she could, but it would make no difference. What's done was done. It had to be done.

It was the cost of thinking Deena was property to be bartered. And that the restaurant was a source of income without doing any of the work.

She bolstered her emotions with thoughts of the crimes and the punishment. He paid the price for his bad decisions and bad actions. It was war but at a personal, individual level.

The Borwyn were coming to liberate their people, but more than that, they were coming to liberate the common Malibor from the likes of that officer.

"You got what you had coming to you," Deena said with stiffened resolve. She drank half the cup and busied herself with getting ready for the day's customers. She walked into the kitchen and froze the second she made it through the door.

The memories of the boss processing the officer like a side of beef were something Deena would never forget. Even reconciling herself with the killing didn't change the memory.

It would harden her soul if she didn't care. She hoped the boss was okay. He'd done the hardest work.

She checked the outside door to find the morning's delivery of vegetables waiting. Deena brought them inside and started the prep. It was a mindless job that gave her too much time to think, but she had new worries that transcended the death. She had to find and detail the targets for the Borwyn attack. She promised them within a week.

She didn't even know where to start, but she could share the good news that Moran was still alive but a prisoner of the Borwyn. She'd have to convince Lanni not to go to the authorities. That would be a negotiation in and of itself, but her husband had survived. That was nothing to take lightly.

Lanni would have to wait out the war until he could be released. In those days, Deena would tell Lanni the truth. Until then, she'd remain undercover. Deena needed to find a way into the base. Lanni could provide that. In two days, they'd have their day off.

Deena would insist as a small gratitude for the information.

After two hours, she'd done as much prep as she was willing to do. The restaurant opened in an hour. The boss and Lanni should be arriving soon and then the cook.

Deena helped herself to a third cup of coffee and drank it while sitting at the bar. The boss was the first to arrive. He looked as bad as Deena had felt.

He let himself in and then locked the front door behind him.

"Prep's almost finished," she said.

"Then finish it," he replied. It was the same banter every morning.

"I'll get to it once I'm on the clock," Deena replied, taking a slow, casual sip.

"Are you drinking my coffee again?"

"I'm drinking *my* coffee. You'll have to get your own." Deena held the cup below her nose. The normality of the banter was a comfort.

"We gonna talk about last night?" he asked.

"Nope. Nothing to say."

"I agree. I better get in the back and finish the prep to cover for my lazy, good-for-nothing employees. Woe is me!" The boss waved his hand and grunted at Deena as if saying 'go away.'

Deena tossed him a clean apron. The one from last night had gone through the automatic dishwasher, twice. It was as clean as it was going to get. He caught it and immediately held it away from his body. "You got a dry one? You may be into wearing a moist apron, but I am not."

"Moist. Nice." Deena put her coffee down and went around the counter to get one of the other aprons. She pulled out the cleanest and turned to hand it to him. He took it with his free hand. The other tipped her coffee into his mouth. "This is good. You might want to get yourself one, on the house."

He waved his fresh apron and headed into the kitchen.

Deena had to laugh at the absurdity of it all. She stared at the balled-up apron sitting on the bar top where her coffee used to be. She hung up the wet apron and prepared herself yet another cup.

Lanni appeared at the front door. Deena hurried to let her in.

"I have news," Deena started.

Lanni's eyes were red and puffy from crying, as they had been the second her husband's squad had lost contact and the base would give her no information.

"You absolutely cannot tell anyone. If you do, you'll get my contact killed and worse, you'll get me killed, too. Do you understand?"

Lanni nodded.

"I need you to agree, out loud. I don't want to die because word got out. No one, Lanni. This is deadly serious."

"I agree. Is my husband alive?"

Deena nodded. "He has been captured by the Borwyn and is safe."

"They have to negotiate for his release!" she shouted.

Deena seized her by the throat and dragged her toward the corner. "What part about you're going to get me killed didn't you understand? Shut up! Shut your mouth. You get to hold this knowledge close to your heart and nowhere else." Deena ended by shaking the smaller woman.

"I'm sorry." She struggled weakly to get out of Deena's grasp.

Deena realized she may have made a huge mistake. "The Malibor are negotiating, but you know how they are. And believe it or not, the Borwyn have no intention of killing him or even hurting him. Calm your mind and your soul. It's the best news you could get because only two survived the attack."

"The Borwyn," Lanni spat now that she'd run through the complete range of emotions. "They're vile."

"What would we do if we captured Borwyn? You know

the answer. They'd be tortured to death. Your husband will be freed. I can feel it in my bones. Have faith and by all that's sacred on this world, keep your damn mouth shut." Deena let go of her.

"I'm sorry. It came as a shock."

"Not another word. But I have a favor to ask. I burned all my bridges to get this information and I'd like to go into the military zone. I know there have to be some tasty young officers in there. Maybe do a bit of shopping, if you know what I mean."

"I thought you swore off men," Lanni countered, wiping her face and composing herself.

"Window shopping," Deena corrected. On the far side was the spaceport, and in the middle, the headquarters building stood unassumingly. It would be impossible to determine which was which from space or on a high-speed pass from close overhead. Deena needed to differentiate and fill in the grid coordinates that Crip and Max had developed. "In two days, we'll be off. I'd like to go then, if we could. Earlier in the morning because that's when they'll be out and exercising."

The corners of Lanni's mouth twitched upward. "Moran would work out early and come home sweaty and gross. *Deliciously* gross." She tipped her head down to stare at the floor.

Deena let her have her reminiscences.

When Lanni raised her chin again, her eyes were clear. "Yes. We'll go walking around. I can get you in there because I have an ID."

Deena nodded. "That's all I ask for. Thank you. You better get to work. We've been missing you."

She furrowed her brow and leaned close. "Is it true?"

Deena shrugged and shook her head. "Is what true?"

"My husband."

"Very much so. The information came at a high price from a source I trust but can never be known. Your husband is alive and being taken care of. There's only one other who survived, a soldier named Raftal."

Lanni nodded, tightlipped. "We know him. That's good news, too. He's single. No one else survived? I've met some of the others. I wish Moran hadn't gone. It's better when these things are someone else's problem."

"It's a dagger right to the heart. I understand, Lanni. Get to work. The boss man is in the kitchen finishing the prep."

Lanni put on her apron and disappeared into the kitchen.

Deena patted the counter with the loaded blaster hidden underneath. If anyone came for her, she wouldn't go without a fight. She didn't think they heard her signal. She didn't think anyone cared enough about the corrupt officer to check up on him. She hoped for a lot of things, but that wasn't the best plan.

Soon, it would all be over. She hoped for that, too.

"I prefer the Malibor rations," Brad said while enjoying one of their multi-bag delicacies.

Jaq ate the microgreens and fungus grown with bacteria. She preferred the Malibor food, too, as much as it grated on her soul. Jaq wanted to be a good example for the crew.

The seats on the mess deck were little used as the ship

had spent well over ninety percent of its life in zero-gee. The rare times it accelerated, it was for short bursts and not a constant one-point-two gees. It was a welcome respite. Their bags stayed on the tables without being netted. The diners stayed in place without locking their boots to the deck and bracing their knees under the table.

"Here." Brad forced a bag into Jaq's hand and relieved her of the one she'd been holding.

She tasted it and closed her eyes to savor it. "We need to eat what we can produce or we'll lose the ability to feed ourselves once the Malibor rations run out."

Brad stared into the distance. "I can never go home. I'll starve. Our food really is garbage."

"But it extended your lives and for that, I'm grateful. Your people are going to make it possible for us to win this war."

Brad held her gaze. "Then we need to win it before we run out of Malibor food. I can't go back to New Septimus."

"Is that the extent of your life? Food?"

Brad looked around, wondering if Jaq was still talking to him. He pointed at his chest.

"Of course I'm talking to you."

"When you're a stud beast like me, you have to send egregious quantities of fuel to the engine."

Jaq slowly ate her Malibor side dish of mashed potatoes and gravy.

Brad took a squeeze from her micro-greens before recapping it and setting it aside.

"What?" Jaq demanded. "*Stud beast*. I ought to send you out the airlock without a suit."

"But my boys just got married and I'm feeling feisty," Brad replied.

Jaq stared at him. "Is this conversation going anywhere?" she wondered.

Brad sobered. "It's a mindless banter to take your mind off the next phase of the operation. It's going to be the big one. We have to win this fight."

Jaq took his hand. "We have to win every fight. There's only one *Chrysalis*. We aren't getting a second chance. Who do we need from New Septimus? I selfishly want the best of who remains."

"And I'm going to poach them for you. How many can we take on board?"

"We can handle about twenty-five. After that, we're out of room. *Cornucopia* is behind us, skirting the asteroid belt to be in position to support extended operations over Septimus. We can't embark any additional specialists on the cargo ship. It's our one ship."

"I can bring a few using *Starstrider*. We can even bring *Starbound* and *Starwalker* into the mix. That gives us three additional ships."

"Unarmed ships, Brad. I can't put them anywhere near a gunfight. The best you could do is make yourselves targets to draw fire away from *Chrysalis*. I don't like that idea at all."

"What idea do you like?" Brad wasn't being confrontational. He suspected he knew her answer.

"Kill them from as far away as possible while traveling as fast as we can travel. The only ships they have left have to be aged with poor targeting systems directing barely functional weapons. I'm not counting on that, but I believe this is the case. We need to hit them hard and finish them."

"What about the ships hiding inside the space station?" Brad stood and collected their food bags.

"We'll come back for them. We'll align the ship and fill the spindle with withering fire. If they're afraid to sally out to meet us, then they'll be targets that don't shoot back or prisoners when they surrender."

Brad nodded. "Give them something they've never given us, the chance to survive. Crip is doing it on the ground, and we're going to do it up here."

"We have limited success in getting people to surrender and then keeping them alive," Jaq admitted. "Which reminds me, what about that boy we pulled off the cruiser, Zinod Weft?"

"He's with the Phillips boy learning how to weld."

"Is that a good idea? He can cut a hole in the hull with one of those things."

"That's the beauty of it. He doesn't have access to a unit without someone else there. Phillips is close enough in age that Zinod can look up to him without being overwhelmed by an adult, and Phillips Junior is still old enough to keep the lad from hurting anyone. We've added an adult to that team to keep an eye out, too."

"I was right in not worrying about it and I shan't think again about it."

They walked to the central shaft, where they pressed the button and waited like normal people. "I used to be someone," Jaq said with a laugh.

They headed to the bridge. Slade Ping was waiting for them. "We have an issue," he said.

"That can encompass the entirety of the universe. You'll have to narrow it down for me."

"There appears to be two ships in orbit over Sairvor."

Jaq looked to Brad for his analysis. "We'll have to deal with them before we can go to Rondovan." Rondovan, the moon over Sairvor within which New Septimus was hidden.

"And we left an intact weapons platform over the planet, too," Taurus added. "Looks like target practice."

"What kind of ships?" Jaq asked.

"Unclear at this distance. We'll gain fidelity as we get closer," Slade explained.

Brad crossed his arms and stepped closer to the front screen that showed Sairvor at the end of their arcing course along the orbital plane.

Chrysalis barreled toward Sairvor. Two unidentified ships were displayed as red icons, where their course ended at Septimus's twin planet. The screen showed ten hours until they inverted and started to slow.

CHAPTER 14

It is the mark of an educated mind to be able to entertain a thought without accepting it.

The refueling had not yet started. And the question of rearming had been kicked from office to office. That had not yet gotten any traction, either. They were told to wait.

Tram wasn't used to waiting with absolutely nothing to do. He'd never been in a commercial dining facility before, either. Tram sat at a café table on the broad walkway. The four had been provided with credits to pay for meals while they were in New Pridal.

They had a menu and were supposed to order what they wanted. Kelvis remembered from decades ago, but neither Sophia nor Evelyn had experienced anything like it before.

They were out of their element. Their escort, Janeece, had to get back to work and had left them on their own.

An attendee arrived and held a chalkboard to write on. She stared at them and they stared back.

"Are you going to order?" she asked.

"We're not from here. We've never done this before. Can you help us?" Tram asked, pointing to the menu.

The server was mildly amused but patient. She explained the entire process and what each named meal consisted of.

Sophia leaned close. "I'm proud of you for asking."

"It wasn't my first choice, but I'm hungry," Tram admitted. "We should put Evelyn in charge of keeping us fed."

She raised her eyebrows. "Why is that? Because it's women's work?"

"No. Because you're not afraid to get answers to our questions. I have to try to figure out for myself." He nodded toward Kelvis.

"I have to admit that I wouldn't have asked. I would have figured it out, plus I'm willing to eat anything."

She smiled. "The men who impacted my life have been less than respectful. It's given me a hard edge. I know my husband forgives me, but I ask for your forgiveness, too."

"Nothing to forgive. It's how we move forward that matters. We can't let the past determine who we can be," Tram said sagely.

Kelvis looked sideways at Tram.

Tram shrugged. "We've all had hard times, but ordering food isn't one of them. I'm sure it's better than anything you had on New Septimus."

"By Septiman's grace, that stuff was foul, but let's not talk about that. Let's talk about how Evelyn is going to help us get projectiles for *Matador's* railgun," Kelvis replied.

"I see your evil plan, but I like it. Yes, we'll enjoy some fine dining and then I suggest we visit the manufacturing facility directly. There are official channels, and then there's the way you really get things done." Tram nodded to the others.

Evelyn watched him from the corner of her eye while leaning on Kelvis.

Two hours later, they found themselves covering their ears in a separate enlarged cave with equipment churning and banging to create a series of similar objects. There were multiple lines, but not enough to produce more than five completed items.

While they watched, the components for a railgun rolled off the line. A worker took them to a table and began the assembly process. Within five minutes, he had it together. It didn't have a power pack or a stock of projectiles, but it was a complete railgun of the combat team's design.

"Do your thing." Tram nudged Evelyn.

"Watch and learn," she said, tucking her hair behind one ear and walking up to the man who had put the weapon together. "That was impressive. Isn't this one of the spacer's weapons?"

He shrugged. "I don't know. I follow my instructions. I put a hundred things together a day."

"Where would we get supplemental materials for a weapon like this made? The soldiers can use the projectiles." She let the thought hang in the air between them.

"I have nothing to do with what's produced. You'll have to talk to Bandele, the production manager, over there." He pointed before moving to another table and assembling the pieces that were there.

"Thank you. I hope to see you later." Evelyn waved over her shoulder as she tossed her hip on the walk away.

"You're a married woman," Kelvis said.

She glanced at him sideways. Tram, Kelvis, and Sophia followed her.

Evelyn stopped to talk with a man who was about her age. He stood at an aged computer terminal and hammered at the keys.

"I'd say I could help, but I don't know the first thing about a computer," Evelyn started. "But I do know about weapons." She pointed toward the cave wall. "Out there, we need more ammunition. Something big is coming up and the production office didn't put us into the queue in a place we consider anywhere near satisfactory. The munitions we're looking for are little more than metal slivers. They're accelerated to a speed that turns them into a molten ball for the remainder of their flight."

"Metal slivers? We get tons of those from the shaping and clearing processes. Do you have the specs, pretty lady?"

Evelyn motioned to Kelvis. "My husband will be able to give you the information you need."

He looked disappointed while giving Kelvis a hard look up and down.

"You need technical specifications? I got plenty of those. Can I use your computer?"

"Do your best. Keys don't work so well."

It took Kelvis three seconds to understand why the man had been hammering the keyboard. Even with the input limitations, Kelvis had the gunship's ammunition detailed on screen.

"We can do that. Steel, not high carbon, but better than rusty iron. Let me allocate a machine. Production office approved this, right?"

"Of course," Evelyn purred. "But they're way down in priority. Do we look like low-priority kind of people?" She stood back and modeled for the man running the line.

He watched appreciatively.

Kelvis stepped between them. "Can you run a sample that we can check?"

"I can run a few hundred using the stripper. Give me five minutes."

"That would be magnificent," Evelyn replied. The four stepped aside and let the production manager work the computer. He pounded the "enter" key, waited until the order was confirmed, then gestured for them to follow him.

They walked to the third production line, where slivers were pouring from a discharge chute. "What do you think of these?"

Tram made to reach in, but Bandele stopped him. "They're sharp. You need gloves." He pulled a glove from his back pocket and put it on.

Bandele reached in and removed three of the slivers. He showed them to Tram and Kelvis. They leaned close, blocking the light and defeating the purpose of their examination. Kelvis backed away to let Tram look at the final product. As the former battle commander, he had more experience with the E-mags and railgun technologies.

"They'll do. Can you get ten thousand of them to us?"

"Is that it?" Bandele joked. "Give me an hour, but you'll need help carrying it out of here."

"We'll find something and get it where it needs to go. You've been amazing," Evelyn said.

The four headed for the corridor. "We need a cart and a pass to go to our ship," Tram said. "Looks like we need to pay Janeece a visit."

"She's responsible for us. I hope she's not surprised that we may have taken things into our own hands. And then we better cancel the production request that has been put in with Magnus," Evelyn said, closing the loop so the New Pridal residents didn't produce something that had already been manufactured. Resources were much better than what *Chrysalis* had access to but were still limited. They didn't want to be responsible for wasting production time.

They strolled down the corridor to get to the Janeece's office. Inside, they found her working away on a mountain of documents. Wood and water were in short supply, even with the forest outside. They couldn't cut down trees in a normal way without tipping the Malibor to their presence.

Everything had a cost. Anything done outside the mountain came with risk. It was why the Borwyn Assault Brigade operated so far away, even though the brigade was little more than a reinforced company. There were supposed to be five companies, but they didn't have that kind of personnel. Glen Owain commanded the first company. Second through fifth were more like observation posts with barely a platoon of soldiers at their command.

The soldiers didn't leave a big footprint.

Janeece looked up from her work.

Evelyn leaned in. "You look like you could use a break." Evelyn nodded toward the door.

"This work needs to get finished," she argued, but her heart wasn't in it. She leaned back and sighed.

"We could use a cart and a pass to get back to the ship," Tram explained.

"You don't need a pass. The guards know who you are."

"We'll be hauling the reloads for the railgun," Evelyn whispered conspiratorially.

"How did you get those?" Janeece looked alarmed. Evelyn winked at her. "I don't want to know. We have our processes, but then, there's the way things get done."

"We saw they were producing railguns for the combat team," Evelyn added. "That is a welcome addition. We're going to give the Malibor what they deserve."

"That is good news, too. You don't need anything from me to do what you need to do," Janeece said.

"A cart to haul ten thousand rounds for the railgun," Evelyn clarified.

"Ah. Next room toward the exit is storage. You'll find something in there."

"You've been a wonderful guide through the winding maze of life in New Pridal." Tram bowed deeply.

They excused themselves. In the corridor, Evelyn stood outside the door to the office while Tram headed for the storage area but stopped when he saw the others weren't following.

"What?"

"We have time. Maybe we can help Janeece." Evelyn looked hopeful.

By Tram's calculation, they had forty-five minutes before

the production manager would complete the job and deliver ten thousand rounds for the gunship.

"Why are you looking at me?" Tram said with a smile. He sauntered back to the group, wrapping Sophia in a hug and kissing her on the top of her head. "It's a good idea. If we're going to work around the system, we need as many allies as we can get."

"You mean, we're helping because it's the right thing to do," Evelyn clarified.

"You know that I just fly the ship. Kelvis fixes the ship. And you tell us what to do."

Evelyn narrowed her eyes to determine if Tram was being confrontational. He held Sophia tightly.

"While we're in the mountain, yes. I understand these people, even if I don't understand any of the technology. I accept it for what it is. Also, most Borwyn women are on their last legs when they reach my age. I'm just getting started."

Tram held out a hand. "Deal."

Kelvis held the office door, and they re-entered to stand in front of Janeece's desk.

"We want to help you. We have forty-five minutes, so put us to work," Evelyn declared.

Janeece didn't know what to say and remained flummoxed for several uncomfortable breaths. Tram and Sophia held hands while shifting from one foot to the other.

"I guess you can put these in alphabetical order." Janeece started to gather the paper, but the stack was too large. She carefully put them down and pointed to the whole stack.

"I'll take care of those," Tram said. Sophia stayed behind

Tram as he moved the pile to the floor, where he sat cross-legged in the middle of it. She rubbed his shoulders as he worked. He realized that she probably couldn't read. She was young. Evelyn was old-school, brought up by the originals who were recently outcast. She had been schooled while they still had books.

"What else?" Evelyn asked.

Janeece remained flustered.

"Have you never had help before?" Evelyn asked.

"I'm the lowest in seniority. I usually get to help others. That's why this happened." She stood and spread her arms wide to take in the piles of brownish papers surrounding her.

"What do you do?" Tram asked.

Janeece laughed and sat down. "I file everything that needs to be filed while recycling that which doesn't need to be retained."

"How do you determine what to keep?" Evelyn wondered.

Janeece shrugged. "I guess?"

"What do they use this stuff for?" Tram said while reading the forms. "These look like requisitions. On *Chrysalis*, people ask for stuff, we write it on the wall, and then erase it when the order has been filled. Are all these filled?"

Janeece nodded.

Tram stopped sorting. "I hear there's a cart next door we can use. If these have been filled, then keeping them adds no value. Unfilled ones need to go into the queue or get rejected. Seems simple to me."

"Not simple at all. It depends who they complain to when they're told no."

"Then we keep the rejected ones only. All the rest get recycled. You know that we have very little paper on board *Chrysalis* and what we do have is for the archives to show us how it was done by our ancestors."

"The ancestors live on in New Pridal," Janeece said.

Tram stood. "I'll get the cart. Nothing encourages me more to win this war than seeing this. Will we devolve into more paperwork if we move into Pridal? By Septiman's good graces, I hope not."

"We'll be right back," Evelyn said.

Sophia and Kelvis stayed in the office.

In the corridor, Evelyn stopped Tram. He expected to get his butt chewed. What about? He couldn't fathom, but it would be clear soon enough.

"We're in a position to usher in new procedures. We have to win this war, Tram. For the health of the Borwyn people."

"I couldn't agree more. Let's get rid of that trash and then pick up our ammunition. I want to see it loaded and ready to fire. Maybe we can encourage the ground crew to refuel us and then we'll let Crip know that we're ready to go. The sooner, the better."

CHAPTER 15

If you do not change direction, you may end up where you are heading.

Jaq crossed her arms and stared at the screen. The ship had inverted and was slowing at a steady one-point-two gees. They had apparent gravity for another twenty-eight hours with the last two hours adjusted based on the posture of the ships over Sairvor.

"What are they doing, and who are they?"

"Recce ships from the surface? Like you encountered last time," Brad ventured.

"Would we see those little things at this range?" Jaq wondered.

"We would. Sensors are five by five," Slade said loudly and confidently.

"Then what are those ships?" Jaq pounded a fist into her hand.

Slade worked his systems.

Jaq tapped her foot rapidly while looking back and forth between the front screen and her sensor chief.

Brad poked her in the arm. "We're still too far away."

"We're not too far to call them. Amie, give me the Malibor channel and configure the directional antenna. Alby, prepare to fire."

"We're twenty-five million kilometers away," Alby stated. "It's not exactly a high-percentage shot."

"Doesn't matter. There's nothing to slow the rounds down. An object in motion and all that."

"Doesn't slow down unless acted on by an outside force. I know. Donal and Dolly, give me a good solution and take into account the planet's gravity at the endgame."

"Not our first impossible-odds shot, Captain. We'll see what we can come up with. It'll help to know if they're the enemy or not."

"They're the enemy because we know they're not Borwyn," Brad said. He knew exactly where the stealthy scout ships were—one in the cargo hold, one behind them, and the last one was still at New Septimus.

"Amie, give me a channel."

"It's open," the communications officer confirmed.

"Malibor ships in orbit over Sairvor. You've probably seen us bearing down on you. You'll move to the planet surface or you'll be destroyed. You have five minutes to respond."

"What are they going to say?" Brad asked once Amie indicated that the channel was closed.

"Don't shoot. We'll comply," Jaq guessed. "I'd tell us not to shoot. How long will it take our signal to reach them?"

"Right around two minutes," Amie replied.

Jaq knew the time. That was why she only gave them five minutes to reply. The whole evolution would take no more than ten minutes, if the Malibor assumed the five minutes was in addition to the time it took for the signals.

"Not you again," a Malibor voice said four and a half minutes after Jaq sent her message. "We hoped you'd been destroyed."

Jaq crossed her arms. "The captain of the Malibor scout ship. Those ships didn't have weapons, did they?"

"No," Alby answered. "We can rip them apart as we approach."

Jaq bowed her head for a moment.

The shepherd filled the silence. "Give mercy to those who are weak. Feed those who are hungry. When Septiman grants us more than we need, we must listen to His voice."

"Dammit," Jaq said. "We need allies, not enemies. There are enough Malibor on Sairvor to cause us real problems, not now but in the future."

"That's the long game, Jaq. This guy remembers your mercy and still wishes you dead." Brad shook his head. "The only thing the Malibor understand is brute force."

Jaq gritted her teeth and snarled her displeasure.

"Maybe we can foment another civil war so they can kill each other off. That'll make our job easier." Jaq looked hopefully at Brad.

"There was a time when I would have advocated exactly that, but a smart captain convinced me that winning the war meant winning the peace. We defeat the enemy when they are no longer the enemy. They will forever be malcontents because they're Malibor, but you knew that when you started this journey from the outer reaches of the system. Remember the radio challenge you issued months ago? May Septiman's star guide you to paradise. What was the right answer?"

"May paradise bring us peace." Jaq waved toward the comm officer. "Give me the channel." Jaq stared at Brad.

Amie tapped a key and confirmed it was live.

"Malibor scout ship. Once again, we find that we have no need to destroy you. We simply ask that you stay out of our way while we conduct operations in support of the liberation of Septimus. Do you need food or water?"

Jaq waited the obligatory five minutes before expecting an answer, but like before, it came early.

"We could use food. There's been a drought on Sairvor. It would mean a great deal for us to take foodstuffs for our ground crew and our crew's families. But why would you do that? You're Borwyn and you must know that we don't trust you."

Jaq nodded to Amie. "Malibor scout ship. We're the Borwyn you don't know. We're not what you've been taught. We'll earn your trust. We'll give you food. I'll need you and your sister ship to come together and power down your engines. We'll arrive at your position in under twenty-eight hours. Please, make no threatening moves. We know your ships are unarmed, but we are not. Our weapons will be powered up because we don't trust you either, but we are the ones who can change that, Captain."

Four and a half minutes later, a single word arrived. "Agreed."

Jaq turned to Brad and slowly shook her head. "I expect duplicity."

"I expect they'll lie about where they got the food from," Brad replied.

"You know what we're going to give them." Jaq smiled.

Brad laughed. "Microgreens and processed algae. We'll keep the Malibor rations for ourselves." Brad headed for the corridor. "I'll let Chef know, and we'll stage the supplies for transfer via the port roller airlock and the starboard standard airlock. I'll get people with stunners to standby. We will still have to show our strength to dissuade them from trying something. I don't trust them, but I believe their sense of self-preservation will keep them from doing anything that will get them killed."

Deena strolled beside Lanni, who pushed a stroller with her baby girl inside. The military compound's streets and walkways had little activity. A small group of soldiers ran by, joking and laughing as they went. The two women drew their attention for no more than a single glance over their shoulders.

They walked toward the heart of the compound two kilometers from the front gate. Deena maintained a dialogue about absolutely nothing to keep Lanni engaged. Gossip, work talk, and the recent weather made it into the conversation. The women were used to being on their feet so the walk was easy, pleasant even.

"How far do you want to go?" Lanni asked.

"To the spaceport and beyond!" Deena declared, raising

her hand in the air. She lowered it and turned to Lanni. "Do you ever dream of the stars?"

"Heavens, no." Lanni shook her head. "I like my feet on the ground with my husband by my side and our little baby held between us."

"I feel you. I like my life, too, but think there's much more, and it's out there." She stared at the blue sky as if she could see outside the atmosphere, all the way to the station and beyond. "I can see the space between."

"We're working girls who deliver the food to those who would go to space. Our lives are down here, Deena."

Deena nodded. She knew the truth. She didn't have to convince Lanni that there was more to Septimus than the Malibor's vision of who deserved a good life. The rest of the population supported the chosen few.

More than the fleet. Deena stared grimly ahead. The headquarters building were surrounded by additional fencing and armed guards. Deena noted the location in distance from the gate and relative direction. She plotted its location on a mental map. The other buildings of concern were close enough that one coordinate would leave the inner compound a smoking hole when *Chrysalis* dropped munitions from orbit.

"We better go around that," Deena said. "Looks like they don't want anyone accidentally going that way."

"That's where the senior officers do their thinking. That's where they issued the orders that sent my husband to the Borwyn."

"Then we definitely want to avoid them. I'd want to punch them in the face for ordering others to take risks that they aren't willing to take themselves. None of them went on that patrol."

"They suck hairy butts," Lanni said.

"Lanni!" Deena exclaimed.

"They made me angry. Do we know if they've made any progress with negotiations to bring my husband home?"

Deena held a finger to her lips. "We mustn't speak of it in the open," she warned. "I burned that bridge. I won't find out anything new. I have high hopes that the next thing we hear is the sound of his voice. I look forward to meeting him."

Lanni smiled. Deena's confidence was infectious.

As it was intended, but Deena knew beyond a shadow of a doubt that Moran was in Borwyn hands and they would see that nothing happened to him. He was safer than if he'd be anywhere near the headquarters building or the spaceport. When the bombardment started, the last place anyone would want to be would be on the military compound.

"It's a walk in the sun," Deena said.

Lanni steered around the fenced-off area, pushing quickly to get the baby's stroller beyond the guards.

"That place gives me the creeps."

"Why?" Deena wondered.

"They hide underground and make decisions that affect everyone. Do we know who they are or what they look like?"

"Should we know?" Deena asked. The highest-ranking person she ever met was the captain of the *Hornet*. She'd never seen his superiors. She chalked it up to her low rank, but Lanni's perspective might have been more on point.

They didn't want anyone knowing who they were. All the power resided below ground. It would be Deena's pleasure to guide *Chrysalis's* ground bombardment to wipe out that facility and all within.

They walked quickly, maintaining a good pace. It took longer than either of them thought to get near the spaceport. It was a solid five kilometers past the headquarters.

They stopped at an overlook with a plaque for a memorial.

The day we drove the Borwyn from this city, Paliman's Day, 3257. Long live the Malibor.

"Long live the good people who love this planet," Deena said softly.

"What does that mean?" Lanni asked.

"It means that we won the planet and to keep it, we need to love it, not just exist on it. Look at that sky? It's cool, but beautiful. Don't you love it here?"

Lanni was taken aback. She studied Deena. "I never really thought about it, but yeah, I guess I do. It's not like we have any other options."

It sounded like a challenge for Deena to talk about the stars.

"We don't. This is our home, Lanni, and from what I hear, there's no place like home."

"I thought you were weirding out on me, Deena, but you just think deeper than the rest of us. I'm proud to call you my friend."

Deena wrapped her arm over the younger woman's shoulder and looked out over the spaceport.

She kept a smile plastered on her face despite counting three gunships and ten spaceworthy shuttles. One was fueling and being readied for space. She'd ridden something similar to the space station for further transfer to *Hornet*. They'd brought the new fleet personnel in a bus with blacked-out windows and rushed them onto the shuttle without windows.

Paranoia, but they allowed visitors to worship at the altar of their *victory* over the Borwyn.

"We better go. They probably don't want observers."

They hurried away as fast as they'd come. Deena fought the urge to look over her shoulder. She tried to take in the blue sky and the warmth of a cool day, but she shivered nonetheless. The strain of the worry was weighing on her.

All the while, she committed to memory the location of the landing pads, the system radars, and control facilities. It was a massive field, and she hoped she guessed the distances right. She'd do the best she could, but the three gunships bothered her. Were they flightworthy?

She'd pass along the information. It would be up to Crip and Jaq to determine how to deal with them.

CHAPTER 16

The whole purpose of intelligence is to turn mirrors into windows.

Tram and Kelvis surveyed their work. The railgun's hopper was half full of the metal slivers it turned into plasma. The railgun, the cannon around which the ship was wrapped. Malibor gunships had one purpose: put a great number of high-velocity rounds into space. Some gunships had two cannons, but most had one. This was the latter.

Matador's sword.

The challenge with using the system during intra-atmospheric flight was in controlling the ship's orientation. To attack ground targets, the ship's nose would have to be pointed at the ground. Strafing runs would be limited before the ship had to pull up.

Tram wanted to practice, but there were no simulators, and flying the ship around the mountains might highlight where they were hiding. Giving the Malibor an idea where they could find the surviving Borwyn wasn't anything Tram wanted to be responsible for.

He was still kicking himself for the pop-up maneuver he executed to get the gunship to the landing pad, even though he'd hugged the mountain as tightly as he could to put the ship into a radar's background clutter.

Tram wouldn't get the chance to practice. He'd have to take the gunship wherever Jaq determined it needed to go. First time would be showtime.

Evelyn and Sophia flopped on the deck.

"That sucked," Evelyn groused.

Kelvis smiled at her. "But we got it done. It only took seven trips up the ladder."

"Times the four of us. Twenty-eight trips. Who knew slivers of steel were so heavy?" Tram asked, but it wasn't a question. He knew the mass but was generally oblivious because of doing manual labor aboard *Chrysalis* in zero-gee. "We powered through the pain!"

Sophia stared at him like he'd lost his mind.

"We celebrate the little victories," he explained. "Did you see the ground personnel?"

"No. I was focused on not falling off the ladder," Sophia replied.

Tram nodded. "They were getting the refueling equipment ready."

Kelvis beamed his approval.

"We'll be ready to go in short order," Tram confirmed.

"Then what?" Evelyn asked the hard question.

Tram hadn't gotten that far in his thought planning. "We wait for word from *Chrysalis*." Tram sounded unsure of himself because there was one minor problem with the next step.

The combat team had the radio, unless they brought the gunship's radio online, and that would be dangerous. It broadcast along a wide spectrum. They couldn't send a directional signal like Larson could using the dish on the portable unit.

"We don't have a radio," Tram said softly.

Evelyn pointed toward the gunship's flight deck.

Kelvis understood the dilemma. The ladies did not. Kelvis explained, "If we radiate from this ship, then the Malibor will know where we are, even if they're not looking. It'll be like sending a beacon and a flare into the sky at the same time. The space station will hear us as well as any Malibor ship in the air or in space."

"We don't want that," Evelyn agreed matter-of-factly.

Tram chuckled for a moment. "No, we don't. Which brings us back to how are we going to find out what, when, and where?"

Evelyn and Sophia raised their eyebrows knowingly.

Tram's face fell with the revelation. "We ride horses or we walk back to the front lines," he stated, "because there's no way I'm going in there to ask those people if we can use their radio."

Kelvis grimaced. "We took a ton of paper to the recycling plant. Maybe we can ask for one little favor? I'm an engineer, and I'm old! I can do without horse riding or walking." He looked at his wife. She made a face at him. "You can do it, honey."

Tram felt sorry that his friend's life hung by a thread, but

Tram was going to stay out of the blast radius and impact area soon to consume the engineer. Tram stepped back to give them room.

Crip and Max studied the terrain map they'd built. It showed the field and the western gate, the one that Deena had gone through. They wanted her insight into what was beyond the gate unless there was an alternate way into the city, but they hadn't heard of any.

"We'd be caught in a crossfire before we set one foot inside," Crip complained.

"We have a gunship that could blast a hole in the wall," Max replied.

"That might ruin our element of surprise." Crip kneeled on the ground to get a better look from what they'd see on approach. Branches represented the city walls, but they had been meticulously placed with the contour, just like the rolling hills leading up to the city. A covered approach was lacking.

"I don't see a way in," Max said, "unless we go in at night, which is what we're going to have to do. Then we could scale the wall at any location. We can pick a spot that will be conducive to our disappearing inside the city with the least amount of grief."

"Four-soldier teams. Two men. Two women. But we'll need to task Deena with finding us the best place to cross the wall."

"On top of what we've already given her. I don't like it, Crip." Max frowned at the terrain map.

"It's not optimal, but we can't fly a reconnaissance flight. That would alert them that the war was close. They'd rally the entire population. They'd be put on alert, and that would be the end of subterfuge. We'd get a lot of our people killed." Crip gripped Max's shoulder. "We just haven't found the right way yet. When we do, the Malibor are going to pay a high price."

Max laughed. "They won't pay too much because we'll be hiding."

"When we're inside the city, we need to unsettle their command structure. It's the whole reason for taking the risk. I have to wonder if we can't do it from afar. The gunship. *Chrysalis*. Bomb them into next week."

"You know what we were taught from the old military training manuals. You can't hold ground from the air."

"We don't need to hold it. We only need to destroy the enemy's ability to resist."

"The Malibor will fight us. They won't give up Malipride." Max threw his hands down in defeat.

"What if they don't have to?" Crip suggested. "Jaq doesn't want to kick them off the planet. She only wants the Borwyn to return and then be in charge, of course, because the Malibor can't be trusted."

"Win the hearts and minds of the people. Is that what we've been doing, Crip?"

Crip nodded toward the medical tent. "Let's check on our prisoners, see if they're still angry with us. We may have made some progress on a small scale."

The two walked across the compound and into the tented medical bunker. They found Raftal, Moran, and a Borwyn guard playing cards.

The guard jumped to his feet, upsetting the table. "Sorry, sir."

"For what? I'm fine with you playing cards. They didn't get away, did they?"

"Well, no."

"Then you did your job. Give us a few minutes, will you?" Crip asked the man. He bowed his head and departed.

"How are you holding up?" Crip asked.

"I have one arm," Moran snapped. He was pale with clammy skin. He blinked rapidly to clear his eyes.

Crip leaned close. "The arm was lost in combat in the middle of a violent storm. We did everything we could to save the injured once the battle was over. What would your squad have done if you had won that engagement?"

"We would have left your bodies to rot and continued with our mission," Moran stated with a sneer.

"Aren't you glad we didn't do that? Can't hold your baby if you're dead."

Raftal stood and gestured to the side.

Crip took the seat next to the bed while Max and Raftal stepped away.

"He's not getting better, and the doc tells me I can't donate more blood," Raftal said.

Max waved a nurse to him. "Does he need more blood?"

"He could use some, but we'll get him plasma, as much as we have, and that will suffice. Your people have been very kind in donating, but we can't process very much out here.

We can barely do samples. If we had..." She stopped herself before saying anything about New Pridal.

Max understood. "We can only do what we can do. Will he survive?"

"He's over the worst of it, but he's still suffered unimaginable trauma and his body is trying to cope. It could take a while. Plasma, fluids, and food. At least he didn't lose his dominant arm so his retraining won't be as hard as it could be."

"Thank you." Max turned back to Raftal. "You heard her. He needs to fight for it. We're giving him everything he needs. Time and attitude will carry him to the other side of health. So what? He's missing an arm. He'll make do because the alternative is unacceptable. We all learn to make do with what we have."

"You have a lot."

"By some measures, yes. We have dry beds and good food. We have people who care surrounding us, but you have people who care surrounding you, too. We don't want to see you or Moran dead."

"Why aren't you torturing us for information?"

"You're both young. What do you know that you think we don't already know?"

"Nice try!" Raftal said. He tried to hide the humor he found in Max's question. "You're right. We don't know anything. They didn't even tell us anything about this mission. Just that we were on it. The guys who knew what we were after got killed first—the Fristen mercenaries and the lieutenant."

"We only saw one mercenary," Max replied.

"The other one shaved and put on one of our uniforms, but if you looked closely, you would have seen the difference. No matter. Good thing that they put Moran on point and me at the end."

"That's the way it works. The important people are in the middle of the formation. It's how it usually is. We didn't need to capture anyone. We only had to keep you from getting into the forest. This is our home now, and having enemies traveling through isn't acceptable." Max took Raftal by both arms. "I'm sorry we're at war. You seem like a good guy. I'd have you on my team any day, but what I really want is for my team to be hunters, or farmers, or engineers, or even construction workers. Imagine building something like a home."

Raftal dipped his head and stared at the hard dirt floor. "That would be nice. I had no choice but to enlist. The second son serves. So here I am. How long will I be here? This isn't a prison camp."

"You two are the only prisoners we have. We would prefer to turn you loose, but I fear sending you back to Malipride by yourselves will not be well received. They'll put you in prison or worse."

"I think you're right. That's why we're not trying to escape. There is nowhere for us to go. We'll be forever in between our two worlds. We can't surrender to the Borwyn and we can't go home to the Malibor."

"You didn't surrender. You have nothing to be ashamed of."

"But I did. I was in the tree. I had you in my sights but didn't fire."

Max clapped him on the back. "I am happy you didn't! My wife is happy you didn't. And my friends, too."

"I'm glad I didn't. I don't want to die. I've accomplished nothing in my life," the young man lamented while baring his soul.

"You're going to help that man back to life. He carries your blood. Let him share your spirit. He has too much to live for."

Max guided Raftal back to Moran's side.

Crip was telling him the story of when the pipes burst in the lower decks and how that was the only "rain" he'd seen until he landed on Septimus.

Moran was listening only because he didn't have a choice. The scowl on his face said he wanted to be somewhere else.

Raftal moved close and took Moran by the hand. "What do you want to do?" Raftal asked.

"What do you mean?" the injured man replied.

"What do you want?" Raftal said it slowly and clearly, emphasizing the last word of the question.

"To have both my arms again."

Raftal shook his head, then he nodded toward the cards scattered on the small table. "We have to play the hand we're dealt. Me? I want to smell the fresh air and have a little deer meat. I think it's better than the bovine we get, when we get it."

Moran stared at the tent above. "Lanni works at a restaurant where they cook really good food. I worried about her getting a job there, but this new woman took her under her wing. She keeps Lanni safe. She makes sure the restaurant runs well. It keeps getting better and better. My wife is happy. I should say that she was happy. I bet she's a wreck with me missing. I hope Deena can help her keep her head up until I can get word to her."

Max's head snapped around. "What did you say?"

"My wife works in a restaurant. So what?"

"Who does she work with?"

"What's it matter to you?" Moran clamped his mouth shut.

Raftal gestured for Crip and Max that it was time for them to go.

Crip moved in between Max and the injured man before he told them too much.

Once outside and away from the medical bunker, Crip stopped.

"That's why she wanted to know who those two were," Max said.

"She's taking a risk if she tells Lanni anything. We should probably work on an exit strategy."

Max vigorously shook his head. "No! You talked about winning the hearts and minds of the people. She's doing exactly that."

"One person out of a million means there's a long way to go, but it tells me that Deena's confidence has increased rather significantly since she met you, Max. She's protecting other women from the soldiers. That's huge."

Max smiled proudly. "I would expect no less. She's incredible."

"And we need to talk with her about an exit strategy. We don't want to offer her up as a sacrifice to the Malibor. Once we have the coordinates of those facilities, she doesn't have to stay there. She can come back to us."

"And that has a risk, too," Max pointed out. "One can't just leave the city, can they?"

"I think they can, but what I think is irrelevant. It's whatever options Deena can find. If we tell her to leave Pridal, will she do it? That'll be her call."

Max walked around with his hands gripped behind his back as he tried to sort it out. "I used to be able to think more clearly."

"Welcome to married life, my friend. I'm glad that I can keep a clear head."

"What are you talking about? You've got two women. I'd rather be me than you, but you're right. Deena distracts me, but it's for the best, isn't it?"

"Makes life worth living, Max. We need to win this war so we can take some time for us, but I don't know what I'd do with nothing to do. Would I get bored and go back to the ship?"

Max shrugged. "I'd like to think you wouldn't waste brain space thinking about that stuff until after we've won the war. We don't even know what we're going to do next. Our FOME is Deena. Focus of main effort. I find that disconcerting, but I have to live with it. You figure out how we can deploy the combat team to help us win this war and get my wife out of that city." Max pointed in the direction of Malipride.

He was right. Crip didn't have the first idea what the combat team could do to help. Their fate was in everyone else's hands.

CHAPTER 17

Do the easy things first and the hard things will be easier.

Jaq surveyed the bulkhead work on the deck below the bridge. Getting the emergency overrides installed had been a priority. It was also for an emergency she hoped they wouldn't have.

Hope for the best while preparing for the worst. It made operating a combat ship easier when the crew had already thought through the worst-case scenario.

"Good work," she told the team. "When's the last time you slept?"

"What day is it?" the elder Phillips asked.

Days in space were a moving target. They manually adjusted the lights according to a twenty-four-hour cycle to give some semblance of a circadian rhythm. It made it easier planning work shifts with a set schedule.

"Secure your gear and take a break. We don't have long before we start the hard decel. It'll be best if you get your sleep before then. Once we arrive in orbit over Sairvor, we could be mixed up in a fight. We'll need you to be ready." Jaq waved an arm to take in all three crew. "We need all of you at your best."

"We wanted to get one more," the junior engineer said.

"Laudable, but no. I need you rested far more than I need a bypass on the next emergency bulkhead. Go on now. Stow your trash."

They gave the captain a hearty, "Aye, aye."

She took the ladder up to the command deck, where she strolled the short distance to the bridge. The bustle of activity was refreshing. Targeting, weapons, navigation, and thrust control. Comms worked the channels.

Jaq helped herself to the sensor pod where Slade was poring over incoming data.

"Are you active?" Jaq asked. Were the radars radiating actively? She used the shorthand they'd grown accustomed to.

"Both," Slade replied without looking up.

Dolly was in her seat, hunched over her terminal. Donal was farther back. He rocked and smiled to music that only he could hear.

Jaq worked her way back to him. The shepherd stood in anticipation of Jaq's visit. She hadn't intended to talk with him but changed her mind. "Be there in a sec, Shepherd."

She tapped Donal on the shoulder.

He jerked as if waking from a nap. "Captain. Fancy you joining me at this workstation of mine. What can I do you out of?"

"I'm sorry..." Jaq reviewed the words she'd heard but couldn't make any sense of them. "What?"

"You visited me, lass."

The originals weren't constrained by anything, least of all a captain that was at least thirty years their junior.

"Did you fix the acceleration gauge?"

"Right as rain, Skipper," Donal replied with a salute.

"What about targeting?"

"Updated. Just waiting on a target to blast out of space. We'll adjust based on flight profiles. We're dialing it in. Margin of error on the shots is under point-three percent."

"That sounds good. Is it good?"

"It's nearly a percentage point in gravity-affected shots. We're close to zeroing in. There will always be error because of gravitic waves and other spatial distortions that we can't see, but for what we can see, we can calculate better targeting solutions. We *have calculated* better solutions."

Jaq thought he wasn't being completely forthcoming. "Then what's the issue?"

"What issue?"

"The one you're not telling me." Jaq raised her eyebrows and crossed her arms in defiance. She would wait as long as it took for him to get past the humor he used to distract her from his unspoken concerns.

He raised his hands in surrender. "The targeting systems on the cannons are less than exceptional. They need a complete rebuild. Volley fire is what it will take to get us to point-three percent. They are told where to fire, but the micro-adjustments to put the cannon down the desired line of fire aren't happening with consistency. It's summertime aiming."

"It's less than one percent, which means at extreme range, we could be off by a lot, but what is summertime aiming?"

"Some of the time it gets where it's supposed to go. See, summertime."

Jaq tightened her jaw, thinning her lips across her teeth. She uncrossed her arms and nodded. "I'm going to talk with the shepherd now, and then probably start drinking."

"You came to the right man!" Donal blurted.

"You better not be making booze on my ship."

"Never, Captain. Not as far as you know."

She pointed to the rear station where the shepherd continued to stand.

"You look troubled," the man said as she approached.

"Not at all," Jaq replied. "How's the crew's morale?"

"We've taken losses that certain crewmembers cannot rectify, but it has brought them closer to Septiman. Only He can bring peace to a troubled soul."

"Amen, Shepherd. We have work to do, and if people are not in the right mind to do it, then we'll have to get the right crew into place who can do the jobs. When we're in combat, there's no time to think. They have to act."

The shepherd looked around before leaning close and whispering, "You should talk with Teo."

"Any topic in particular?"

The shepherd stared back without giving any hint what his concerns were.

"On my way," Jaq said with a nod and a quick step

around the sensor pod, through the battle commander's area. "You have it, Brad. I'll be down in Engineering."

She hurried off the bridge, nearly running in her haste. She hammered the button for the lift when she arrived, glancing furtively over her shoulder to check if anyone was following. The shepherd knew something she didn't. Jaq wanted to find out what it was without Brad or someone else making Teo feel uncomfortable and unwilling to speak.

The elevator arrived, and Jaq rode it alone all the way to the engineering level. She strolled into Engineering to find Teo by herself.

Jaq walked around as if inspecting the various interfaces, panels, and equipment.

"You're here for a reason," Teo said.

"Astute, but I would expect no less. What's getting you down?"

"Down? Nothing. Up? If I could get a couple days with those Malibor power plants, I think we could double their output. I've been running the numbers. We need to fabricate two reflecting plates and new regulators, but that'll be easy."

Jaq sighed in relief. She expected a heavy conversation about how Bec was stifling her initiative and his interference would end with an implosion that would turn *Chrysalis* into a cloud of expanding plasma. Or something as egregious.

"I hate to tell you no, but we don't have the time. We have belligerents over Sairvor that we have to deal with before we can attempt to go to Rondovan and New Septimus. We won't be able to linger at any of these locations. Not two minutes longer than we have to. We're here to get missiles, and that's it. Then we'll be on our way to Septimus. The combat team is biding their time, and that can't be good for their health. The longer we leave them down there without support, the more the Malibor can focus on them."

Teo nodded. "We can make *Chrysalis* sing a new song. All I need is two days, Jaq."

"You'll have priority if I can get you those days. Can you break them down one at a time so if we have to power up, we can do it with one until you can bring the other online?"

"I'd prefer not to do it twice. I need two days uninterrupted time."

"I hope we don't need to give you that time. We're going to clear the space above Sairvor, then we're going to rearm, then we're going to Septimus to lay down the law. The Malibor are going to feel the full weight of the war they started."

"I'll do the best I can with what we have." Teo tipped Jaq's chin up. "You seem upset."

"I thought there was something wrong. I'm pleased to find out that there isn't."

"I'm tired, but I can make do."

"Then get some sleep. Put the engineering watch on duty. We'll be decelerating soon. I want you well rested when we get to Sairvor. We pulled the bulkhead teams off to rest, too. They're our damage control in case anything happens. They're better off rested than having a couple extra manual overrides on our emergency bulkheads."

Teo pursed her lips and gazed over her domain. The ion drives continued to operate with the bio-packs instead of circuitry. It was an experimental process that worked. It had been the only choice.

The damage they'd suffered from a myriad of attacks had been extensive.

"I'm amazed we're still flying," Jaq said what Teo had been thinking.

"Frankly, Captain, I am, too. Sometimes, we exist by force of will alone. My dad told us about the early years of New Septimus. Sometimes, we have no reason to survive beyond the refusal to accept defeat."

"That's us." Jaq held out her hand and Teo took it, shaking firmly.

Jaq whistled while she walked away.

She listened to the thrum of pumps moving fluids around the ship and the soft vibration of power coursing through massive cables.

Jaq thought the ship was already singing.

Deena looked around her before unlocking the door, hurrying inside, and locking herself in. She stepped to the side to peek through the restaurant's front windows. Was anyone watching her?

She slowed her breathing while standing still.

After five minutes, she was confident she hadn't been followed.

Deena poured herself a drink. She took a long swig and then headed upstairs, into the bathroom, and secured the door.

She dug out the radio and set it up. Deena looked at it for a long time. Her finger hovered over the power button.

Instead of growing more confident with each transmission, she felt an overwhelming sense of dread.

Deena pulled the antenna down, bundled the unit into its carry bag, and put it back. She turned on the shower as hot as she could stand it and stood under the water for a long time. When she climbed out, her fingers were wrinkled. She dressed in a bathrobe she'd purchased for living with Lanni and opened the bathroom door.

An insistent tapping on the glass of the door shocked her senses. She eased onto the stairs and looked toward the front. A new officer waited there. They'd replaced the old one already or they were looking for him. She contemplated sneaking back upstairs, but this time, she had something she didn't before.

A blaster hidden under the bar.

She walked down the stairs, making a show of drying her hair. She turned on the inside lights, all of them. She didn't want there to be anything that couldn't be seen from outside.

"Can I help you?" Deena asked through a partially opened door. She blocked it with her foot to keep him from pushing it open.

"I'm looking for the man who is supposed to be on duty. He talked about a hottie working in this place. I can only assume he meant you."

"He tried to get my attention to let him in for a drink, but I declined his rather gracious invitation."

The man studied her from head to toe, but not in a creepy way. He struck her as a man conducting an investigation. "Are you staying here?"

"No," Deena lied. "I'm showering here to save Lanni and Moran's water. I'm staying with her a few blocks away."

"All the lights were off," he countered.

"So random guys wouldn't think they could get a drink with a *hottie*, isn't that what you called me?"

"I did not. Make sure you're out of here by ten. I wouldn't want anyone else to be mistaken about someone living here. You have a good evening, ma'am."

"That's a lot of pressure, but I'll do my best." She didn't remind him that he hadn't asked anything about the officer.

Deena locked the door behind him. She turned out all the lights and went upstairs, where she promptly got dressed. She didn't take anything with her because she was supposed to already be staying with Lanni.

She wondered if she was going to have to get her own place. Skirting the rules wasn't going to serve her. She needed to fly under the radar. She trudged down the street, head down but wary, glancing left and right while stopping occasionally to look behind her. It was what she'd grown accustomed to doing. The officer was working his way down the street, looking for anyone who had seen the man who was supposed to be on duty.

Deena didn't look directly at him. She didn't want more questions. She didn't want him searching the restaurant to find the unlabeled meat packs in the back of the freezer. That would lead to a whole series of uncomfortable questions.

CHAPTER 18

Keep your feet on the ground, your face toward Armanor, and the darkness will stay behind you.

"Recommend we maintain one hundred thousand KPH," Jaq called across the bridge.

No one disputed her.

"Bring us around the planet in a lower orbit than the weapons platform. We'll take it out from below before we move into position with the two scout vessels. Can you get a good scan of the planet during our pass?"

"Major power sources, general population centers, but that's about it. Only the big stuff. We won't be able to perform any detailed radar sweeps of the surface on a single high-speed pass."

It confirmed what Jaq already knew, but she had hoped with Donal and Dolly's tinkering that they'd have refined the capabilities of the sensor systems. But it wasn't to be.

"Twenty minutes to zero-gee," Ferd announced.

At five-gee deceleration, the ship's aft end faced Sairvor where two scout ships waited. A weapons platform was halfway around the planet, but primed and ready to fire, as far as they knew.

They would have liked to recover its components, but Jaq was pressed for time. The combat team had been on the ground for nearly two months. The longer *Chrysalis* stayed away, the more the Malibor could prepare.

The Malibor were no longer fooled into thinking Sairvor was rising against the leadership on Septimus. The high-speed run against the ships in orbit over Septimus confirmed that it wasn't the Malibor.

The Malibor fleet had taken direct action by sending an old cruiser carrying five gunships to Farslor. That was a well-designed attack meant to destroy the Borwyn cruiser.

But they failed and were left nearly toothless. Jaq was betting that one more trip to Septimus could be their last. With the space around the Borwyn home planet cleared, Jaq could talk to the Malibor about bringing peace to the Armanor system. It would be easier to talk with the successors after the entire leadership was forcefully removed through targeted bombing and precision attacks. The combat team could conduct even more refined attacks, if they were in a position to not get overwhelmed.

What kind of chaos would ensue once the attack started?

That was the biggest unknown. Jaq continued to let her mind wander until the engines ended their run. Thrusters brought the ship around nose first to better engage the weapons platform.

"Offensive systems online. Nine minutes to optimal firing solution," Alby announced.

The ship accelerated toward the upper atmosphere owing to Sairvor's gravity, but the friction of the exosphere would slow their headlong rush around the planet. Jaq wanted no more than twenty-five thousand KPH when they pulled the nose of the ship away.

She watched the numbers, ecstatic with a power system that showed their storage at eighty-eight percent, even after two hours of hard deceleration.

Jaq released herself while the rest of the bridge crew stayed in their seats. She floated toward the overhead. The friction provided enough resistance to add apparent gravity of twenty percent. She inverted and stood, facing the group upside-down. She walked gingerly, pulling herself along the upper rail.

She nodded to Alby, and he gave her the thumbs-up.

Slade did the same.

Brad unbuckled and joined her on the overhead. He checked the time. "A couple minutes and we'll need to be back in our seats."

"Yep. I like spending as little time as possible in that thing. It's restricting."

"It's supposed to be. The human body is frail. Space is a vicious beast with a voracious appetite."

She checked his expression to see if he was waxing poetic for some reason, but he gave nothing away.

"Space will hurt you, if you let it," Jaq replied. "I don't intend to let it."

"Me, neither. Let's take out this weapon platform, then

we'll spank us a couple Malibor upstarts. The food and drinks are staged on both port and starboard sides. Close cargo bay door four so they don't see our Malibor power plants. Also, shut them down so we don't burn through the shielding. We have four stunners with two groups of two. I'll be one of them down there, observing and ready to take action. We'll be suited and the corridor blocked off. If they have blasters, then we will execute an emergency disconnect and send them into space, where we'll ping them with our defensive weapons."

"Ping, meaning blast them into that void you were talking about."

"The end result is equally dramatic, yes. I don't want to do it, but by preparing for the worst, we can hope for the best."

"One minute," Mary reported.

Jaq jumped from the overhead to catch the mid-rail near the captain's chair and pulled herself into it. She struggled with the belt because she kept floating upward. Jaq activated her boots to hold herself in place until she could align herself with the seat. The second try planted her where she needed to be. She strapped in quickly while noting that Brad made it on his first try.

He snickered silently.

She shook her finger at him in caution.

"Acquiring targeting data," Alby said. "Fire."

Taurus mashed the buttons with great zeal. The ship vibrated from the barrage, which started and ended in under a second.

The hits on the weapons platform were nearly instantaneous. The platform shattered under the onslaught, but it didn't explode.

"Inverting to slow," Mary said. "All ahead standard."

"Two-point-nine minutes to full stop," Ferd added.

Acceleration reached three gees while the ship slowed.

"Two targets locked. E-mags are hot," Taurus called out to reconfirm that they were ready to shoot the targets if they did anything other than wait for *Chrysalis* to arrive.

The energy gauge had ticked up to ninety percent before the E-mag barrage. It was back down to eighty-eight percent with the three-gee deceleration, which was nothing more than accelerating in the opposite direction.

"One minute," Ferd said.

The Malibor ships maintained their position.

"Looks like they're going to play nice," Brad said.

"Looks like," Jaq repeated. "It's good to see how overwhelming firepower cows the most stalwart souls."

"Thirty seconds." Ferd stared at his controls while the main screen showed the approach.

"Inverting." Mary adjusted the ship's orientation.

"Engaging thrusters for final deceleration and station-keeping. I'll put us in between the two scouts."

A ka-thump reverberated through the ship.

"What was that?" Jaq demanded.

"We've destroyed a lot of ships over Sairvor. There's probably significant debris out there," Alby ventured.

Jaq nodded as she clicked the safety buckle and freed herself. She pushed out of her seat as another thump sounded from overhead, the forward section of the ship. A massive blast threw the nose off its vector. Red lights flashed on the board. Emergency bulkheads slammed into place when the hull breach registered.

"Report." Jaq looked to anyone for answers.

"We hit a mine," Slade said.

The battle commander whipped around. "How?"

"Active sensors are focused close to the ship," Slade said, leaning close to his screen.

"Get us out of here," Jaq ordered. "Target those scouts."

"Belay that!" Slade shouted.

"Full stop," Ferd noted.

"Explain." Jaq kicked off her seat and flew across the bridge, over the battle commander's pod to the sensor section.

"On screen." Slade leaned back and pointed. "Ugly status quo."

Dots showed where the mines were. It wasn't unmanageable. A total of six remained, including the one they bumped that didn't explode. Five active mines surrounded the ship with one near the aft end.

"Gil?" Jaq asked her defensive weapons officer.

He shook his head. "They are danger close. Another blast could hurt us worse than what we already are. Recommend we don't fire."

"Are those two scouts ready to die?" Jaq looked at Taurus.

"They are, but they're sitting still just like us."

Jaq clenched her fists, looking back and forth between the screen and the crew.

Brad jumped up and headed for the corridor.

"Employing damage control. I'll report when we know the extent of the damage."

He disappeared off the bridge.

"Amie, open a comm channel to those ships."

"Roger." She tapped her keys and delivered a tight nod to the captain.

"Malibor scout ships. We've hit a mine and are counting six more surrounding us. Would you know anything about that?" Jaq counseled her tone, but she was furious. She expected the Malibor to be contentious, but they'd damaged the ship. The forward sections weren't manned during movements because those decks were closest to impacts during high-speed transit, whether the source was natural or artificial.

"We're trapped out here, too. We dare not move because one of those mines will destroy us. Your monster ship weathered the impact well. We didn't see any Borwyn bodies ejected into space. Shame."

Jaq growled before replying. "I think you should watch your smart mouth. We have our weapons trained on your ships and are more than happy to arrange your meeting with Septiman so He can judge you harshly."

"Your threats are meaningless. What are you going to do about those mines so we can all get out of here alive?"

"You seem to think that I care about your lives," Jaq snapped. She took a breath and exhaled before speaking again. "The mines are between our ships. We can't detonate them without risking us both. How did they get here and why? Seems convenient that you're hiding among them."

"We stopped here because of them. We were shooting for the zero-gravity point between Rondovan and Sairvor."

Jaq drew her finger across her neck to close the channel. "If it wasn't those two, then who?" She looked at Brad's empty seat. No one knew this space better than him. "Alby?"

"Not even the slightest idea. Could that ship that tried to ram us have dropped them? A gunship, maybe? We fought a lot of ships in this area. They didn't have a chance."

"And they would do whatever they could. Mines are a weapon the Malibor would use. Then again, we dropped two missiles in space and put a few landers out there filled with explosives. May Septiman forgive us." Jaq shook her head. "Give me the channel again."

"Go," Amie told her.

"Do you have any ideas on how we can disarm the mines?"

"They're not ours. We don't have anything like that. You'll have to ask the Malpace. That's their kind of garbage. Pollute space so no one can use it."

"Then we're in this together. Can you move at all?"

"No. We move. They follow. If we stay still, they remain dormant."

Jaq thought for a moment. "We'll work on it. We'll be back in touch."

Amie closed the channel.

"We have three landers that we could use to draw them away," Jaq proffered. "But I don't like that idea because it would leave us with none. We also have *Starstrider*."

"*Starwalker* is at New Septimus," Alby suggested.

Jaq shook her head. "And that would show the Malibor

where the Borwyn have been hiding. I don't want to reveal anything about New Septimus." She looked toward the corridor. "I'm going to check on the damage. In the interim, get Teo, Bec, and anyone else up here who might have ideas on how we can deal with those mines. I want as many ideas as I can get so we can come up with the least risky way to get out of this mess and back to Septimus. We have people on the ground who need to know that we're coming."

While Jaq was taking advantage of zero-gee and flying off the bridge, she heard Gil start an interrogation of Donal about targeting the defensive weapons systems for danger-close fire.

Jaq wasn't sure where Brad was, but she knew where the damage had occurred. Her heart skipped a beat at the unexpected damage with the possible loss of life. The added delays put Crip and the others on the ground at risk. She had to stop to collect herself before reaching the central shaft.

It wouldn't do for the crew to see her distressed. She was the central spine of *Chrysalis*. If she warped or broke, the ship would fail. *We're so close*, she thought, *but obstacles keep punching us in the mouth.*

She wanted to vent her frustration on the Sairvor Malibor, blast them with a full broadside. They might be responsible, no matter that they claimed the opposite, but that wouldn't solve anything since they were trapped as much as *Chrysalis* unless they could deactivate the mines.

Her team would search the scout ships once they were able to board whether the Malibor liked it or not. Trust but verify.

She would shake their hands and send them on their way

loaded to the overhead with food for their people. And she'd watch them return to the planet surface, where they could share the goodwill with Borwyn labels on everything.

Jaq thought about what it would take to defeat the Malibor when a single mine could stop *Chrysalis* dead in its tracks. She needed the Malibor to stop fighting.

She pushed off the wall and continued to the central shaft, heading up toward the ship's nose. She pulled herself out on the second level where the worst damage had been highlighted in the immediate damage report. She found Brad in the corridor adjacent to the damaged area.

"How bad is it?"

"We don't think there are any structural issues. Blasted a series of outer panels from the double-hull structure. It's not horrible. We need to reskin about two meters by five meters on the outside and one-by-two meters on the interior hull. Phillips Senior and Junior are heading outside to take care of it."

Jaq screwed up her face. "Is that safe?"

"They are going to keep an eye on the mines as they move to the damage. If the mines don't pick up on the people, then we'll be good. If the mines move, we'll know right away and they can come back inside."

"Will they have time?" Jaq wondered

"The alternative is that they freeze in place and wait for us to figure something out that doesn't involve blowing up a mine and showering them with shrapnel." Brad frowned. "They have that as an emergency action. They can do the super-slow crawl across the hull to get back inside."

"There's no way we can fix this from the inside?"

"Only the inner hull. That leaves us exposed in what is supposed to be a hardened part of the nose. We need that for the debris we tend to leave everywhere we encounter the Malibor. Also, we didn't get the manual override installed up here."

Jaq laughed. "Of course we didn't, but that was by design. No people up here to override. We just occupy the next section wearing suits and then activate the bulkhead. Once the pressure between the two sections equalizes, the bulkhead should open. That would give us access to the internal part. We can fix that first so we can fly if needed. We push back the hull breach to the space between the outer and inner hull."

"I knew that, but wanted the biggest fix first, but your priority is better. I need to intercept those two before they go outside. They're in their suits. We only need to stage them in here and activate the next emergency bulkhead." Brad rushed off, leaving Jaq standing there.

She deactivated the magnetic clamps on her boots to check the emergency bulkhead. It was scarred from previous impacts. The corridor walls were also discolored. A railgun projectile hole in the deck had been welded, and the repair stood out against the deck's texture. Scars were a testament to the resilience of the ship and its crew. Burned and punctured but not broken.

Jaq felt rejuvenated despite the work before them and the mines surrounding the ship. It didn't take much to breathe new life into her soul. They were close to winning. She could feel it.

That meant they were close to losing, too, but the

Borwyn crew wouldn't allow it. Phillips and his son were willing to go outside the ship to repair the damage, outside where six mines hovered, waiting to activate. Jaq didn't curse her bad luck at hitting one mine, she thanked Septiman for their good fortune that it was only one.

CHAPTER 19

The ship is no more than the life and desires of its crew.

Brad intercepted the Phillips boys, rerouting them away from the airlock and into the bulkhead section. He released the lock and the bulkhead slammed down behind him.

He contacted Engineering to vent the atmosphere from that space. After Teo confirmed the location and then reconfirmed, the panel showing the status of the next space turned from green to red.

At that point, the automatic bulkhead should have raised. Brad used his portable radio to contact the welders.

"Phillips one and two, status, over."

"Bulkhead is up, and we are moving in," the elder Phillips reported.

Zero-gee made it easier for them to get into place with their equipment and metal patches. The storage areas had secured scrap metal for such use. They'd recovered tons of it from *Butterfly*, their sister ship, but they had used much of their stock. The damage from the attack that drove *Chrysalis* into hiding had been extensive. Phillips Junior nearly losing his life had been a motivator for his father to drive himself even harder.

The two made a great team and that was how Brad intended to deploy them, especially when there was only a single glaring wound to the ship. He would leave it in their hands.

That left the rest of the crew on alert with nothing to do.

"Cutting the patch to fit the interior hull," Phillips said casually. "While you're out there picking your nose, why don't you get us another patch for the outside? Two meters by five meters or two by two and a half times two. We can weld them together if need be."

"We can pre-position them, but once we've restored atmosphere, we'll probably take care of those mines before you two go outside. It's a mite dangerous out there."

"You need to know if those mines will follow someone in a suit, don't you?" Phillips asked.

Brad wanted to know. "I'll test that theory myself."

He headed to the central shaft and down, pulling himself as quickly as he could. He passed Jaq, who had not heard his exchange. She was too busy talking with the crew to keep them motivated. She had been sending people to eat in small shifts. Most of the crew remained on station, except for the ten percent hurrying to the mess deck for a snack.

Brad approved. Good food always made him feel better. He would have loved to join them, but he didn't have the time.

He reached the bottom deck where the majority of the

environmental suits were stored. He picked one that was recently cleaned and fully charged. There weren't very many ready to go.

There was only two crew working in the area. "Do you guys need help?" Brad asked.

"We could use an extra set of hands." They looked hopefully at Brad.

He made a face while shaking his head. "I'm going outside to play chicken with a mine, but I'll send a couple people to you. We're in between engagements at the moment."

"Are we going knee-deep into another battle?"

"Soon. Right now, we're staring down a couple Malibor scout ships, but they're unarmed. The problem is the six mines. There were seven, but you know what happened to one."

They nodded but didn't press Brad for a further explanation because he was already getting into the suit. He locked the gloves in place before putting the helmet on.

The suit prep crew double-checked the fit and gave him a thumbs-up.

"I need a mobility pack, too," he said.

The crew took one off the bulkhead. "It's served us well," the crewmember said.

Brad examined it. Like every other mobility pack, it was scraped and discolored from use and abuse. He remembered it well. It was the one he'd used when they moved the power plant away from the dead Malibor cruiser.

"I like this one," he told them.

Brad headed for the central shaft and flew upward. He

intended to use the port roller airlock. He hoped the bumper would provide some protection if he could hide behind it.

He wasn't sure it would help if a mine came after him, but it was better than nothing.

Brad flew down the corridor, past the pre-staged supplies for the Sairvor Malibor, and into the airlock. By procedure, they kept the interior hatch open to prevent a hostile from using the airlock until *Chrysalis* was ready. Brad closed the hatch and cycled the system. He popped the outer hatch and pulled himself outside the ship. The airlock closed once Brad was clear.

He clung to the hull, pulling himself hand-over-hand aside the roller.

"Brad, is that you outside the ship?" Jaq broadcast to his radio.

"It might be. Would I be in trouble if I were?"

"Better you than our welders," Jaq replied. "What do you hope to accomplish out there?"

"I would like to determine if a person in a spacesuit will trigger those mines to follow."

"So you volunteered to use yourself as bait?"

"If I had asked, what would you have said?"

"That you were the best choice for this job. Lead from the front. It's what we do, Brad. Don't get yourself killed. I was just starting to like you."

"I shall endeavor to survive this little adventure. Sorry, gotta go. I need to concentrate."

Brad twisted himself around to look at space. He had a hard time seeing the mines. One of the Malibor scouts was outlined against a backdrop of the planet. That's how Brad saw the first mine, looking for where it was little more than a shadow against the planet. He knew where the others were in relation to it. He looked for the one he thought was the closest.

He finally located it, but when he took his eyes off it to watch where he was walking, he spent just as long relocating the mine.

"I need your help," he radioed.

"Your wish is my command," Jaq replied.

"I doubt that, but I need second-to-second feedback on whether these mines are moving. I'm having a hard time keeping my eyes on them."

"I think it's intentional that you can't see them. Standby. Chief Ping will talk to you directly."

"Hey, Captain. How's it hanging?"

Brad chuckled. "It's floating, but we'll leave that alone for now. I'm going to walk upright along the hull. Let me know if I need to duck."

"I doubt you'll be able to duck fast enough if one of those mines goes off."

"I mean to hide if it starts moving. Okay, I'm upright."

"No movement. Still no movement. And it's not moving..."

"Funny. Can you put the nice guy on the radio?"

"Nope. Captain's orders. Still nothing. Seems like it doesn't differentiate a person in a spacesuit."

Brad stopped walking. "I'm going to use the mobility pack and fly a short distance off the hull. While I'm out here, I might as well check the damage up front." Brad released his magnetic clamps and touched the pneumatic jets to accelerate at less than a meter a second. He angled along the hull. "Moving with the pack. Distance to the hull is two meters, traveling parallel."

"They are not moving, Captain."

"I like hearing that. I'm going to extend to five meters from the hull." Brad angled away, maintaining a steady speed.

"We have movement. The mine closest to you is on an intercept course at slow speed."

"Moving to the hull." Brad accelerated enough to hit the hull in less than two seconds. He grabbed a projection and hung on, cycling the mobility pack down.

"It's still coming directly at you."

"Crap. I'm moving away from the ship." Brad pushed hard off the hull with both feet to fly free of the ship without engaging the mobility pack. He could see the mine change course to intercept him. Brad fired the jets at one hundred percent.

The mine accelerated to match him.

Brad shrugged out of the pack, aimed it away from the Malibor scouts and *Chrysalis,* and turned it loose. He maintained his speed while the pack accelerated. He relaxed his limbs and turned around to watch the mine. He floated free, making no extraneous movements. The mine came directly at him.

"Brad, get out of there!" Jaq ordered helplessly.

Brad turned off his radio, but spoke as if it were on. "The pack is headed toward deep space without me. I'm a slave to physics, Jaq. There's no changing course for me. Damn. Not how I wanted to go, just when things were getting good. Bye,

Jaq." Brad stared at the mine as it approached. It was picking up speed.

He arched his back to get out of its way. It passed less than a meter from him. He forced himself to keep his eyes open, see what there was to see on the Malibor weapon. A rough, non-reflective surface. Protrusions, probably contact triggers. Rudimentary propulsion.

The mine accelerated past him.

Brad held his breath while the mine shrank into the distance.

He reactivated his radio. "It appears to care nothing about me," Brad said. "The damage to my ego may never recover."

"I bet it will. Brace yourself, feet first toward the explosion," Jaq advised.

"I'll do my best, but I'm moving away from the ship at an alarming rate. The delta between its speed and mine is not as great as I would like."

Brad put his feet toward the mobility pack and the mine racing after it. He straightened to show as little surface area as possible while wishing for the mobility pack to maintain its course and acceleration.

Time slowed while Brad waited for the inevitable. "I think we could outrun the mines," Brad said. The mine could barely out-accelerate the mobility pack and its two pneumatic thrusters. "Get a jump on them and go."

The explosion started as a white flash. In space, there was sound, but it was miniscule. A low growl, like a vibration, swept past along with fragments—the lethal part of the mine. A small shard caught the fabric on the arm of his suit.

Atmosphere immediately vented in a narrow stream. He slapped a hand over the tear and held it shut.

"Brad, are you okay?" Jaq sounded concerned, almost desperate.

"One little tear. I'll slap duct tape on it when I get a free hand." Brad laughed at his own joke.

Jaq didn't reply. He expected she was making faces.

Brad continued, "Looks like we have a method to lead the mines away from the ship."

"You want me to donate five mobility packs? Maybe you can wave your arms to get the attention of a second mine, then we'd only have to sacrifice four more packs."

"That's harsh, Jaq. I thought you liked me."

"Tolerated without disdain was what I meant to say," Jaq replied. She leveled her voice to deal with the reality of the situation. "You'll need to shepherd your power and air. I don't know when we'll be able to come get you. Turn off everything except your heat and radio. We'll contact you when you need to turn on your beacon."

"Heat's already at a minimum. I think my eyelashes are frozen. I'm showing three hours of air, Jaq."

"Looks like we'll have you picked up in less time than that, then. Get some sleep. I'll be back in touch."

"Sleep. Yes, that's what I feel like doing." Brad didn't transmit his last. He'd already turned the microphone off. He checked his power systems to find he had five hours of juice. He turned the heat up to above freezing.

They'd learned valuable information, but was a lingering death worth the price?

CHAPTER 20

Trust no one, even when you have to trust somebody.

Deena glared at the laughing men. One of them had just pinched her butt. She turned quickly, but not fast enough to see which of the two closest to her had done it.

"Get out," she said.

"We're still eating, and dessert isn't far away," one of them replied with a lurid lick of his lips.

Deena backed up until she was out of reach and then blocked the boss. "One of them grabbed me."

"Then punch him in the face." The big man shrugged.

"I didn't see which one did it. Can't punish the innocent for the crimes of the guilty."

The boss scoffed. "They're all guilty. Look at them." He turned back to the paperwork he was buried under.

Deena put the dishes down and headed back to the table. "Boss said you gotta leave because you're jerks."

"Nah." Before the man could finish his denial, Deena

slapped him across the face. He came out of his chair in a fury. Deena was already in motion with a front kick that landed square in his groin the instant he was upright. He doubled over and fell backward. The next closest soldier demonstrated his indignance by reaching for Deena.

She turned and delivered a heel strike to his nose, exploding it over his face in a spurt of blood that reminded her of a squashed tomato. She jumped back, hands raised and ready to fight the other two soldiers at the table.

The man with the shattered nose dropped to his chair while the blood flowed through his fingers and down his chin.

"I said don't touch me!" Deena shouted. "I demand to know who your commanding officer is so I can report your misconduct."

The soldiers at the other tables put their heads down and focused solely on their meals. That was exactly what Deena wanted from them. Compliance through fear.

"You're going to have a hard time explaining how a girl beat you bloody. You're in over your heads, gentlemen. Your behavior is unbecoming. We're going to stand up to you and you will suffer greater and greater until you understand. We're not your property, and we're not your toys. Now, pay your bill and get out of this restaurant."

"We won't come back!" the first assailant grunted while he continued to hold his twig and berries.

"Then the class of our clientele will definitely rise. We don't need any customers who demean the uniform along with all of the Malibor. Put your money on the table and walk away before you get yourselves hurt."

"Where'd you learn to fight like that?" asked a soldier from a neighboring table.

"A stepfather who thought everyone in the house was his property. He walks with a permanent limp nowadays. I can't imagine where that came from." Deena smiled and took herself into the kitchen.

The cook cowered. "Holy bejeebies. You don't care, do you?"

"I care too much about the sanctity of my own body. You should care about yours, too."

"I do," he said.

"You take drugs. You do not care about your body."

"Hey!" He straightened for a moment before ducking his head. "Don't hit me."

"Why would I hit you?" Deena looked curiously at him. A minor commotion came from the front when the soldiers tipped their table over on the way out. Deena barely gave it a glance. "So?"

"Because you hit people for no reason?" the cook ventured.

"You know that's not true. I hit people for the valid reasons of modifying their malicious behavior. No one should act like that. No one should tolerate those who act like that."

The cook checked the grill. He flipped a burger off it and directly onto the bun. "Order for table four."

Deena laughed. "You're all right when you're not acting the fool. I'll get this right out to them." She grabbed two plates and walked them into the seating area, stepping carefully through the mess on the floor.

She delivered the order with a smile and a call to enjoy their meal.

The soldiers in the restaurant clapped. Deena bowed to them, then turned to cleaning up the mess.

"We'll do it," a young soldier offered. "They're from my unit. We feel obligated to make it right, but we'd appreciate it if you didn't report it to the commander. I don't think you'd like what he'd do."

"Put the restaurant off limits and bring me up on charges?" Deena knew the type.

The soldiers at the young man's table laughed. "Sounds like you served."

"Brother served. I got the stories secondhand," Deena lied. "I appreciate it. I'll get the mop."

Four soldiers had the area straightened in less than a minute. Deena mopped up the mess. The young man handed over the money that had been scattered. "I think they shorted you."

"Add stealing to their inauspicious record. Do you want those guys anywhere near you in a war with the Borwyn?"

Their faces dropped. "How'd you hear about the upcoming war?"

Deena hesitated. She wanted to hear what they were planning, but she didn't want to expose herself as a spy.

"Aren't we always at war with the Borwyn? They're trying to steal our land." She had a hard time saying the words.

"There's a hard push to recruit soldiers to go to space, join the fleet. The smart ones are already gone, but they didn't volunteer. They were reassigned. It doesn't say much about us that we weren't chosen, or at least their impression of us."

"Keep your feet on the ground. This is a good place if you let it be. It doesn't have to be like what they're trying to make it. Malipride is a beautiful city. We need to enjoy it, all of us together, not just the men while the women hide. We're supposed to be equal, aren't we?"

"A feminist," someone from a nearby table said in a low voice.

"A pragmatist," Deena countered. "Why should half the population be held down? Have the men defeated the Borwyn yet? I heard they've destroyed a great number of fleet ships. Is that true?"

"It's classified. Soldiers shouldn't open their big mouths when they're not on the compound." The soldier glared at Deena. He was the next rank higher than the others. A corporal, Deena thought.

She bowed her head. "I'm sorry. I've not told anyone. I work, I sleep, then I come back to work. I have no life besides this restaurant, and I despise getting grabbed. Reminds me of my stepfather. I will always fight back," Deena explained. "Half-price for everyone. Settle your bills. I think we'll close early today. I'm a wreck."

"If you want to do something else, I'd be happy to go to a museum with you," the young soldier said. Deena was young, but this man was still her junior.

"I'm not ready to date anyone, not yet anyway, but you've been very kind, and that's how you do it. That's how you create a respectable relationship." Deena headed to the closet to put the mop away.

She reset the table and picked up the cash left there. It was less than their bill but more than the food cost, so it was better than a wash. She went to the restroom and cleaned up. By the time she made it back to the restaurant, the crowd was lined up to pay.

They nodded to her and checked out with the boss.

When the last one was gone, the boss turned the sign around to show they were closed and locked the door.

"Sorry, Boss man," Deena said softly.

"They're not going to boycott us. I've had spies checking out our competition, and they report that there is no competition. We are the cleanest and best within walking distance of the front gate. They'll be back. There's no way those guys are going to tell anyone they got beat up by a girl. Four on one and they lost. I'd be careful going out, if I was you. They're going to want some kind of payback."

"Next time, I'll break more than a nose, but I can't stay here, as you know. I have to get my own place, so that's what I'll do this afternoon. There are a couple places I want to check."

"Go on then. We'll take care of closing the shop." The boss waved her away. She dropped her apron on the counter and waved on her way out the door. The boss relocked it behind her.

She went straight to the bus stop. She had no intention of staying anywhere near the restaurant, which was too close to the military compound and spaceport. Deena needed the separation, to not be a fixture in this part of the city. She'd thought she could tolerate the challenges because it was only going to be for a short time, but it was dragging on.

I miss you, Max, she thought while waiting. She kept checking around for soldiers to intrude, but only civilians milled about.

She needed to find a place and then she needed to call Crip and Max. The Malibor admitted they were starting a war with the Borwyn and that they were recruiting assets for the fleet. If *Chrysalis* had destroyed nearly all of their combat vessels, where were they sending the transfers? What did the Malibor have that Jaq didn't know?

Deena frowned while thinking about it. The Malibor had a surprise in store. Crip needed to know. Jaq needed to know.

Where was *Chrysalis*?

Deena liked it on the ground. The free space, the air, the sky. Even the city.

She'd take the first place that was even close to reasonable. All she had to do was afford it. Moving in would be easy. A backpack and a bag. That was it.

Would she want to keep the apartment after a Borwyn victory? Would it be possible to stay?

Probably not. Once anyone learned she worked with the Borwyn, her life would be in jeopardy, no matter how well the Borwyn treated them compared to the corruption of the Malibor government.

The bus arrived, and Deena climbed on. She threw coins into the register and took a seat in the back so she could keep an eye on her fellow passengers.

Over the next half-hour, riders got on and off without rhyme or reason. When they entered the residential district, Deena left the bus. She followed the directions to a rental agency. They were easy to find since they displayed more signs than should have been reasonable.

"Looking for an apartment. Will pay with cash. What do you have?" Deena told the first agent.

The woman's eyes brightened.

Deena slipped her a hundred pfennig bill. "For you. I can't emphasize enough that I want to secure a place today."

She checked her listings and skipped past the cheaper places to the high-end ones.

Deena shook her head. "Middle of the road."

The woman scrolled back. "Next door. Second floor. Controlled access. You running from someone?" Deena stared at her. "No matter. This is the right place. Let's take a look."

They strolled to the next building on the block, a property owned by the leasing company with the apartments they'd show off before sticking people into other apartments scattered throughout the area.

Close to the bus stop. Away from the military. And secure.

They went to the top floor. "The second-floor apartment will be ready later today," the agent explained. Deena visualized an eviction team ready to throw a deadbeat tenant out on the street.

"This is an identical layout." The agent opened the door to an apartment that was far more than Deena needed.

"This is pretty big. It's just me."

"You could grow into it with a long-term rental."

"What's the premium for this place?" Deena asked.

"Twenty-five percent higher than the second-floor apartment."

Deena didn't have to save any of the money she was earning. She didn't even need food.

A furnished apartment on the top floor. It was between two other apartments, but she could turn on the included video system to mask a radio call.

"I'll take it on a three-month contract."

"We need six."

"Done."

Deena followed the agent back to the office to finish the paperwork and make the payment for the first two months. Deena handed over cash. The agent waited for another *tip*.

"There's a limit to paying someone extra for doing their job. It is your job to rent apartments, is it not?"

"Sure, but it can be the easy way or the hard way."

Deena trapped the woman's wrist on the desk and squeezed. "I already gave you an extra hundred for no reason whatsoever. How much extortion do you get away with on a daily basis? And don't tell me none, since you seem well-practiced. Don't be the second person I've had to beat senseless today. Well, third, to be honest. And because we've come to an understanding, I don't want any problems with that apartment. If I have to come back in here, you'll be sorry you ever saw me walk through that door." Deena smiled until the woman nodded.

She hustled through the paperwork. Deena walked out of the office ten minutes later with two keys to the apartment and two keys to the outer door. She walked around the neighborhood to get the lay of the land. A small grocery store was less than a block away. A liquor store was next to it.

Deena bought a salty snack, fresh fruit, and a can of beer. She helped herself into her new apartment and placed her prizes in the refrigerator. She tried the video system and was pleased to find it was operational. Watching news or what passed for entertainment was novel. It had been forever since she watched anything like average Malibor television.

Forever. That was three whole years. It felt like two lifetimes ago.

She took one last stroll through her apartment and left. She needed to get her stuff from the restaurant, and that meant the radio. She had to make a call.

CHAPTER 21

Life and death are one thread, the same line viewed from different sides.

"Max, it's Deena. She wants to use voice again." Crip shook Max. The urgency in his voice and the contact with his wife was enough for him to vault off his cot. He threw on his uniform shirt and ran barefoot from the bunker. Crip was right behind him. "You know you're in your underwear."

"No time," Max replied while glancing down. He looked sideways at Crip, but the commander was all business. They needed the coordinates to pass on to *Chrysalis* and *Matador*. They hoped she had them.

Max sat at the radio where the operator had already copied the burst transmission with a series of seemingly arbitrary numbers.

"There we go!" Crip declared. He took the numbers and ran toward the command center.

Max took the microphone. "We have voice," he said.

"Great to hear yours," Deena replied. "They are recruiting for the fleet and have already sent what they called their best and their brightest to space."

"What does that mean?" Max wondered.

"I wish I knew." Deena passed on the information. She'd leave it up to those with more information to decide what it meant. "There are three gunships at the spaceport."

Max nodded to the radio. "Three gunships, roger. Are you doing well?"

"I am holding it together, but I'm ready to leave. Please tell me it'll be soon. Also, tell me Moran is okay."

"It'll be as soon as we can make it. Moran is recovering, albeit slowly. He lost his arm and that is taking some getting used to."

"He lost his arm?"

"But not his life. We need to close this channel. Keep your head down. As soon as we can, we'll be there or you'll be here."

"Next comm in three days," Deena confirmed. "I look forward to seeing you."

"Yeah, me, too." Max handed the microphone to the radio operator, who closed the channel.

"I hope they aren't using radio direction finding equipment. She'll be found out." The radio operator's expression was grim.

Max blew out a hard breath. He shared the same fear. He stood but leaned heavily on the table.

"You don't have your pants on," the radio operator observed.

Max looked down and recoiled in mock surprise. "I must

have run over here so fast, I left my pants behind. That's going to make for a long and embarrassing walk back to my cot. I better get going, then."

Max had to find Crip. Three gunships. That changed the dynamic. It begged the question of whether they were operational or not. He assumed they weren't, believing they would have already deployed if they could.

Or were the gunships hiding?

Fleet personnel, recruited. Would they take the gunships to space to intercept *Chrysalis*? Ambush the Borwyn flagship when it appeared in the skies over Malipride. Ambush. Three gunships were no match for Jaq and *Chrysalis*.

The combat team had their own gunship. They could hit the enemy ships while they were on the ground. They wouldn't have a chance. What air defenses were active over the spaceport?

Max detoured to the command bunker to talk with Crip.

He found him with a grease pencil at the map of Malipride. He'd marked the locations of the headquarters building and also the locations of the key targets at the spaceport.

"Deena said three gunships. Did she identify any radar installations or air defenses?"

"One building that she identified as traffic control, one radar, and three enemy ships. She said those were gunships." Crip chewed on his lip while he studied the board. "They're staggered. We could hit two with one pass from *Matador,* but they'd have to swing around for a second pass to take out the third."

"She didn't say anything about air defenses?"

Crip shook his head. He handed over the paper with the codes.

Max read through it twice. "Does that mean she didn't see any or that she couldn't look for them?"

Crip shrugged. "Welcome to the unknowns of planning for a battle where our very existence is at stake."

"Where are your pants?" Eleanor asked as she walked up.

Max looked down, annoyed that people cared that he was only partially dressed. "Too busy." Max tried to read between the lines of code, but it was simple and there was no hidden message.

"You have nothing to be ashamed of," Eleanor replied.

Crip snickered. "We have our targeting information, but we're missing one thing. Air defenses."

"That's not a big deal for us, but your people flying the gunship could find the information useful so they don't get themselves shot down."

"Our thoughts exactly. Have you made any calls to the mountain recently? Can we request a call with Tram?"

"Once the gunship went airborne, we implemented radio silence. Just in case the Malibor turned on their radio direction finding equipment. We can't risk giving away the location of New Pridal."

"And Deena's been using clear voice on the radio."

"You need to stop her from doing that. Hopefully, it's not too late."

Max closed his eyes and groaned. "She's trying to do the right thing. She's privy to what's going on in a way we never suspected. We never had codes for that stuff. I'd think the Malibor could break a simple replacement cypher. She could carry nothing with her." Max ran through a series of excuses in his mind, and none of them added up to increase her safety.

"She's taking a risk based on her assessment of the information's value. I don't agree with it, but she's on her own and it is her decision," Crip explained.

"Request permission to put together an extraction team. We have Malibor clothing we can wear."

"We don't look Malibor, not even a little bit. Max, we can't go running into the city. We'd wreak havoc, and then we'd die. Borwyn in Malipride! That would unite them against us like nothing else could."

Max wasn't buying it. "We'll move at night. They won't know we're there."

"Next call, we'll tell her to get out. We'll transmit the recall code and cut the channel. Then we'll go to the edge of the forest and wait for her."

"She's going to need help," Max insisted.

"Go get some sleep, or at least put some pants on. You'll think about it and realize that the only thing we can do is make things worse. We have to wait. Might as well add *pray* to the few options available."

Max nodded. "I'll be in my bunk." He walked away with a heavy cloud hanging over his head.

Eleanor waited until he was gone. "You need to watch him."

"He's upset, the most I've ever seen, and I've known him his whole life. He's worried about Deena."

Eleanor agreed with the obvious. "Still. You don't want him to get hurt because he's distracted."

"No live fire. We need to contact our people in the mountain. They need instruction on employment of the gunship. That includes coordinates and when to go. How do we get in touch with them?"

Eleanor held her hand up and made a walking motion with two fingers.

Crip shook his head. "That's what I was afraid of."

Brad had lost oxygen when he wrapped duct tape around his arm, but not much. He tightened the fabric and started at the hole itself. After that, he had nothing to do but wait.

He'd slept, oddly, but once he woke, all he could see was the countdown until he'd be out of air.

He was a long way from *Chrysalis*, which both surprised and amazed him about distances in space. Something as large as the cruiser disappeared quickly into the darkness of the void. He was on the wrong side to see reflections from Armanor's beams. No one cast a shadow in space. They only created a deeper darkness.

Twenty minutes.

He activated his radio. "Jaq, tell me good news."

"We deployed five mobility packs, but the mines didn't follow them. We don't know why."

"Now we're down six packs and the ship remains trapped. You have time. Save yourselves by saving the ship. Form an alliance with the Sairvor Malibor. Let me say that again to be sure you got it: don't be in a hurry."

"How much time do you have, Brad?" Jaq asked.

"Fifteen minutes of air and two minutes of gasping the last bits. I'll turn off my radio. Actually, let me save a little bit of power now so I can at least be warm. Turning up the heat. I guess it wasn't meant to be. Save your words. Think kindly of me, and tell my daughter she's the best of everything I am. For my sons, I wish I had the chance to meet their wives. Okay, that's enough. See you when it's all over."

Brad turned off his radio before anyone could reply. Fifteen minutes. Watching himself die hadn't ever been an option he was willing to accept, but physics had worked against him. *A body in motion remains in motion unless acted upon by an outside force.* He was traveling inexorably into space and would continue to do so. Maybe they'd collect his body later.

He'd be blue. A song came to mind, and he chuckled briefly. Blue and frozen solid. *I guess I've lived long enough,* he thought.

Brad stared into the blackness behind him where he couldn't see the ship or anything else. Armanor cast light but there were shadows...

He slammed backward into a solid object, bounced, and started to tumble. He flailed with both hands, looking for something to grab onto. He was too close to see what he'd hit. The object slipped beyond his grip and he continued to spin away, but he had slowed.

Coming around, he recognized the shape behind him. A Borwyn scout ship. He turned his radio on. "You are a glorious sight, *Starwalker*."

"Who are you talking to?" Jaq asked. "We see nothing on our scopes."

The ship eased toward him using thrusters only. The side hatch popped open, and a spacesuit-wearing individual leaned out with a rope. The ship slowly overtook Brad until the rope could be tossed. He caught it and gripped it like the lifeline it was. He pulled himself toward the hatch. The individual inside pulled him rapidly toward the ship.

Brad was dragged inside, and the hatch was secured. He started to remove his helmet, but the figure stopped him, drawing a line across his throat.

"I have less than five minutes of air left," Brad nearly screamed. His breaths were getting harder to draw into his lungs. Five was optimistic.

So close, he thought. He wanted to pull his helmet off but was stopped once more. He floated freely within the cabin while a pilot worked the controls to hold the ship steady.

Doing nothing to draw the attention of the mines, and that included not transmitting. Getting blown up would be a lousy way to end a rescue.

A green light flashed on the panel, and the figure unlatched Brad's helmet and pulled it free, bouncing the rim off the back of Brad's skull in his hurry to let Brad take a deep breath.

He immediately choked and gasped as the air was still at an extremely low temperature. Brad exhaled clouds of vapor in rapid succession while he tried to slow his breathing. The figure who helped him took off his own helmet.

"Cold, no?" Bill Macturno said casually.

"Bill. You dragged your wrinkly old ass out here to save me?"

"I wanted to give you a hard time because that's what I

do. What did you think you would accomplish out here? I never took you for suicidal, but you always had some mental health issues going on. It was inevitable that your self-destruction would become apparent for all to see. I've known it for the past fifty years."

"Of course you did." Brad slowed his breathing, taking the air in through his nose and out through his mouth.

The pilot was a younger member of the New Septimus citizens. "You're Bill's nephew?"

"That's right. Wellesly."

"It was coming to me," Brad lied.

"I'm afraid there's a problem with the heater and we won't get the temp above freezing. If you have power left in your suit, maybe turn up your heater."

"It's already up," Brad replied. "I was going to die from a lack of air, not power. I decided I wasn't going to shiver my way to the afterlife." Brad looked to the two men. "How did you get out here without attracting the attention of the mines?"

"Thrusters and no emissions. You were hard to find," Bil admitted. "We'll accelerate slowly until we can take a spin around Rondovan."

Brad pursed his lips. "I have a different idea. Stop scoffing. At least give me a chance to articulate my suggestion."

CHAPTER 22

The oxen are slow, but Septiman is patient.

Tram paced along the main thoroughfare of New Pridal. It cut a line down the center of the cavern where the majority of the city was located. The only traffic was foot traffic as people went about their business. People glanced at the strangers as they passed.

The women wore tanned hide outfits that made them stand out, but the locals were kind enough not to stare. Tram and Kelvis wore their coveralls. They hadn't dressed for ground operations.

"Maybe we can get different clothes. I expect that's a different requisition form funneled through two different departments. Or we could let Evelyn handle it."

Evelyn gave Tram the side-eye look of doom. He didn't wither under the spotlight.

"I'm starting to get a reputation, and I'm not sure I like it."

"You've gotten us everything. The gunship is refueled, rearmed, and stocked with snacks. We only need a 'go' order."

"Are clothes your priority, or do you want to talk with Crip?"

"Well, if I have to choose, I'll go a direct comm channel to Crip and the combat team."

"Then let's focus on that." She pointed to a tunnel. "Is that where we can find the radio operators?"

Tram nodded.

Evelyn held out her hand and Kelvis took it. They walked together while Tram draped his arm over Sophia's shoulders.

"What do you want to do?" Tram whispered.

"I want to win this war so we can go home."

"You mean the village life," Tram replied. "I'm good with that. Maybe grow potatoes." He laughed. "Can you see me growing potatoes?"

"Yes," she replied sincerely.

Evelyn walked with a purpose, quick and with a heavy tread. She slowed to read the signs at offices along the way. Two armed guards stood outside an office ahead. Evelyn glanced over her shoulder and shook her head.

The radio room allowed no casual visitors so people couldn't do what they were attempting.

The sign behind the guards read 'Strategic Communications.'

"We need to send a message," Evelyn said and pointed at the door.

"No communications," the guard said. "We're exercising radio silence because of the gunship's arrival. We can't highlight ourselves while the Malibor are looking this way."

It was what they were told before. Tram was opposed to the alternative.

"The Malibor are that good with RDF?" Tram wondered.

"Do I look like a radio knob?" the guard shot back.

Tram understood the words but not what they meant. "I feel like the right answer is no, but I can't be sure."

"Go on. Off with you." The second guard waved them away.

Tram walked away, chin on his chest as he stared at the floor. "You know what this means," he started. "We're on foot back to the others."

"Maybe we can catch a ride. Let me see what I can do. You wait at the café. I'll meet you there."

Jaq floated around the bridge. If they had gravity, she would have been pacing, stomping back and forth. "What happened to Brad?"

The last transmission had been cryptic, and then his radio went dead.

"I will continue trying to raise him," Amie said. She hunched over her console and spoke softly into her microphone.

"Get me firing solutions on those mines! Repeaters, chain guns, crew with tasers. I'm done being stuck here, a helpless target for whoever can take a shot at us."

"Captain!" Amie interrupted. "It's *Starwalker*. They have recovered Captain Yelchin."

"How'd they get out here?" Jaq shook her head. "It doesn't matter. The stealth scout was able to navigate the minefield?"

"*Chrysalis*, this is your favorite human being on board *Starwalker*. How's it hanging?"

"Brad, you gave us a scare." Jaq didn't go further into her emotional turmoil. "Did the scout ship find a way through the minefield?"

"Afraid not. They refused to fire the main engines or the radio, drifting in with thrusters only. We used thrusters to clear the area. I suggest it's a combination of thrust and electromagnetic emissions that triggers the mines. One or the other might be okay, but not both together. That's why your mobility packs didn't trigger them. Once it locked onto me and the pack, it continued after the movement. Good thing I stopped talking."

Jaq looked at Alby and Slade. "Can we turn it all off? Stop radiating everything?"

"Sure," Alby replied quickly.

Slade hemmed and hawed. He didn't want to shut down his systems. "We'll be blind. We won't know if the mines are following us."

"Better that than blown up. Shut everything off. All electronics, including computers. The only thing we'll keep active is thruster control. We'll thrust our way clear then fire up the mains."

"With everything powered down, it'll take a while to bring the ion drives online," Ferd said.

"Then we'll use our thrusters for that much longer. Get a bearing because you'll be flying blind. I don't want to end up getting sucked into Sairvor's gravity well."

Ferd got to work. He pulled out a pad and made notes, writing vigorously on an erasable page.

"Amie, give me ship-wide." Jaq could have dialed up the intercom herself, but she felt it was more profound when the comm officer did it. She'd bring her an extra Malibor dessert ration later.

Amie nodded that the channel was live.

"All hands. To remove ourselves from this mess, we need to power down all emissions. We will take everything offline except thruster control. We'll use them to move us out of the impact area. Once we are sufficiently clear, we will bring the engines online first to more expeditiously move us away from the mines. Then we will blast them from existence."

Alby raised his hand. "Once we move clear and have a decent stand-off distance, we can blow the mines."

"If we take too long bringing our systems online, they could run us down. I don't think they're fast enough to chase us down, but I don't know for sure. Let's go lower risk and fly away first, then come back shooting. We'll need those Malibor scouts out of the way, too. Amie, give me those two ships, please."

"I have them on speaker."

"Malibor scout ships. Power down all radiating systems like your radars and communications. De-energize anything that radiates and move away on thrusters only. We will be doing the same. We've had a successful test that this works, and that's good enough for me. We'll be moving away from the minefield momentarily. You won't be able to reach us during the transit. As soon as we're clear, we're going to return with our E-mags making short work of those mines. Then we'll reestablish contact with you. Please move out of the blast area, for your own safety. Also, we have the food and water pre-staged by our port and starboard airlocks. Let's clean up the mess left by the Malpace, and then get to work."

"We will watch you move from the area before we de-energize anything. We don't trust you," the Malibor captain replied.

"Have it your way, but don't be here when we come back, otherwise the consequences could be extreme. *Chrysalis* out." She waved to the bridge crew. "Power us down and, Ferd, prepare to get us out of here. Wait for my word."

Alby ordered Gil and Taurus to go through their targeting systems one by one to take them offline. As much as it bothered him, the alternative was less savory. Stalemate was no way to conduct a space battle. *Chrysalis* maintained an advantage when it was underway.

Slade turned off the active emitters. "We can keep passive receptors online with zero emissions," he announced.

"I don't want to take any chances. Give us ten minutes of movement, then turn on the passive collectors. Maintain visual on those mines as long as you can." Jaq hung onto the pole next to her seat. She lounged off the mid-rail while watching her crew work. Systems winked off the main board as they were powered down until only the external visuals remained.

"They'll disappear into the darkness right quick and in a

hurry. They're not exactly designed to be seen," Slade replied.

"Gil, how long will it take to power up defensive weapons?"

"Ten seconds to get one set of repeaters operational. Unleash the fury of the chain guns!"

"I love it when people embrace their job."

"A minute for the E-mags, Captain," Taurus added.

"We'll need to be farther than a minute away at a mine's top speed. It caught up to a mobility pack at maximum acceleration, so it's faster than that." Jaq wasn't sure what the top speed would be. She expected to move for thirty minutes at least to be sure the ship was well away from the minefield. "While you're watching those mines, keep an eye on those scout ships. We'll blast them just as readily as we'll take out the mines. I'm not convinced they knew nothing about them."

"Preparing to send our enemies into oblivion. Roger," Alby declared. "It would make me happy to turn everything in this area into space debris."

"I figured. That's the battle commander's job, but restrain yourself for now. There's something unholy about shooting unarmed ships. And get me the status on the repairs in the forward section."

"They're finished. The Phillipses are waiting at the airlock for the word to head outside," Alby reported.

"Tell them to stand down for the time being. Belay that. I see that internal comms are offline." She looked around the bridge until she saw someone with nothing to do. "Donal. I see you trying to hide. You're a runner. Go the forward airlock and let the Phillips family know what we're doing. Make sure you heap praise on them while they go get something to eat. We might need them in about an hour."

Donal popped out of his seat and flew upward until he slammed into the overhead. He grabbed the upper rail with one hand and saluted awkwardly with the other. "I was just looking for something to do." He pulled himself along the overhead until he reached the hatch to pull himself out of the bridge and kick down the corridor.

Jaq smiled and shook her head. She wasn't used to seeing people who weren't familiar with zero-gee.

The board showed clear. "Are we ready?" she asked.

Alby and Slade both confirmed that systems were offline. Mary and Ferd confirmed they were flying blind.

"Give me thrusters, Ferd. Course, mark two, orientation minus one."

It was the course Ferd had already plotted away from the minefield. The thrusters fired, but the ship movement was imperceptible.

"Are we moving?" Jaq wondered.

"Visual confirms we're moving away," Slade said. "Unable to calculate speed."

"Is your computer on?"

"Hard to access the visual without it, Captain," Slade replied without looking up. "No movement from the mines."

Jaq nodded while leaning against her chair. Only Slade could see outside the ship. Other systems were off. Ferd sent commands to the thrusters and they responded, but without external sensors active, he wasn't sure what was happening. The ship's ancient gyroscope had been calibrated before the systems were taken offline. It provided a limited resource for navigation based on angular momentum and inertia.

"Estimate one meter per second," Ferd said.

Jaq was tense. She wanted to believe that they'd come up with a way to defeat the mines, but she expected one to follow them and then the rest to chase down *Chrysalis* and destroy the ship.

"Keep us sideways to the mines. I don't want to show them our vulnerable sections. Not the aft end and not the open cargo bay with the power plants."

"Power plants are offline, and the cargo bay doors are closed," Alby reported, taking over what Brad would have tracked.

She nodded. She'd seen that but still wanted the power plants on the other side of the ship from the minefield, once they were away from them.

She pulled herself across the command deck using the mid-rail until she reached the sensor pod. She stared at the back of Slade's head until he looked up.

"Not moving," he said and returned his attention to the mines.

"Two meters per second and increasing," Ferd announced.

"Still nothing," Slade said before Jaq could stare at him.

Jaq moved to Gil's station. "When I give you the word, bring up the defensive systems. Let me know when you're ready to fire."

She moved to Taurus's side.

"When I ask Gil to bring his systems online, I want you to energize the E-mags, just in case the defensive systems don't get the job done. I think we'll have enough distance between us to hit them with the big stuff. We'll see if Donal and Dolly's adjustments can zero us in on such small targets."

"I look forward to seeing them disappear," Taurus confirmed. "As many shots as it takes. Those two want more data. I'm happy to oblige."

Jaq smiled. She loved the morale on the bridge.

"Thrusters at maximum. Five meters per second," Ferd said.

Jaq returned to her seat but didn't climb in. She had time to kill and energy in abundance. Waiting wasn't in her nature, but she had no choice. She had to wait as long as it took. Would thirty minutes of thrusters-only propulsion be enough to buy them the time for the defensive systems to power up and lock on to the targets?

Too many unknowns. Once the ion drives were running, they'd accelerate away from the minefield. In seconds, they'd be far enough way that the mines would never catch up.

Nothing but time to kill. Patience had saved Brad's life. Jaq tried to daydream and be thankful for his delivery, but she needed a tactical assist.

"Shepherd, give us a prayer of thanks for Brad's rescue."

"Lo and behold, the magnificence of Septiman! His hand reaches into the cosmos to save our captain's beloved, her dearest sweetheart, he who makes her whole..."

Jaq interrupted. "Yeah, yeah. We get it. Thanks for the blessing, Shepherd." She expected something a little less personal and more big-picture. That was the last time she'd ask the shepherd to help kill time.

"In Septiman's name, we pray," the shepherd finished.

Jaq started to go to Slade's station so she could see what was going on, but he wouldn't let her have his terminal—appropriately so. He had a job to do.

Jaq stopped herself and returned to her seat, where she crawled in. She closed her eyes and made like she was sleeping. Time moved even slower. The lesson of patience would be hammered into her very soul, no matter how much she fought it.

CHAPTER 23

To realize that you do not understand is a virtue; Not to realize that you do not understand is a defect.

Crip rose later than usual. He hadn't slept well, bothered by dreams of horrible events happening in the city. He could do nothing about that, but he could make sure they were ready whenever the battle would be fought. In the city or out, his combat team had to be tight.

He looked for Max, but his cot was empty. "I expect you didn't sleep either, my friend." Crip went to the mess bunker for coffee, eggs, and meat. He snagged his coffee and scanned the few faces under the tent. He asked the cook making eggs to order, "Did you see Max?"

"Hasn't been in yet. Do you want something?"

"Not yet," Crip replied while looking elsewhere. He hurried from the tent to the command bunker, where Glen and Eleanor were studying the new information that Deena had provided.

"Have you seen Max?" he asked.

They shook their heads. "Is there something you want to tell us?" Glen wondered.

Crip held up one finger. "Wait one."

He circled the camp before returning to the combat team's bunker. Crip took a closer look at Max's cot. His pack was gone, as was his pulse rifle. He'd taken his pants, too.

"At least that's something," Crip told the empty space.

He returned to the command bunker, head down and dejected. "Max is gone."

"We figured," Glen replied. "That means we move to an alternate camp so he can't inadvertently give up our position. We'll go to a place he hasn't been to."

"It's the only thing we can do. The good news is that he's more likely to fly under the radar by himself, if there can be any good news out of this."

Glen scowled. "There isn't any good news here. Being married to an operative changes the dynamic and not in a good way. This is why we don't condone it or support it. Let's hope Max comes around before the Malibor find him."

Evelyn batted her eyelashes and smiled her best smile. The dispatcher was having none of it.

"You're not getting any horses. A caravan is going out tomorrow. You can join them. It's the best I can do. Take it or leave it."

"We'll leave with tomorrow's caravan, and thank you. You have been very helpful. We wouldn't know what to do with the horses anyway, so you're right and we're much better off." Evelyn gripped the man's hand for a moment before strolling away.

In the tunnel outside the dispatcher's office, Evelyn lamented. "I must be losing my touch."

"I don't like horses," Tram admitted.

"Everyone knows this," Sophia said, piling on to Tram's discomfort.

He frowned and strolled away from the group. He motioned for them to follow. "We better grab something to take with us to eat. Two days on horseback. Maybe I can get an extra blanket."

"Me, too," Kelvis agreed. "I was made for riding on spaceships."

"It's not that bad," Evelyn groused.

"We'll check in with the caravan lead and then we'll get our stuff from the ship," Tram said. "And then let's find a place to make ourselves sandwiches. I like sandwiches. We never had anything like that on board *Chrysalis*."

"Men..." Sophia looked to Evelyn for confirmation. "Motivated by their stomachs."

"We're fighting to free Septimus for all the Borwyn. That rates a sandwich, doesn't it?"

"What if we have to turn around and come right back to the mountain?" Sophia wondered.

"Then that's what you'll do," Kelvis said. "Evelyn and I will stay here to make sure the ship is in perfect condition."

Tram stared at the old engineer, who smiled beatifically.

"I see how you are. I'll hold you to that. While you're at it, make sure the ammunition hopper is filled. We don't know what kind of death and destruction we'll have to deal. Running the gun wide open might be critical."

"You just want to torture us running up and down that ladder."

"Hook up a pulley. Kelvis is an engineer."

"Can you do that?" Evelyn asked

"Sure. There's an attachment for one because even the Malibor aren't keen on ladder climbing."

Evelyn looked down her nose at Kelvis.

He shrugged and tried to look innocent.

Tram held out his hand and Kelvis shook it. "Take care of our ship. Sophia and I will find out what we need to do with it."

Deena was hyper-aware. She saw the men in every shadow, behind every corner. It was wearing her down. She walked in fits and spurts, stopping to watch to keep anyone from sneaking up on her.

Nothing had changed beside getting the new apartment. She decided to get off the bus one stop early to foil anyone who would be waiting to ambush her.

Except now she had no one with her, and the blaster was at the restaurant.

The security provided by superior firepower. She decided to steal it, and that meant she needed to start carrying a purse.

No, not a purse, a bag for groceries that was mostly empty. No one would angle to steal such a meager prize. She vowed not to make contact through voice. She'd use the digital burst only with the minimal code she'd memorized.

It was insufficient but would have to do. She'd drive herself into an apoplectic fit if she kept taking extreme risks.

The question she needed answered was, what about the invasion of the forest to secure the gunship? With the loss of the Malibor reconnaissance team, were they still going to execute the mission?

She wanted to know but reconciled herself that she wouldn't learn what the assault brigade was going to do. She'd sent the information that she was tasked to provide. And more. Now it was their turn.

Two and a half days to the next radio message. If anyone had been listening in, they would be geared up to find her. She would make one burst call that night and then stand down the radio for a while unless events dictated otherwise—like an aerial attack on the city that would signal *Chrysalis's* return.

A grim satisfaction warmed her soul. The evil was to be expunged. The toxic culture of the Malibor was about to suffer a critical loss.

She walked with her head held high.

Hands grabbed her from behind and stopped her mid-stride. She was picked up and propelled into a wall at the edge of the sidewalk.

She spun and crouched. Two men. One with black eyes from his broken nose.

"You," she snarled. Her fear had been replaced by hope only to be replaced by anger. "It takes two of you to handle li'l ole me. You are pathetic examples of what our soldiers have become. Are you the ones who are going to defeat the Borwyn? I'll be shocked if you survive the first battle," Deena taunted.

The men outweighed her greatly, and they counted on their mass to dominate her.

She did what they didn't expect. She screamed bloody murder.

They surged in to stop her. Deena had learned to deal with one enemy at a time, pick the weakest one and take him out.

She faked right and jumped left. She ducked and brought a vicious uppercut under the second man's chin. His head snapped back as his momentum carried him forward. He staggered another step and fell face-first into the wall. His arms hung dead at his side as he crumpled to the sidewalk.

"You know you can't take me," Deena said. People across the street had stopped, but no one was coming forward to help.

The man produced a folding knife with a blade as long as his hand.

"Really?" Deena had practiced disarming an opponent. She longed for the grocery bag that she planned to snag from the restaurant along with the blaster. Even an apple would help her distract him, but she had nothing. She maneuvered to keep the unconscious man between her and the broken-nosed soldier. Trip him up. Make him take his eyes off her.

Deena screamed again. The fire behind his eyes had turned incandescent with rage. He could no longer be reasoned with or cajoled into leaving. He would fight unhinged until his fury was spent.

"Mister," a voice came from behind the soldier. He didn't hear. He was beyond that.

A hand seized the soldier's arm, and he slashed it. The soldier roared and launched himself at Deena.

She focused the entirety of her effort on the hand holding the knife. Deena let the knife stab toward her. She blocked the hand and redirected the momentum along her side. She grabbed the arm and twisted, kicking her hip out to pull the soldier over.

He bumped against her but didn't go over. He pulled back with all his might, ripping his knife hand free. The blade cut through her palm, and the soldier stood.

Deena grabbed her hand as a lightning strike of pain shot through her body. She dodged backward.

A shadow passed over his head as the club came down. The dull thud sounded wet and hollow. The soldier's eyes rolled back, and the knife slipped from his fingers.

An old man stood there with two hands on a heavy wooden cane, holding it like a bat while blood streamed from the back of his hand.

"Damn youth of today with no respect for the kinder folk."

Deena took the opportunity to kick the soldier in the face. She held her hand. "Twins," she said to the old man. "Thank you."

"I wasn't doing anything. Retirement isn't what it's chalked up to be when there are good barfights to be had!"

"We better get a bandage on you. I'm afraid I don't have anything with me, but we have something where I work, that restaurant right down the block."

"We better wait for the police. They'll need to lock these two up."

"Are you sure they'll do that? They're soldiers and tend to get away with a lot."

"I might have some pull," the old man said. He waved at someone Deena couldn't see.

Since they weren't immediately going to the restaurant, Deena helped herself to the sleeve of the soldier's shirt. She used his own knife to cut it off. She wrapped it around her hand and then cut off the second sleeve.

"Let me see your hand." She gestured for the old man to lift the hand that he'd been pressing against his other. "To the bone," she observed before wrapping the sleeve and double twisting it with the knot pressed up against the worst of the cut.

"That looks familiar. You serve?"

The hair on Deena's neck prickled. "Brother served. We're always competing, so I promised to learn everything he was supposed to know."

"You learned well. That's good military triage. Stop the bleeding so you can get back into the fight."

"Did you serve?" Deena asked, trying to redirect the conversation away from herself.

"Forty years' worth. We failed, you know."

Deena shook her head and held her hands up. Her cut throbbed. She winced.

"Hold it up." He held his hand at shoulder height. "But that's neither here nor there. The soldiers of today aren't like the ones when I joined. We had just won the war and moved into Malipride. Then we started fighting among ourselves.

That meant the Borwyn were able to escape. Did you know that they've come back?"

The old man pointed at the sky. "They're up there wreaking havoc. I voted that we negotiate, and they ran me off the council. I'm sorry. I'm just an old man now and rambling about how good I used to be. You know that, right? The older we get, the better we used to be." He laughed a deep bass.

"General!" a voice called. "What the hell?"

"Two of our soldiers attacked this young woman and had to be put into their place. Is there anything you can do about them? We can't have this young lady walking around in fear."

"They won't see the light of day," the man replied. He removed a comm unit from his pocket and made a hushed call. He looked up. "That's a lot of blood."

"Always looks worse than it is, but I feel like I donated blood and should be given a treat and ranji juice."

"I'll take care of you, General. Join me in the restaurant."

"Send the medics to the restaurant," the general ordered. It wasn't a request. He had easily slipped back into his military mode. The police officer saluted. "Shall we?"

He held out his arm and Deena took it.

"You fought well. Learned that from your brother, too?" the general asked.

"Brothers, am I right?" Deena replied cryptically.

She unlocked the restaurant and left the door unlocked. It was early and she was the first one in. She turned on the lights and pulled the medical kit from the closet.

"We have gauze and tape, but I think we both need stitched up."

"A rag will be fine. I was led to believe there would be pastries and ranji juice?" he quipped.

"You're charming," Deena told him on her way to the kitchen. "Anyone who drummed you off the council was grossly mistaken. I'm sure you see with greater clarity than those running on pure emotion."

She returned with bread, jam, and two glasses of juice.

"What would make you say that?" the general asked with narrowed eyes.

Deena was left to walk on eggshells. He had disarmed her and of all the people she needed to be careful around, he was the most dangerous she had yet encountered.

She sat next to him at the bar and nudged the bread, jam, and knife toward him.

"Ladies first," he said.

She prepared a slice and handed it to him.

"Saviors of the innocent first. I insist."

He bowed his head. "I asked a question."

"I want to live my life free from threats. That means the likes of those guys as well as from the threat of the Borwyn. We've fought how many civil wars in the past forty years? We've fought ourselves until we just fight for no reason. Are we weaker than the Borwyn? Is that why the soldiers are distraught? The feeling of hopelessness is dangerous. It is destructive to a once-proud force."

"Maybe you should be on the council, but as I look at you, you're a half-breed, aren't you?"

"My mother was brought in from the Borwyn survivors hiding in the forest. Was she a captive or was she well-loved? I regrettably don't know the answer to that."

"Why'd you scream? You could have handled those two. You *were* handling them."

Deena sighed, took a long drink of her juice, and put her glass down. "I want to believe that there's good in the world. That there are people who will help when someone is in need, even if that someone is a half-breed."

"It's barely noticeable," he said, making a face. "Maybe you should be on the council to convince those people of that. Get them to embrace something other than their own power."

"The only power you have is what others give you," Deena said, quoting Crip and Max.

"You definitely need to be on the council. I should introduce you, but alas, they'll look askance at your youth and demean you until you quit. You won't stand a chance. It's like attacking a fortified position from the open."

"I don't know what that means," Deena said.

"You get yourself killed. I wouldn't do that to you."

Two medics knocked on the door. Deena waved them in.

"I hear you had an exciting morning, General." The two set their bags on the bar. Deena was nudged out of the way.

"It makes it more painfully obvious, young lady, with every window you open."

"General?" one medic asked.

"There's an injured lady. You will treat her first, and you will treat her with respect. You will also apologize for discounting her." The general left no room for disagreement.

"We're sorry, ma'am. We didn't see that you were hurt. Of course we'll treat you, but we can treat you both at the same time."

"That works for me," Deena replied, mind racing at how to leverage her new relationship. She appreciated the respite.

"He got you good," the medic was saying.

Deena nodded while holding her hand out. The blood gushed from the slice that ran the length of her palm.

"Looks like he got a tendon, but lucky enough, we can get that, too. We've training for this." The medic was far more cheerful than he should have been. He injected a numbing agent in two different places, then got to work repairing the tendon.

Deena couldn't watch. She started to feel nauseous. She flushed and sweat poured off her. She started to fall, but the medic caught her and eased her to the floor. He finished his work while she remained passed out.

The general's cut was deep but didn't affect any tendons. He refused the injection and told the medic to get straight to stitching. The medic was quick with stitches that weren't too small. He'd have a healthy scar, something he'd earned a few times during his years of service.

He took a knee next to the woman whose name he didn't know and waited. Once the internal and external stitches were completed, one of the medics helped himself to the small refrigerator under the bar to get two cans. He put them on the sides of her neck to cool her down.

Deena groaned long before she opened her eyes. "That sucked," she grumbled.

"I thought you were tougher than that. I may have to revise my opinion of you," he quipped while helping her up. "Take a seat and relax."

The general shook both of the medics' hands with his left hand and thanked them profusely.

"Let me buy you a drink," he offered.

"We're on duty," they countered.

The general returned behind the bar to deliver a flavored soda water to each. "Where'd you boys sign up?"

"West side," they replied in unison. The police officer watched from outside. The medics saw him, downed their drinks, and made their farewells.

After they departed, the boss arrived. He took in the massive bandage on both Deena's and the general's hands. "What happened to you?"

Deena waved her club hand. "Those nice gentlemen from yesterday attacked me. They'll both be going to the brig for an extended stay thanks to the general who saved me from their tender mercies."

The general waved his bandaged hand. "General Yepsin, at your service."

"I'm much obliged," the boss said. "This is my place. I'm Dintle, but everyone calls me boss man."

The general laughed. "Do you have many problems with our boys?"

"Rarely," the boss replied. "Those from yesterday got handsy, and we can't have that. She broke a nose and probably removed his ability to reproduce. I'm not sure that's a bad thing."

"You should have reported him," the general stated. "Next time, save yourself the grief. Report them up the chain or just tell me and I'll take care of it. She needs to rest. She's lost a lot of blood."

"And you, too, General," Deena said. "I hope you'll be able to join us again soon. I'd love to sit and talk. Too many don't understand the finer points of governmental relations. We could solve a lot of problems over a beer, and probably all of them over a bottle of wine."

"I'll take you up on that. If I had a granddaughter, I'd want her to be just like you. I never got your name."

"Deena. Just Deena."

"Call me Max. General Max Yepsin, at your service, fine lady."

A chill ran down her spine. "I most assuredly am not going to call you Max," she said without thinking, "but I will call you Pap."

"Deal." He scanned the restaurant up, down, and side to side. "Nice place you have. I'll be back."

A new plan appeared in Deena's mind. An audacious and beautiful plan.

CHAPTER 24

Silence is a source of great strength.

"Fire!" Jaq shouted and punched at the main screen.

Taurus pressed the button and said softly, "Firing."

The E-mag batteries launched a devastating broadside at the tiniest of targets. The ship vibrated and hummed with the onslaught.

"Should have been me," Gil complained.

Alby argued for greater standoff distance, and the mines hadn't followed *Chrysalis*. That gave them the range to deliver withering E-mag fire.

The first mine blew right away in a small fireball that was quickly extinguished. Then the second until all six were blasted out of space, even the dud that had hit the ship but not exploded.

"Nice work," Jaq said. "Rendezvous with those scout ships and then we need to collect my deputy. He's been goofing off long enough."

"If they took him back to New Septimus, then he'd have to eat and drink their food. I bet he's as eager to get aboard as you are to have your love muffin," Taurus said.

"Upstart!" Jaq shook her finger at her intransigent offensive weapons officer.

"Coordinates laid in," Mary announced.

"Decelerating and turning around," Ferd added. "Three gees for a couple minutes, Captain. On your command."

Jaq eased into her seat. "Ship-wide, please, Amie. All hands, three gees for two minutes. Into your acceleration seats or bunks. Brace yourselves. Executing in thirty seconds." Jaq watched the timer on the main screen. When it hit thirty seconds, she gave the signal. "Command is given. All ahead standard."

The ship's engines delivered a solid three gees of thrust. It slowed to a stop and thrusters changed the ship's heading to an angle to miss the debris field they'd just created. The Malibor scouts had adopted a new station, not far from their previous location but out of the blast area and line of fire from the E-mags. They were at a full stop.

"They seem to be playing nice," Jaq said. "Gil, you have your opportunity. Keep them covered in case they try to pull something. Slade, paint them red with everything you have."

"We've been pounding them and that area the second the mines were destroyed. I'm surprised they aren't glowing from all the radiation. They won't be dragging us into another minefield," Slade confirmed. "Area is clear."

Jaq waited until the ship was inverted and slowing before she moved out of her seat. "Rally the airlock teams, stunners, axes, clubs, prods, nets, and anything they can think of in case the Malibor try to pull a fast one. They are not to go beyond the airlock. We'll hand the supplies in. I don't want to see their ships, and I don't want them to see the inside of ours."

"Roger," Alby said. "You have it, Taurus. I'm on the port-side team."

The ship transitioned from minimal acceleration to zero-gee. Jaq and Alby flew to the central shaft, where the elevator was locked out. They dropped inside and pulled themselves down. "I'll take starboard. No one gets on board my ship!" Jaq stated in no uncertain terms.

Alby laughed with a dark smile. He was angry with the Malibor for everything they'd done. He wasn't likely to get over it anytime soon, but he would follow Jaq's orders. She'd gotten them this far and had his full confidence. He wouldn't betray her trust, no matter how much he hated the Malibor.

Alby was first to arrive. He put on one of the pre-staged spacesuits. The others arrived while he was still dressing. They carried a myriad of tools that could be used as weapons.

One of the maintenance team dragged a plasma torch.

"What are you going to do with that?"

"They'll feel the flame of my fury!"

"Do not fire up the plasma torch. Take a net." Alby shook the net holding the supplies.

"But...plasma torch." The man pointed at the system magnetically attached to the deck.

Alby shook his head. "Good initiative, but let's go with something a little less dangerous to anyone who might be caught in the wrong place. Catching them in the net will keep them from getting on board *Chrysalis*. That is your guidance. No Malibor sets foot on our ship."

They rogered their agreement and took positions around the airlock. The two most important crewmembers were beside the hatch, where they could interdict a transgressor without being seen.

"I'll toss the boxes at them from down here, working back to front," Alby said. He clamped his boots to the deck and waited. A gentle thump announced the initial link-up with the Malibor scout. The external hatch cycled and opened. The airlock showed green. The two ships had equal pressure.

The Malibor crew were not wearing environmental suits, but the Borwyn crew were. Alby waved, and the Malibor opened the internal hatch.

"Stay right there. We'll send the supplies in."

"Why are you in suits?" the Malibor asked.

"In case of duplicity, we'll vent this section to space. We're not convinced you had nothing to do with those mines."

"I don't care what you're convinced of. You said you'd provide food."

"We did, because you and I are fighting the same enemy. You call them the Malpace, the Malibor who have taken over Septimus and Alarrees. We seek their surrender or their destruction."

"If you get it, what will you do with us?" the Malibor asked.

"Not a thing. We're not like you. We're happy to not be at war. Can you live without fighting?"

The Malibor rubbed his chin but didn't answer.

Alby tossed the first nets filled with micro-greens and processed algae.

"We just want to live," the Malibor said in between bundles.

Alby stopped tossing the bags. He unhooked his helmet and removed it.

"That's the smartest thing I've ever heard from a Malibor," Alby said. He clumped up the corridor and held out his hand. The Malibor looked at it.

"Don't make the mistake of thinking we're friends. I hate you with every fiber of my being, but I hate them more." He nodded in an indistinct direction to reference the Malibor on Septimus.

"Eat my shorts, Malibor scum," Alby said with a laugh and returned to tossing the nets with the food bags. When he was finished, he closed the interior hatch. He waved to the Malibor captain, and surprisingly, he waved back before securing the external hatch.

"You can take your suits off," Alby said. He hadn't put his helmet back on. It was floating down the corridor. He watched it mindlessly.

The Malibor had taken Septimus away from the Borwyn and driven *Chrysalis* deep into the Armanor system. They were the enemy. Alby wondered how many who had participated in that attack were still alive. Were any of the planners or leaders still around? He shook his head. The Malibor descendants didn't bother to give it back, right the wrongs of their forefathers.

No. He hated them all.

"Break's over. Back to work." Alby looked at the maintenance crew struggling with the plasma torch. "Next time, just bring a wrench."

Jaq headed toward the central shaft. Her group had handed over the supplies without saying a single word to the Malibor crew. They had buttoned up the airlock and gone on their merry way.

It was anticlimactic.

Jaq caught Alby coming her way. She floated free in the central shaft, a place she liked because it gave her access to the whole ship.

Alby shrugged and did a somersault. "They took the food and left without so much as a thanks. At least they waved."

"Ours didn't even do that. They seemed like angry people, unhappy to receive charity, and unhappy that it came from Borwyn, but not too proud to deny the help."

"I'm sure others would tell you it was the right thing to do, but I'm not one of them. I know you want to win the peace with these people, but there will never be peace with the Malibor. They won't accept us. Period."

"Their loss. I can sleep at night knowing that we did everything we could as well as killed any Malibor ships that crossed us. We're giving them the choice in how they want to die. It could be old age or in the glory of a senseless battle. Which reminds us why we're here. I hope they have our missiles. I want those tubes filled."

Alby nodded vigorously, which made his whole body spin. "Missiles will be good."

"Let's go get my deputy."

"Be there as soon as I turn in my suit," Alby said.

Jaq shook her head. "We never put them on. I had a feeling they weren't going to try anything."

"Procedure! What about planning?" Alby grunted in mock disgust. "I'm appalled."

"Ditch your suit. Once those scouts enter the atmosphere, we're gone."

Jaq flew up the central shaft and deftly pulled herself out on the command deck level. She continued to the bridge, where she checked the status board for any change. Energy gauge showed ninety-eight percent. She loved that she didn't have to worry about the energy storage. The gross Malibor power plants took up too much space, but the tradeoff was worth it.

"Set course for the far side of Rondovan. Wait until those scout ships are clear before you engage."

Ferd nodded while Mary input the coordinates. "Acceleration planned for one gee."

"Roger," Jaq confirmed.

Slade continued to radiate at full strength, lighting up the two scouts until they entered the upper atmosphere on reentry. "Shutting down active systems," Slade said.

"Engage," Jaq ordered.

The ship swung around and accelerated at a single gravity on its way around Sairvor. It pulled up and around the moon, inverting and slowing to a stop once out of sight of the planet surface.

"Get those landers ready to go, Benjy!" Jaq called out. "I'll be on the first one in."

"Captain? I could go," Alby said. At Jaq's look, he withdrew his generous offer. "Or I could stay here and watch the gauges and the Phillips boys slap a patch on the outer hull."

Jaq gave him the thumbs-up and walked briskly down the corridor. One gee versus zero-gee was enough to add a spring to her step. She punched the button and waited for the elevator.

She couldn't remember if they'd removed the explosives. Brad was supposed to take care of that. He wasn't here to chew on if he'd left it. Then again, he'd been busy fixing the major damage to the ship and using himself as bait for a mine. Jaq wanted to tear into him for being so inconsiderate, but it's what she would have done if she had the opportunity.

Maybe she'd say nothing.

In the bay, she found one lander had been emptied and only half of a second. The third was still packed. "Benjy, get that second lander emptied and send it after me. I'll ride in the first one. Take me to New Septimus!" She pumped her fist in the 'hurry up' gesture.

"I got you, Captain. Next stop, paradise."

She laughed. "That reminds me. Let me get a drink off your water stash before I go. There's no way I'm drinking anything in that place."

Jaq drank half his flask, thanked him, and hurried into the lander. Benjy had already prepped it. The ship took off within a minute of Jaq getting seated.

The lander raced away from the cruiser and through the camouflaged entrance. Jaq was oblivious, but for Benjy, it was disconcerting to fly the lander into what appeared to be a solid rock wall.

The lander continued down the tunnel and to the

landing area, where automated systems helped guide it in. The craft touched down, and the engines faded until they were off.

Jaq popped the hatch and stepped out to find it empty. "You son of a..."

Brad popped out of a nearby building and jogged to the landing area to grab Jaq, pick her up, and swing her around.

"It's nice to not be dead," he told her.

"I thought about how I was going to chew you out for doing something I would have done and decided to say nothing. You should be proud of me for not airlocking myself when I thought you had died."

"You'd do that?" Brad put her down and leaned back.

"Don't be insane. I'd be angry with you for the rest of my days and if I was a corpse, I wouldn't be able to curse your name."

"That's what I call true love!" Brad declared and kissed her.

"I came for missiles," Jaq said.

Brad made a face. "Ooh. I have bad news and good news. There aren't any missiles."

"None?"

"None. They couldn't handle the complexity or the mass, so they made a bunch of pulse rifles instead. We can arm most of the crew."

Jaq didn't see the efficacy. "Are we going to put them in spacesuits and line them up in the cargo bay to shoot at our enemies?"

"No. We're going to take over the space station. The

station controls the shipyard. We want to see what's inside the spindle, don't we?"

"You had way too much time to think, but yes. We want that space station. We want the shipyard. And we want the Malibor fleet to surrender, whatever ships we have the mercy to leave alive, if any."

Jaq and Brad shared a moment before others from New Septimus joined them. "How many volunteers are going with us?" Jaq asked.

"As many as you can handle. Thirty? These will be younger and less specialized, but they are motivated."

"Which means they're the ones who will be carrying the new pulse rifles."

"They've been training for a couple weeks now," Brad replied.

"A second lander is coming, once we clear the explosives out of it." She raised her eyebrows at Brad, but he shook his head.

"I wouldn't know anything about that," he lied. "I'll get them lined up and lined out. Time's wasting."

"I couldn't agree more. We have our combat team on the ground, wondering what we're doing out here." Jaq noticed the scout ship on the pad. Only one was there. *Starbound* was still providing oversight and comm relay.

"You should replace *Starbound*. He's been out a long time."

"He doesn't want to come in. He feels the end is near. I do, too, Jaq. Endgame. We fly to Septimus and bring this war to an end."

"There are a thousand ways for us to die between now

and then," Jaq replied. She scanned the eager faces hurrying toward her and Brad. "Pulse rifles instead of missiles? You guys are killing me."

"We couldn't produce them. That was a tall order, Jaq, and you know it."

"I got my hopes up," Jaq admitted. "I guess we'll take the pulse rifles. Better start loading up your people."

Brad waved for the group to assemble. Bill Macturno, a former nemesis turned ally, approached. "I'll send them in, one by one."

"They can shoot the weapons, but can they operate as a single unit?"

"That's the question, isn't it? The answer is, we'll see. They're going to be good fighters, Brad."

"I hope so, because I'll be right there with them. You know I'm going, too."

"Not me," Bill replied. "I know better than that, but you still think you're young."

Jaq looked at Brad. "What do you think you're doing?"

CHAPTER 25

Mastering others is strength. Mastering yourself is true power.

The darkness was nearly complete once the group had been ushered outside. Tram and Sophia were along for the ride with the others, who were horse wranglers. They would take the caravan into the woods to a rally point where they would be further directed to the camp.

Pre-dawn was the best time to avoid detection. They would be a long way from the mountain before the light of day showed them to the world, if anyone was out there looking. They took a slightly different route every time to avoid wearing down a single trail that would point directly to the mountain entrance.

A voice spoke softly from a shadow. "Grab a horse in the middle of the line. Both of you on one. Don't want anyone getting lost. If you get distracted together, you'll be better off."

"Hard to argue with that logic," Tram replied. "Could you point us to the middle of the line?"

Everything was black. The body that followed the voice took Sophia's hand while Tram held the other. They walked almost fifty paces before he guided Sophia's hand to the warm side of a large animal.

"Hairy beast," Sophia said. "The horse, too."

"Hey!" Tram lifted Sophia into the saddle. The guide had already moved away, leaving Tram to help himself. "I got it. No problem."

He heard "shh" from the darkness.

Sophia giggled, which made Tram laugh.

"I'm doing my best," he told her. He lifted himself into the saddle on the second try. "I'm much better with a spaceship."

"What are we going to do?" Crip asked.

Glen looked up from his shovel. "Nothing. Max is a grown man. I trust that he won't give anything away about us. I guarantee he won't give up Deena to the Malibor. So, the only person he's going to hurt is himself. I wish it were different, but what we learned over the past fifty years is that we don't need to punish our own. There's a lot to be said for learning the hard way. And don't you think you're taking your squads out there to look for him."

"What else are we going to do?" Crip countered.

"We're going to finish digging these bunkers." Glen

glanced around to see half the company digging while the other half had spread into the woods to provide security.

"We can let him know he's not alone, even if he hides from us," Crip explained.

"He's got a full day head start. You'll not catch him."

Crip took a halfhearted shovelful of dirt and tossed it aside. "We have to."

"I know, I'd do the same thing, but please don't go to the city. Max is no problem. The rest of your people, I'm not so sure that none of them would crack."

Crip wanted to argue but couldn't. He had full confidence in Max, too, but not all of the others. "We won't go beyond the edge of the forest."

"Run a full reconnaissance and good luck. Do you know your way well enough to get there and back?"

Crip had been studying the landmarks and the key terrain features enough to be comfortable. He had built numerous terrain models showing it all while he, Max, Glen, and Eleanor discussed the strategy of defending the woods from a full-scale incursion. They had to guess what the Malibor force composition would be because no one knew for sure.

They hadn't tasked Deena with getting the information because an incursion hadn't been contemplated when she went into the city. The first they suspected one was when Deena told them, but it was because of their actions. The gunship had drawn their attention. Now that the gunship had moved, would it be of even greater interest to them?

"We'll check all avenues of approach. We won't let the Malibor get past us."

"May Septiman guide your eyes and ears," Glen said.

"I thought you weren't a believer?"

"But you are, my friend," Glen replied.

Crip appreciated the gesture. "We'll be back as soon as we can. We'll leave our comm system with you in case *Chrysalis* calls. We won't be able to set it up on the fly, and we need to travel light." He handed his shovel to Glen and hurried away, rallying the combat team to join him in the central area of the new camp.

With everyone accounted for, Crip gave them his mission objective.

"I'm sure you all know that Max has gone in search of Deena, or we think that's what he's done. He could have slipped into the slit trench. In any case, we're going to look for him. We will not enter the city, but we will send a small team through the infiltration corridor where we ambushed that Malibor squad."

"What about the prisoners?" Danny Johns asked. "They could help us."

"Or they could give us away in case we run across the enemy," Crip argued. "They'll slow us down, and we need to go fast. Fantasia and Danzig on point." He pointed at the couples and gave them their place in line. Single file because speed was of the essence. If they saw something, they'd fan out into a more appropriate formation based on the enemy. "Danny Johns with me."

Danzig shouldered his pack and made final adjustments with the straps. He checked his pulse rifle before balancing it across his chest. Fantasia made a show of checking her bow and small quiver of arrows. Her pack was smaller but carried everything she needed.

They stepped out in the direction Crip pointed. He moved in behind them. The others followed silently until the Finleys brought up the rear. They seemed to be best at the back of the line, watching out for those in front while also making sure no one was behind them.

The combat team moved quickly. That was the whole point. They didn't stop for seven hours. Crip estimated they were halfway to the forest border.

"We get there tonight," he said. No one argued. They were on a mission to save their teammate.

They took a short break, only ten minutes. Long enough to change their socks. Crip and Danny Johns took point for the second half. They should have changed those on point every hour so they'd always have fresh eyes, but they didn't. Crip accepted the risk.

They jogged to establish the initial distance between them and the others before they slowed to a quick walk. Crip wasn't going to look for Max in the woods. He was going to look for him at the transition to the fields. It hadn't rained in a few days. Max would be smart enough not to leave any prints, but inside the cut that led into the fields, there'd be less room to avoid that.

It was late when they arrived. "Spread out. Ten-meter interval," Crip instructed. "Settle in. Half on watch, half off. Two-hour shifts. Pass the word. At first light, Danny Johns, Fantasia, and I are heading into the cut."

"Me?" a small voice questioned.

"You're good. You're fast and you're as light as fog. I think we'll need someone of your ability and stature."

"I'll do my best," Fantasia promised.

"I expect no less. Get some sleep. Dawn will come before we know it."

―――――

Deena made a valiant effort with her one hand, but she couldn't keep up. The boss put her on the register and at the bar while he grumbled about having to wait tables.

"Listen, knucklehead," Deena said softly, "if the general puts out a good word about this place, we'll have more business than we can handle. We want to be on the most favored restaurant and bar list. It will be where all the soldiers come, and if the general is in here? They will behave themselves. It's a win-win, and all you have to do is wait tables for a couple days until this bandage comes off."

The boss frowned. "Is there a limit to how many people we can put in here?"

"A to-go line. Make them wait outside and they can pick up their orders. We'll need another cook, a prep chef, and then double our food orders. We're already running out of supplies each day."

The boss hurried through the tables to take orders and clean up as soon as possible. Occupancy and throughput were principles he preached. Why keep four tables occupied by the same people for two hours when those four tables could host four different groups for sixty-four meals with drinks instead of sixteen? He liked the math.

The servers and cook weren't enamored of the extra work, but it made them a lot of extra pfennigs. No one complained about payday.

Deena poured drinks with one hand but efficiently so. She tossed them on the bar, and the boss and Lanni delivered them and returned empty glasses to the automatic dishwasher. Deena glanced at the door as it opened. She found the general walking in. He skipped past the counter and went straight to the bar. He used his cane almost as an afterthought. It made Deena wonder if he needed it at all or if he liked carrying a weapon in plain sight.

"How are you doing, young lady?" he asked.

"I feel about how you look," she shot back.

"Old?" he quipped. "I get it. Probably pale and tired."

"The latter. What can I get for you, Pap?"

"A bowl of soup?" he said.

"Coming right up." She called the order through the window, adding that it had priority.

"No. Never eat before the troops," he argued.

"They'll eat just fine." She chased two soldiers away from the bar who were happy milking their drinks and not spending money.

The general took a seat. Deena poured orders while contemplating the conversation she wasn't sure she wanted to have. If the general dug into her past, he would quickly discover it was a fabrication. She'd be discovered. He didn't seem like the type who would overlook a Borwyn spy.

No matter how likeable she was. She smiled at her own joke.

"You didn't go home? Do you live too far away?"

"Something like that. You know I don't tell anyone where I live. It's a security issue. Shame it has to be that way."

He thought for a moment. "I don't blame you. It is a shame." He committed to nothing else. At least he didn't press her.

"Did you do anything else during your day? Maybe you saved a litter of puppies from a burning building, or was it only a damsel in distress?"

He laughed. "I have to admit that I like puppies but will never have one myself. I went to the compound and talked with a few commanders. I think you'll see a change. Not all the way, but a little bit. And you won't see those two again. They'll get to enjoy five years of hard labor—as soon as they get out of the hospital, that is."

She nodded and poured two more drinks.

"I thought you'd be pleased," the general added.

"I am, and don't tell anyone, but I got a neat pocketknife out of it." She obliged him with a smile. Deep down, she was thinking how to leverage this new friendship. A bored man who wielded significant power in a previous life and still had friends on the military compound. "What I hear you saying is that you've been our greatest advocate and that we will soon be inundated by new customers."

"It was the least I can do. You know the old saying. No initiative goes unpunished. Good work gets you the opportunity to do more good work."

Deena moved to the register and pulled out the help-wanted sign from under it. She set it on the counter. She grabbed a pen to add to the sign, but her writing hand had the stitches. She looked dumbly at the big bandage.

"I'll write it. What do you want it to say?"

"Military spouse preferred," Deena replied. The relationship with Lanni had yielded high-value intelligence. Being in a position to influence the community was a benefit to the coming fight. *The Borwyn aren't your enemy as much as the men sending you to die,* she thought.

The general wrote it, and then added in small print, "Endorsed by General Yepsin."

"What are you doing with my sign?" the boss asked. He took it from the general, scowled, and put it in the window. He grumbled under his breath on his way to pick up the next order.

"You should buy the restaurant from him. You can make a difference among the soldiers, different from when you gave orders."

He laughed. "I fear you misunderstand the pay structure and that I have any money whatsoever. I should probably be one of your new hires. Add the pay to my retirement and I'll be able to take the bus instead of having to walk."

"That bad, huh?" Deena laughed. "Your bandage isn't as bad as mine. Get back here, Pap, and let me show you the ropes."

The general laughed. "We'll see how long I last taking orders from soldiers."

The boss cast sidelong glances in Deena's direction. She stuck her tongue out at him. The general pulled beers and served sodas but refused to mix drinks. "Straight up or beer," he would tell them.

Deena checked customers out using her one good hand. The boss and Lanni turned the tables over quickly and kept them filled through the dinner rush. The boss flipped the closed sign around while they encouraged the last two tables to finish eating and leave. Lanni gave them hard looks during her frequent stops until they took the hint and checked out.

The boss was happy to lock the door when the last one left.

He flopped into a chair without clearing the dirty dishes.

Deena took the opportunity. "Morale is good, Pap."

He looked sideways at her. "Ours or theirs?"

"The soldiers. They seem happy to not be at war."

"Where'd you get that idea? I told you earlier, we're at war. Maybe this was their last chance to remember what they're fighting for. Our way of life. A good meal served by a beautiful woman. Who wouldn't fight for that?"

"Lanni's married to a soldier, and I think the boss man wasn't showing enough leg to get the good tips."

"I heard that," the boss said without turning around or getting up.

"They're coming here for you."

"You said 'good food' wrong," Deena countered. She held up her bandaged hand. "I'm a real sight, Pap. Soldiers are messed up."

"I didn't say they weren't." He laughed. "Is there any chance of getting something to eat?"

"No!" the cook shouted from the kitchen.

"I'll make you something," Deena volunteered. She went into the kitchen, which was a wreck. "We're trying to get you another cook."

Sweat had left streaks down his head. A black pallor from the grease and grill smoke covered his face.

"You did a good job today," she told him.

A cigarette appeared in his hand and he lit it.

She was about to tell him he couldn't smoke in the kitchen but thought better of it. There was no food left, so she went to the freezer.

The breath caught in Deena's throat and her heart skipped a beat. There was little left, and half of the sausage made from the officer was missing. The quickest way to be found out was to bring it up, so she let it go. She pulled out two burgers with freezer burn and tossed them on the still-hot grill.

"That was some day, huh?" she said while her mind raced. The cook didn't reply. He appeared to be asleep.

She cooked the burgers from frozen to ready in three minutes. That was how the line worked. She tossed the remaining fixings on the broken remnants of two buns deemed unsuitable for customers.

Paying customers.

She brought out the food with the remainder of chips that the cook had been helping himself to.

"Good thing we're closed. We're out of business back there when it comes to food."

The general was a good soldier. He didn't care about the appearance of his food, only that it tasted good enough. The bun fell apart with the first bite, and he proceeded to finish it using a knife and fork.

Deena ate the other burger but took her time. "The last hurrah, huh? Just when we thought we were going to take this old dive to new heights."

"This old girl has a lot of life left," the boss said, even

though he also looked like he was sleeping. Lanni continued to work, clearing the tables.

"What does your husband do, little lady?" the general asked.

"Reconnaissance. He went out with last week's patrol." She looked to Deena, who shook her head ever-so-slightly. Her look warned Lanni they were walking on dangerous ground.

"My condolences. That patrol never returned, if I'm not mistaken."

To Lanni's credit, she played the game. "I'm hopeful that he's out there still. He's a warrior with a family. He'll find a way."

"That's the spirit," the general said halfheartedly. He'd probably dealt with too many grieving families over his decades of service.

"What were the worst losses you had to deal with? One of the civil wars?"

The general narrowed his eyes and tightened his lips across teeth until they turned white. "All of the civil wars. Malibor killing Malibor until neither side had enough troops to keep fighting, then the fleet..." He didn't continue. "But now the Borwyn are back and killing our ships, but you knew that."

Deena felt the accusation to the core of her being. She tried to shrug it off. "Soldiers talked about the fleet recruiting efforts. Sending the best and brightest to space, where they haven't been heard from. The soldiers are afraid."

The general nodded. "They shouldn't be talking about that stuff. Not out here. Nothing against any of you, but I'd appreciate it if you didn't share their words with anyone else. I believe I'll continue working here to make sure our people don't spill too many secrets. And you, Deena. You need to join the ranks. I'll walk you through the process myself."

Deena froze where she stood at the bar. She slowly forced herself to take a bite and chewed deliberately to marshal her response.

"If that's a joke, it's not funny. If it's not a joke, then we're done here. I'm not joining the fleet. You called me half-breed. I can take that from you, but it sets me on edge when my supposed peers look at me like that. A piece of meat and not an equal. No, Pap. I'm not subjecting myself to that. You wondered where I learned to fight. Well, I've been fighting my whole life."

"You're part-Borwyn?" the boss said. "Damn! I need to get the lighting fixed in this place." He laughed. "I'm kidding. We're not fixing the lights because then they'll see what we're feeding them."

The group joined the boss in his mirth.

"I don't care, Deena," he continued. "You're a good worker. That's all that matters to me. Lanni is good, too. And you, how much do you think you're getting paid to stand behind the bar like the big man around town?"

"A fair wage, Boss man," the general replied. "That's all I ask. A fair wage. I'll leave you to it. I have matters to attend to."

"Like what?" Deena pressed.

"*Sleep*, young lady. I may be the big man around town, but I'm not used to standing this long, especially since I'm OLD!" He strolled past, using his cane as intended. His hips and knees seemed less than cooperative, the soldier's reward for long service.

"Thanks for coming in, Pap," Deena told him and waved.

He tapped his eyebrow with a finger in a quick salute. He unlocked the door and stepped outside. Deena locked the door behind him.

"If he's going to work here, he needs to understand that we clean up before we leave."

The boss dragged himself upright. "Lots to do before we call it a night."

Deena waited for the opportunity to show the boss the freezer and where some of the evening's dinners had come from.

He shrugged. "It was inevitable."

That had been his plan all along to get rid of the evidence. It made Deena wonder about him. He had done things that she couldn't and did them without batting an eye. Then he'd turned soldiers into cannibals and remained nonplussed.

"Where'd you learn to process meat like that?" she asked.

"Cook, second class, aboard the troopship *Remstall* until I was transferred to that compound right there to finish out my twenty years."

"I didn't think you were that old," Deena told him.

"It's because I didn't eat my own cooking. And you shouldn't either." He winked at her and got back to work.

CHAPTER 26

Being deeply loved brings you strength, while loving deeply gives you courage.

Jaq looked over the corridor crowded with newcomers who struggled to remain upright in zero-gee. Jaq's boots were locked to the deck. Brad handed out puke bags to everyone in the group. They wouldn't be able to fight it, no matter their youth and vigor.

Bill had come along, too. Brad's contemporary. An original. Jaq wondered what unique skill he brought to the party.

Maybe it was only his support for Jaq and Brad.

The group each carried a pulse rifle but at Jaq's insistence, the power packs weren't installed. She didn't need any negligent discharges ripping holes in *Chrysalis*.

"Welcome to the flagship of the Borwyn fleet. We have three ships at our disposal—a Malibor gunship, a Malibor freighter, and us."

"Six if you include the three surviving scout ships," Brad

said softly. It saddened him that they'd lost a ship with its crew when they got too close while the hornet's nest had been stirred up.

"Plus the scout ships," Jaq added. "Has *Starwalker* recovered our mobility packs yet?"

"They could only find three of them," Brad replied.

"Better than nothing. We'll need them. Patch status?"

"Welded in place," Brad confirmed. "The Phillips family is on mandatory rest."

Jaq nodded. She turned back to the group from New Septimus. "You're joining a ship that has been through the war and is still fighting. We've been rigged, re-rigged, worked around, experimented on, and we're using power plants that were ripped from the heart of a Malibor cruiser. We're flying while they are not. They have a few more ships, but we'll destroy them as soon as we can until they have nothing left. And then we'll dictate the terms of their surrender. You have my word that we're going to win this war. After fifty years, it's about time we gave the Malibor what they deserve."

"Hear, hear!" the group cheered until someone yakked into their bag. The others moved away to put distance between them and the smell.

"Our crew will direct you to your quarters and other areas where you can find an acceleration seat. We'll run it up to five gees on our transit to Septimus. We'll be leaving momentarily, accelerating at one-point-two gees until we can slingshot around Sairvor and pick up speed without reducing our energy reserve."

She dipped her chin to them, unclamped her boots, and pushed herself toward the central shaft.

"I'll stay here to get them settled. I'll be up before we hit the upper atmosphere."

"Make sure you do. The last thing I want is for you to be splattered at the bottom of the elevator shaft."

"If you love them, let them go. If they return, then they're yours."

Jaq snorted. "I might have to airlock you to show my commitment. We'll see if you return from that."

"Ouch!" Bill called. "I think I'm going to enjoy this, Yelchin."

Jaq flew as fast as she could pull herself down the midrail. She headed up the central shaft and straight to the bridge, where she found the crew going through the final preparations.

Alby frowned, staring at his screen.

"Still angry about no missiles?"

"It takes an arrow from our quiver," Alby said. "But we have fourteen of sixteen E-mags online. The Phillips boys took care of us while they were out there."

"But they aren't calibrated."

"We took ten test shots at the moon. The repaired E-mags are close enough to be employable with some effect."

"There's some good news. We'll make do without missiles. They weren't that effective anyway, but they did provide a distraction."

"We have three landers filled with explosives," Alby stated.

"Only one is filled. The others are empty. We just brought two loads of people and gear from New Septimus, but we can reload the landers if needed. Do you see a need?"

"Another arrow in the quiver, Captain."

"We'll reload one of them with explosives. Puts two at your disposal and one for our use to transport people and equipment. I see a potential need for both. I'll pass it to Brad for action since he was the one who loaded them in the first place."

She needed her deputy. He carried much of the day-to-day burdens. No wonder he flew off to lead the mine away... She chuckled at her joke.

The reality was that he wanted to win the war, no matter the cost. That was a sobering thought for them all.

"Battle Commander, what's your targeting plan for this run?" Jaq knew what they had discussed. She wanted it delivered back to her so that all hands knew exactly what was going to happen. "Ears, people."

The bridge crew popped out of their seats and faced Alby to listen.

Jaq remembered the air handler that would drone for ten seconds. They'd replace that a while ago to dispense with the interruptions. She wondered why she thought of it now.

"We accelerate to a million KPH, we hit the cruisers in the shipyard while passing, as well as any ships attached to the space station. We destroy any weapons platforms we can find. We'll ping active from two minutes prior to arrival. We'll immediately decelerate at seven gees for sixty-seven minutes. We'll travel about five hundred and fifty thousand kilometers. We'll return at three gees acceleration for half the distance and then decelerate for the other half to arrive at the space station, where we will dock on the captain's order."

"And that's when things get hairy," Jaq said. "We'll have

to make a slow circuit of the station to make sure they don't have any external weapons. We may send a few rounds into the spindle to dissuade any ships inside the cylinder from venturing out. I want sensors to paint me a picture of what's inside. If we are able to dock, then our combat teams from New Septimus will board and secure sections until they can take over the command center. That's where we'll engage with negotiations to bring about the surrender of the Malibor. If we're right, they will have no remaining combat power. They'll be at our mercy."

"What about resistance on the station?" Alby wondered.

"We've seen their blasters and they aren't anywhere near as powerful as our pulse rifles, but I'm counting on their civil war paranoia. The space station could challenge the leadership on the planet, so I think they will have minimal weapons on board in case the Malibor on Septimus had to put them in their place."

"Is that when Crip hits the military base?" Alby asked.

"They'll hit the base and take out those three gunships before we start radiating. They'll see us speeding in, but they won't be able to do anything about their ships in space. You saw what they did last time. They ran and they hid. They tried to ambush us and got themselves shot up. No. They won't stand toe-to-toe with us. They'll stay on the ground. They'll be far more dangerous if we're docked. They'll be able to destroy us at their leisure, and that's not a thought I'm willing to entertain. They need to die on the ground. The leadership needs to be cut off from space, too. Kill the gunships and take out the comm station's antenna."

Brad pulled himself to his seat.

"Reviewing the battle plan?" he asked.

"Yeah. They have it down. Not too many moving parts, but we need you to load one lander with explosives, giving us two to deploy as bombs if needed. We'll leave one empty. We'll get word to Crip tomorrow while we're flying toward Septimus. I calculate they have just under sixty hours before they need to hit the spaceport."

"Sixty hours to the biggest battle of the war," Brad said.

"Only forty because we're not slowing down until we're past the station."

"That's intense. I better get those explosives loaded while we're still in zero-gee. It'll make my life easier, especially since I have a lot of volunteers standing around. We should be able to finish it in ten minutes."

"Call me when you're finished. We'll head out as soon as you're ready."

Brad vaulted over his seat, did a somersault, caught the mid-rail, and pulled himself to the corridor.

Jaq checked in with Slade to verify the timing of the active radar to give them the best advantage while also denying the Malibor information that could be gleaned from the active system's powerful transmissions. At what point wouldn't it matter?

Slade suggested an hour, but Jaq was inclined toward two minutes.

"Let us radiate for a couple minutes when we're an hour out. We can change course at that point. Less than two minutes away, we can do nothing."

"I'd like to think that *Starbound* will keep us apprised of anything that might come as a surprise. I expect to be updated on the order of battle throughout our journey."

"One hour out, Jaq. Let's confirm with our active systems what *Starbound* has seen with their passive arrays."

"Don't forget visual observation."

"And that. Active systems. Confirmation and targeting. One hour from the station for three minutes. Then two minutes out for final targeting solutions."

"Go ahead. One hour. And let us know if we need to change course or only orientation. We're going to put a world of hurt on the Malibor fleet. All things being equal, I expect to erase the remaining ships from existence. They'll be more likely to negotiate when they have nothing left."

Slade made a fist and held it over his chest. "Power, Jaq. It's what they understand. Bend them to your will."

"Once we've destroyed their fleet, we won't need to take any more kilos of flesh. We'll tell them what the terms are."

Slade smiled briefly and then turned back to his systems.

Jaq slowly circled the bridge, touching each of the crew on the shoulder as she passed.

The end was in sight. Would they need to bombard the planet? Jaq didn't think so, but she wasn't sure if the combat team was going to be enough to impact the Malibor leadership. She'd discounted the average citizens. This wasn't their fight. She probably needed the entirety of the Borwyn Assault Brigade to make the necessary impact.

Controlling space would lead to controlling the air, and that would help control the ground.

Jaq climbed into her seat and buckled in. She steepled her fingers and rested her chin on the point. She stared at the status board. Everything was green. The ship was bruised but not broken. They had power in excess. They had speed. They had fourteen E-mags operational and dialed in.

"The battle is ours to win," she whispered to the board. She fidgeted so much she almost jumped out of her seat, but she was trying to be more patient. There was nothing else she could do.

"Amie, prepare to send a message to *Starbound*. Destroy any gunships and cruisers and one comm station at spaceport...and give the exact time as soon as we have our arrival. We need those ships destroyed one hour prior to our arrival. The second we paint the shipyard with our active systems, we want the chaos on the ground to begin. We want them separated so they can't receive instruction. We want them to flail."

"As soon as I have the time on target, I'll pass the message to *Starbound* to be forwarded to the ground team," the comm officer confirmed.

"Mary and Ferd, shout out the time on target when you have it, and that will be a hard time for us to radiate as well. I want the ground attack to happen one minute before we radiate, if they can manage that level of precision. Battle Commander, confirm the times, please."

"Will do, Captain! Woohoo! Forty hours to starshine!"

"May Septiman grant us the victory of peace! May we arrive with our souls intact. Lose no more people in this righteous crusade to return Him to the planet named in His honor. In Septiman's name, we pray," the shepherd droned loudly enough to drown out other conversations on the bridge.

In the silence that followed, Brad returned. "Two landers loaded and ready to launch. New personnel are secure. We're ready to go."

"Take us out," Jaq ordered.

Mary guided the ship while Ferd activated the thrusters. He already had the calculations, he only needed the start time. He sent the time estimate to Alby, who confirmed the numbers.

"Spaceport attack to commence in thirty-nine hours and four minutes. Sensor systems go active for three minutes starting at thirty-nine hours and five minutes. Attack on the shipyard commences at forty hours and five minutes. Mark."

"Transmitting," Amie stated. It took four minutes before she received the confirmation. "Received."

Jaq leaned back into her chair. "Ship-wide, please." As soon as the intercom was active, Jaq spoke. "All hands, we're beginning our run on Septimus. We are going to complete the destruction of the Malibor fleet. We are going to attack the spaceport on the ground at the same time. The combat team is going to engage the leadership there while we attack the station and secure the leadership in space. We're going to finish them. Thirty-nine hours before things get exciting. In the interim, secure yourselves for a slingshot maneuver around Sairvor. We'll hit five gees or more. Don't leave any loose tools or body parts hanging out. Newcomers, welcome to *Chrysalis*. Now, hang on. It's going to get bumpy."

Amie closed the intercom.

"Sounded great, Jaq. We'll double-check our systems a dozen times between now and then. We'll be rested and well-fed. I'm not sure what else we can do."

Jaq leaned out of her seat to catch his eye. "We pray, Brad, that Septiman will deliver us our daily bread and a resounding victory."

"Nothing to worry about, Jaq. You've got this."

"That's what worries me. We don't have anything until an hour prior when we get the final disposition of the Malibor fleet. If they run, we're going to have to hunt them down, and that will be miserable. I don't want to chase them all over the system. If we try to take on the space station with their ships ready to make hit-and-run attacks on us, we're going to have real problems."

"We'll bring the gunship into space to help us hunt them down. We'll get the Malibor leadership to surrender. They will have no backbone when their own lives are at risk. I suspect they're power-mad cowards."

CHAPTER 27

Nature does not hurry, yet everything is accomplished.

Tram slid off the horse. "Is that dinner cooking?" he asked with a smile. He lifted Sophia off and held her close. Riding with her for the past two days had been a greater pleasure than he thought possible.

Glen and Eleanor intercepted the resupply team, asking for Tram and Kelvis.

They were directed to where Tram and Sophia stood.

"Glen. We brought pulse rifles to arm the rest of the combat team."

"They're not here," the commander said. "And neither are you. You have thirty-seven hours to get back to the gunship and then attack the spaceport." Glen checked his timepiece. "Thirty-seven hours and eight minutes to be exact. Where's Kelvis?"

"He's at the ship making sure it's ready. What did you say? We have to go back?" Tram checked his watch and noted the time. He told Sophia to memorize a number—the time on target. "We don't have enough time to get back to the ship."

"You do, but you can't stop." Glen waved over the horse master. "They need to be back in the mountain in thirty-six hours, not a minute later, and sooner if you can manage so they can get some sleep."

"We can make it in twenty-four, but I'll need three fresh horses. I'll take them myself on the shortest route. We'll get there tomorrow night. We'll sleep in the saddle. Minimal breaks. No problem."

"Problem!" Tram declared. "Back on the horse?"

"No problem," Glen replied. "This is it, Tram. This is the big fight. You're going to blast the spaceport and open the way for *Chrysalis* to return. It's been fifty years, and we're here to see it! Get on your horse, and get on your way!"

Sophia hugged Tram. "Duty calls," she said matter-of-factly.

Tram looked back and forth from her to the horse master. "We'll be ready to go when you have the fresh horses. Thank you."

The man rushed into the darkness.

"You're right," Tram told Sophia. "This is it. This is when we all sacrifice for the greater good of all Borwyn. I've grown too comfortable down here."

"And you'll be comfortable again," Sophia replied. "You'll fly magnificently and then we'll return to watch the others do what they need to do. Will I get to see *Chrysalis*?"

"I hope so, even if we have to take the gunship to space and meet it up there. You deserve to see my home, just like I saw yours."

A clumping and whinnying preceded the arrival of three horses, saddled and ready to go.

"I'll miss riding with you in front of me."

"No one said we had to ride separately," Sophia replied.

Tram found it easy to agree with her. He should have thought of it, but his mind was a mess. He had to focus. "The combat team is gone. With *Chrysalis* on its way, they must be getting into position for the infiltration. All hands on deck, Sophia!"

"Fight to win. Isn't that what Crip and Max say?"

"Yes. I almost forgot we were still fighting, but thank Septiman for people like them who keep us all in line."

The horse master didn't say a word when they climbed into the saddle together. A spare horse in case one of the others turned lame. They could turn it loose and keep going.

Tram thanked the man and with no fanfare, the horse master led them back into the woods.

———

Dawn arrived with Armanor casting long shadows across the fields that stretched from the forest to the city. Dew glistened on cobwebs scattered to the horizon.

"Move out," Crip said softly. Fantasia went first, almost dancing as she jogged across the open space toward the cut, a trench-like area between a field and a pasture. It was natural, but it served its purpose to keep the animals out of the field. It also provided cover for anyone who used it to move.

They didn't know how far the cut went, but Crip

intended to take it as far as he needed to confirm if Max had passed that way.

Crip went second, and Danny Johns brought up the rear. The jog turned into an all-out sprint as they got into the open. They weren't used to being that exposed.

Fantasia disappeared into the cut.

Crip entered it and was surprised how the sounds changed within. Birds kept them company in the woods along with the wind rustling leaves. Inside the cut, there was an uncanny silence.

Fantasia had stopped and crouched. Crip nearly ran into her.

"Trying to get used to the sound of the dawn."

Crip didn't understand what she meant until he took a knee and listened.

The drone of a channeled wind. The grasses straightening toward Armanor.

Danny Johns stopped next to Crip. "Anything?"

"Ground is still too hard." Crip glanced around and saw nothing out of place.

Fantasia popped up and moved at a deliberate pace. She studied the ground as she passed. Although blanketed in shadow, their eyes grew accustomed until Armanor rose high enough to bathe the cut in bright sunshine.

When daylight showed the way, they didn't move faster. They were far more wary, on alert for Malibor who should have been defending the way through the fields. The workers would come out shortly, but would they get close enough to see three bodies moving quietly below the level of the field?

Fantasia kept moving. Two hours. And then three by the

time she raised her fist to head level, signaling a stop. She pointed toward the ground.

It was indistinct, but tracks led through a dusty patch of barren ground toward the city. The tread was the same as what Crip had on his boots.

"He's well ahead of us," Crip whispered.

"Do we need to continue?" Danny Johns asked the hard question.

Crip wanted to catch up to Max, but there was no way they would reach him before he reached the city since he was probably already there.

"Best we can hope is that he hasn't been seen," Crip suggested. "Time to go back to the forest." Crip was crushed. He would have rather not known than have clear evidence that Max was headed into the city.

As fast as they'd gone, Max had been faster.

"I'll take point," Danny said, "after a quick look-see." He crawled up the side of the cut enough to peek over the top. He immediately jumped down. "Gotta go. Workers are right there."

He ran in a crouch, hugging the side where he'd seen the workers to lessen the chance that they'd spot him. Crip and Fantasia mimicked his stance and ran in his tracks. Danny ran for thirty minutes before stopping.

He was breathing hard, harder than he should have been.

"A little bit of an attention-getter, no?" Crip asked.

Danny motioned toward the ledge above. "Maybe check things out?"

"I'll do it," Fantasia said.

Crip nodded. The young girl scampered up the side and

lifted her head so just her eyeballs were above the level of the field. She climbed down while standing straight up.

"Easily a couple kilometers behind us. They don't seem to have any concerns about us. I don't think they saw anything. They're up there, tending the fields. No one is acting like the Borwyn are attacking."

"Sounds good to me. How about you, Danny?"

The original was pale and sweating profusely. He had both hands on his chest and held tightly.

Crip kneeled close to him. "Now's a real bad time for this, Danny."

"I'm old, Crip. It was bound to catch up with me sooner or later. The shock of seeing those Malibor that close was a bit much."

"We could have stopped."

"No, we couldn't." Danny's body spasmed, face contorting. "Leave me."

"Not a chance in hell, Danny Johns," Crip said through gritted teeth.

The struggle for breath ended as quickly as it started with one final exhale. Crip bowed his head while holding his friend's hand.

"What's wrong? What's happened?" Fantasia pleaded.

"Heart attack. Danny's gone," Crip said. "Take our rifles."

Fantasia took them without question. Crip leaned into Danny and folded him over his shoulder. It was only one gee, but Crip had gotten used to it and that made Danny seem that much heavier.

Still, he wasn't going to leave his body behind. "Make sure we didn't leave anything behind," Crip said softly.

Fantasia checked the ground while Crip walked away. The sun was climbing and although the early morning chill of a fall day should have kept them cool, Crip started sweating. He didn't risk stopping because he didn't know if he could get up again. The loss weighed on him.

"At the very least, you'll be buried on Septimus."

It came as a surprise when Crip reached the end of the cut and stepped into the open for the last hundred meters.

Fantasia appeared beside him, lugging the two pulse rifles and Danny's pack.

Danzig was the first to pop out of the forest and run toward them, then Hammer and Anvil burst from the woods. They met Crip halfway and relieved him of his burden. The group returned to the forest before the questions hammered him.

"What happened?" They wanted to know.

Crip wasn't a doc, but he'd seen all the originals on board *Chrysalis* die. Cancer got most of them, but a few died of heart attacks. It was almost always the same. It had been a hard life for them. They were much younger when they went.

"Danny was doing what he wanted to do. He died of a heart attack while scouting the Malibor on Septimus. He'll be buried where he was born."

"Did you find any sign of Max?" Binfall asked.

Crip nodded.

Fantasia answered. "He went through to the city. We couldn't catch up with him."

Larson sighed. "What are we going to do, Crip?"

"We're going to wait here while we send a runner back to the camp to check in. They need to know where we are in case the Malibor get uppity."

"And in case Max is running from them," Larson added.

"Just in case," Crip agreed. "I'll dig his grave."

"You'll do no such thing," Hammer stated. "We knew him the longest. We'll take care of his final resting place."

Hammer, Anvil, Ava, and Mia moved into the woods to search for a spot that they would make Danny's own.

Crip leaned against a tree. He closed his eyes to grieve in silence. A small arm wrapped over his chest as Fantasia hugged him and softly cried.

"We have to go," Glen said. "We'll take First Platoon, and the others can follow one by one. If *Chrysalis* is back and attacking the city, then we can't be in any camp. The Malibor will do something. They're not ones to ignore their pain. They'll take it out on everyone."

"We have pulse rifles now. At least enough to arm First Platoon. The Malibor won't be able to stand against us."

"We have two power packs each. That's forty total rounds. If we don't make a good first impression, the Malibor will overrun us," Eleanor offered.

"A risk I'm willing to take. I think if we engage them, they'll know that something has changed. If the city is under attack, I think the last thing they'll do is send their soldiers into the field. I would think they'll keep them closer to home.

Dig in and fight a defensive war." Glen picked up his pack. "Time to go."

"I'll rally the troops. Do you want me to bring the rest along?"

"No. I want you to join First Platoon and me. We're going to lead this parade. Let the platoon sergeants and lieutenants join us a few hours apart so we're not traveling as one big mob. Everyone else can hunker down here. This is a new camp that I'd like to think the Malibor don't know about."

Eleanor hurried away to pass the word. Glen stopped by the mess bunker. "I'd say to keep dinner warm, but I don't know when we'll be back. Button up and keep your heads down."

Those who were in the tent wouldn't be heading to the front. They were the rear echelon. They included the two prisoners, who were getting lunch. Moran's color was improving and he was already learning to eat one-handed.

"Take us," Raftal said. "We want to go with you."

"Why?" Glen asked

"So we can get turned over to our people. How long are you going to keep us?"

"That's a good question. I'm not sure we can spare anyone to guard you if we take you with us. If we get into a firefight, will you be quiet and keep your heads down?"

"Of course," Raftal replied.

"I doubt it, but you're probably better off here." Glen wanted to give the rear echelon something to do. "The doc hasn't cleared you to travel."

"I'm Malibor. I don't need Borwyn approval for anything."

Glen ignored Moran. "And you need to rest, too. You've given a lot of your blood to save your friend's life."

"I don't need your approval, either," Raftal said with less enthusiasm than Moran.

"But you do. You're still prisoners even if we're not treating you like the Malibor would treat a Borwyn prisoner." Glen didn't know how they treated Borwyn prisoners. No Borwyn had been captured for as long as he'd served. "You're not coming with us. You'd be a distraction. We'll send for you if there's an opportunity to hand you over to your people. You have my word."

"Your word!" Moran scoffed.

"When have I not done what I said?" The two prisoners tried to glare. "Exactly. My word is good. You want this to be worse than it is. We saved your lives once the fight was over. We've done nothing to harm you since. Quite the opposite. If you want us to put you in a hole in the ground that's too small and not feed you, we could do that, but we prefer not to, especially since we've never done such a thing. We don't have any holes to use as prisoner cages."

Raftal looked away. "We won't tell you anything."

"I know. We don't need any information from you. Have a good day, gentlemen." Glen walked away before wasting more time. A hand caught his shoulder.

Raftal.

"That's a good way to get yourself killed," Glen snapped.

"But you didn't. Thank you for helping us. I don't want to die, and you don't want to kill us. Why are we fighting?"

Glen faced the young man. "That's the most intelligent thing I've heard in a long time. You have to keep Moran from trying to undermine us. He can't be shouting or trying to take a weapon. That wouldn't go well for either of you. That's not a threat, but if you *try* to kill us, we *will* kill you."

"I agree. I'll talk to him. We just want to go home."

"What will your people do to you if we can hand you to them? They're not going to treat you as heroes."

"No. We'll get interrogated. They'll discount what we have to say about how well we've been treated, and then they'll send us to get un-brainwashed."

"It's better than them killing you for having gone over to the enemy."

"That is an option, and then you will have been right about them. I fear this is probably the first choice so our superiors can save face. No one wants to be the one who gave the enemy Malibor soldiers. At least Moran can say he was in a coma when he was captured. I surrendered. They will be far less forgiving of that."

"And you still want to go back to them?"

He shrugged. "I'm Malibor, and Malipride is my home."

"I understand. I have no home." Glen spread his arms wide. "That is why I fight. Get your stuff. You're both coming with us."

CHAPTER 28

The best preparation for tomorrow is doing your best today.

Tram rolled off the horse and hit the ground with a heavy thump. One of two guards at the entrance to the mountain ran to help. Sophia slid down and nearly collapsed herself. Tram groaned.

The guard helped him sit up.

The horse master walked stiffly, hurrying as much as he could. "I don't blame you, Tram. That was the hardest ride of my life. Maybe we can all sit down while these good people bring us sandwiches and get your spacer pals to join us."

The guard assessed the horse master's expression under the waning daylight.

"Bring help, please," the master requested.

The guard let Sophia take over holding Tram upright while he rushed into the tunnel.

"Are we there yet?" Tram asked.

"We are," Sophia replied softly. She kissed his forehead.

Tram struggled to rise. Sophia helped him up. "These are the benefits of marrying a younger woman," he mused.

"You're so bad." They stumbled toward the entrance to the mountain.

"Wait here," the horse master called from where he was leaning against a tree. "They'll get help. No need to be in more pain."

Tram snorted. "That's weird coming from you as the source of that pain."

"I was only doing what I was told. And here we are. You have a lot of hours left before you need to do your thing. You can rest and then get that ship of yours ready to go. If we had taken another twelve hours to get here, you would feel just as bad but would have no time to recover."

They moved to the side of the entrance and sat on an outcropping that had been shaped like a bench.

They waited in silence, nursing their tired and sore backsides until a small group of helpers arrived with a stretcher.

"It'd be embarrassing to ride in the stretcher. I need to walk slowly, that's all," Tram told them.

"Let the doc take a look at you," one of the men replied.

A woman stepped forward and checked his pulse and eyes. "Exhaustion. Nothing that can't be cured with water, a good meal, and lots of rest." She took in the horse master and Sophia. "Same goes for you other two. Get some rest." She waved for her team to return to the mountain. They took the stretcher with them.

Tram laughed. "I guess we have a long walk ahead of us."

They stood on shaky legs, but arms around each other, they tottered toward the entrance.

"I'll join you," the horse master said. He walked without a limp.

Tram and Sophia watched him. "Hey!" Tram pointed.

"I didn't want you to feel special," he replied. "Come on, lets get you to your friends who can get you to a bunk."

They made it to the end of the tunnel when Kelvis and Evelyn ran up, out of breath from their efforts.

They wanted to know what happened, but there was only one thing that mattered. Tram checked his timepiece. "We have to attack the spaceport in eleven hours and thirteen minutes."

"Well now, I guess we're in the right place," Kelvis replied. "The ship is ready. All we need to do is fly out of here. The question is, when are we going to ask the elders for their blessing?"

"I think we'll skip that part and go straight to the flying," Tram replied. "I thought about it long and hard. They don't get to tell us no, but after the attack, we won't be able to come back to the mountain."

―――――

Jaq toured the bridge. They were at one-gee acceleration because it replicated the apparent gravity in the outer sections of the space station. Brad was training with his boarding team. They were doing their best with manuals that the combat team had used, but they had no time.

She waved at Alby. "You have the bridge. I'm heading down to check on Brad."

"Can I go?" Taurus asked. "I never watched anything Crip did, unfortunately."

Jaq gestured for her to follow. Taurus had to run around the station to join Jaq at the back of the bridge. They walked down the corridor together. Taurus jammed the call button for the elevator.

"How do you think he is?" Taurus asked.

"He and Max are having the time of their lives, but it would have been better if you went with them, especially since they added all these women to their team. Is that what you wanted to hear?"

Taurus smiled and shook her head. "That's not what I was looking for at all, but it's probably what I needed to hear."

"He misses you," Jaq added. "We're on our way to end this war, Taurus. Then we can all go where we need to go, be who we were meant to be. Borwyn on Septimus, where we belong."

"I'm not sure I want to go to the planet. *Chrysalis* is my home."

"We can talk about that later. It's going to be a long, hard road. We still have a lot to do."

The elevator doors opened and they stepped out, only to immediately stop. Two soldiers in training ran by and dove to the deck when they reached the next intersection. Two soldiers at that intersection popped up and ran down the side corridor.

"Not bad," Jaq said. "They call it overwatch, or something like that. I didn't pay attention to what they were doing either."

Jaq and Taurus followed the group as they worked their way through various corridors and into storage spaces.

"Communication is critical! You need to know what everyone else is doing so you don't shoot each other," Brad screamed. "Stop! Just stop."

Jaq almost clapped but didn't want to subvert his authority or control over the training exercise. They had less than twelve hours before the attack began. Eleven hours until they needed to be secured for the final approach. If they had to make any radical maneuvers based on last-second Malibor disposition, then they could do so without hesitation. They expected the Malibor wouldn't cooperate by remaining still and being good targets.

"Take five," Jaq said as she strolled through the group. She nodded toward a doorway a few steps away. They went through to get some privacy, where she tried to console him. "You've had no time."

"We've had enough time to destroy any confidence I might have that we can pull this off."

"Give it another hour. Have them get some rest so they can think about what they're supposed to know, and then bring them back for a couple more hours before we have to secure the ship."

"Thinking is what they need to do more of, but the physical challenges of higher gees and combat operations are wearing them down. You're right, Jaq. They need to rest more than they need me beating on them, but they need something they can hold onto, a quick phrase to memorize. In the training manuals, there were dozens."

Jaq wrapped an arm around his waist and together, they

stared at the bulkhead. Brad was lost in thought. Jaq let go and stepped toward the hatch. "If we don't leave soon, they'll think I'm in here knocking off a piece."

"What?"

"Young people talk for *getting some.*"

"Some what?"

"Never mind," Jaq told him. "It's all yours. They'll do fine because the Malibor aren't going to be well-practiced in repelling boarders. They'll be lucky to have weapons because the Malibor don't trust each other. The only thing the Malibor are united in is their unnatural hatred of the Borwyn."

"It's because the Borwyn are everything the Malibor aren't. They hate us for being better than them, so they have to tear us down. It justifies their existence."

"Sad but true. You have to take over the station. No casualties would be best, but your people have to be ready for injuries and possibly deaths. They need to understand the mission and execute it to the exclusion of everything else."

"And what's that?"

"Secure the command center. Everything else is secondary. Find the quickest and easiest way to get there, then take it over." Jaq had no doubt about the goal.

"We might need plasma torches if they drop bulkheads in front of us," Brad suggested.

"Then bring them as part of a follow-up. I bet they'll have left the command center where it was when the station was built. That's the benefit of being the flagship."

"We've looked at the plans. We know which airlock to use. Everything after that will come from our willpower versus the Malibor's ability and desire to resist. I bet they never planned for the Borwyn to attack the station."

Jaq shook her head. "Civil wars. They've probably thought about defending the station from intruders, but have they done it recently?"

"We'll find out as long as we can get there. They'll have about three hours to realize that we're coming for the station. What will they be able to prepare in that time? That's what we have to prepare for."

"Talk to your people. Keep it simple." Jaq kissed him on the cheek and walked out of the small space.

Brad followed her out. He twirled his hand in the air. "Listen up," he called down the corridor. Everyone moved in, filling the space between them. Twenty-five "soldiers" plus Brad, who wasn't exactly a soldier either. "We're going to mentally prepare, then we're going to take eight hours of downtime followed by two hours of training. After that, we'll be accelerating and decelerating and you'll have to remain strapped in.

"The mission is to take control of the command center. Observe, shoot, talk, and move. That's it. Yes, shoot first. If a Malibor comes up against you, they are the enemy. We'll airlock into the level with the command deck. That means we shouldn't run into non-combatants. Assume everyone is a soldier. Observe, shoot, talk, move, then do it all again. Short sprints. Bounding overwatch. The faster we can get there, the fewer of our people who will be exposed. Once we're there, we'll be able to control the station and most importantly, any other response to *Chrysalis*. *Matador* will attack the ground site while we're securing the station." Brad looked at their faces, trying to gauge understanding. "The command center. Observe, shoot, talk, move," he reiterated.

One of the new crew raised her hand. "Aren't we worried about decompression?"

"The station had self-sealing technology fifty years ago. We expect they still have it. Shoot at viable targets and don't use automatic fire. One shot at a time or we'll find out if the Malibor have let the systems atrophy sooner than we want. Go get some food and sleep. See you back here in eight hours. We'll run through it again, but two things I want you to remember. The command center. Observe, shoot, talk, and move." He raised his hand and waved.

The individuals hesitantly moved away. They were unsure of the ship. They were unsure of themselves. A familiar old face appeared from around the corner.

"Doc Teller. I hope we don't need your services."

"You will. Some of these pups are going to get themselves hurt. You know it, and I know it, but don't tell *them* that we know it."

"Dark Cloud Teller bringing the rain."

"We haven't seen rain in fifty years, my friend. You're showing your age."

"Are we really that old?" Brad was amazed that they were still upright. "The younger generation was supposed to be carrying the load by this point in our lives, and we were supposed to be enjoying retirement."

"Ifs and ands were pots and pans and mushrooms grew out of my forehead, or something like that."

"We'll appreciate you coming with us when we breach

the station. I need to rally the welders too, in case we need creative station redesign."

"I'll be ready with a nurse, who also happens to be an engineer. I should probably let her know." Doc Teller strolled away as if he didn't have a care in the galaxy.

Brad took himself to the combat team's space and studied the station's schematics, including the levels above and below the command deck. He wished he had a deputy who had experience as a soldier, but there wasn't anyone. Danny Johns had gone with the ground combat team. He had been a soldier. Brad resigned himself to the fact that they'd do the best they could while hoping the Malibor would run from the overwhelming firepower brought by the pulse rifles.

CHAPTER 29

Health is the greatest possession. Contentment is the greatest treasure. Confidence is the greatest friend.

Deena ushered the last customer out the door. She hadn't called Crip when she said. With the general spending time at the restaurant, she felt like she was being watched. Deena wondered if it was time to leave.

That's where it got tricky. She found she was loyal to her new friends while also understanding that she was part of the Borwyn combat team. She'd done what she had to do, delivered information on the Malibor troop movements and installations.

"Pap," she said to the old man at the bar. "You could probably get going. We're almost cleaned up for tomorrow."

The boss sat on a barstool behind the register with his arms crossed.

"You could help," Deena told the boss.

"I could." He didn't budge.

Lanni laughed. Between her and Deena, they had the chairs in place and the floor mopped in short order. They ran cleanser and rags over the surfaces and put the stuff away. The two men never moved.

"Are you going to hire someone who will work?" Deena asked as she walked past and poked him in the shoulder for emphasis.

"Probably. I think we'll get a couple applicants soon."

"Soon needs to be yesterday, Boss man." Deena jammed her fists into her hips and gave the boss her most intimidating look.

He smacked his lips and yawned.

"Fine." Deena looked to Lanni for support.

She mirrored Deena's sentiment. "Fine!"

The boss took note. "I'll work on it. You have my word," he replied. "Tomorrow."

"We're done for today," Deena said.

A covered figure stood outside the door, watching through the glass. "I'll chase him away," the general said. He walked stiffly, using his cane for support. "Go away, you vagrant!"

The figure ducked his head. The clothing looked familiar beneath the blanket worn as a shawl in the cool evening air.

"I think I know him." Deena's heart raced from excitement as well as terror. What was Max doing at the restaurant? He was too close to the military compound. She needed to get him out of there.

"Watch yourself, Pap. Coming through." She strode out. She leaned close to the figure. "Come with me." Deena rushed past on her way to the bus stop, where she stood with her hands in her pockets.

"I have some money," Max said softly.

Deena shushed him. They waited, side by side.

Lanni arrived to check on her friend. "Who are you?" she demanded.

"An old friend. I'm not a threat to Deena, I assure you."

Deena nodded. "An old friend indeed. He was injured in a farming accident so stays covered up, but he could be the best person I know."

"You never talked about him." Lanni tried to get a better look, but Deena stepped between them.

"I'm fine, and you'll have to trust me on this. Better than fine, actually."

"I will interrogate you mercilessly tomorrow," Lanni promised. "Especially since you're not going to introduce me."

"I expect no less, and not tonight. We'll talk tomorrow."

Lanni ambled away, looking over her shoulder every two steps while the general and the boss waited on the corner.

The bus arrived and they climbed aboard, paid their fee, and sat in silence while holding hands. Max gripped her hand tightly.

"When did you last eat?" she whispered.

"A couple days, I think."

"I don't have anything, but I'll get something. There's a store close by."

He dipped his head and fell asleep almost immediately. Deena pulled him close and held him.

A few stops later, Deena roused her husband. They

climbed off together and went to her apartment on the top floor. She hurried him inside and locked the door behind her.

He threw off the cloak that had hidden a thin pack and, more importantly, his pulse rifle. Deena looked at it in shock.

"You're in the city with that thing? How did you get here? How did you find me?"

"Raftal told me how to get to the restaurant. I told him that I'd speak with Lanni personally. I won't because you already have, haven't you?"

"I told Moran's wife that he was alive. I didn't tell her about his arm."

"As for getting here, I climbed the wall. It's in a horrible state of disrepair. Once inside, it was easy to cover up and move through the city."

Deena checked her supplies, of which she had very little. She ate all her meals at the restaurant.

"I'll be right back. Don't open the door for anyone."

She locked the door behind her and almost ran down the stairs. She hit the street and walked fast to the nearby grocer. She picked up things she thought Max would like. She wasn't sure since they'd mostly eaten rations when together. She looked forward to cooking something. She spent the last of her pfennigs and shoved her prizes in a bag. On her way back, she slowed to a stop. The officer who had talked to her about the officer she'd killed was leaning against the wall outside her apartment building.

"You want something," she said without preamble.

"A few follow-up questions. There's a chill out here. I think we'll be much better off in your apartment."

She smirked. "I do not. We'll go to the diner on the

corner. A single woman doesn't allow strange men into her apartment. I'm not a working girl, if that's what you're thinking."

"I was not. I only want privacy."

Deena looked left and right. "Then out here is acceptable to me."

The man caught her arm. "Your apartment. I insist. I believe you're on the top floor."

"You know where I live. I have no doubt about that. No need to play coy. If you try anything, I will fight you with every fiber of my being."

"That would be ill-advised, young lady. You know you're in trouble. Just how deep? That's what I'm here to find out."

"I don't know that." Deena shook with anger. They wouldn't give her a moment of peace. She opened the door and headed up the stairs. He followed two steps behind. When she reached her floor, she hurried ahead, hoping she'd be able to get in and slam the door in his face, but he was wary and caught up to her. "Get your hands off me!" she shouted, even though he hadn't touched her. "I said, get away."

She heard a rustle from inside and pounded on the door to cover it. It was unlocked and slightly opened.

"Inside," the officer growled.

She pushed in, not opening the door.

Max was moving. A small gesture and he changed his angle to get behind the door.

Deena stopped to block the officer's way. He shoved her hard and stepped through, throwing the door closed behind him.

Max hammered the officer in the side of the head with everything he had, but the man was far too adept to take the full force of the blow. He was dodging as Max was swinging. He came around with a left hook that skimmed past Max's head.

Deena's foot impacted the backward-dodging officer. He staggered.

Max caught him and rode him to the floor, where he couldn't escape a series of furious blows.

"Kill him?" Max grunted.

Deena nodded. "We have to."

Max rolled him over and thrust his arm under the man's throat then pulled back, leveraging with his left hand to crush the vulnerable windpipe. The man struggled and kicked, trying to get his hands under himself to push off and topple the one behind him.

Deena jumped in to grab a flailing arm. She held it with both hands and leaned back to keep him from getting free.

He soon stopped kicking, and then he stopped moving. Max pressed even harder until he was certain the man would not take another breath.

Max pushed away and crawled across the floor to lean against the wall. "Not how I expected our reunion, my love."

"The Malibor authorities are vile creatures. This isn't the first one I've had to kill, which is why he followed me. He suspected I knew something about the disappearance of the other guy."

"Did they deserve to die?" Max asked, then shook his head. "Of course they deserved it."

Deena snuggled up next to him. "They did. The first guy

was blackmailing the restaurant owner because I had been staying there, but then he wanted more. He wanted favors, so the boss and I saw the last of him, but it gets worse." She dropped her voice to a whisper. "The boss ground him into sausage and then we served it to the soldiers. I didn't know we'd done that. The cook ran out of meat and the dead guy been packaged in the back of the freezer."

She hung her head.

Max chuckled. "It's not funny, but compared to our boring non-adventures, it's something bizarre. I don't think we'll repeat that story to anyone."

"What happened with the squad that Lanni's husband Moran was a member of?"

"Thanks to your warning, we were in position when they tried to infiltrate the forest. We caught them in the open and hit them hard, but we killed the Fristen mercenaries first. The others ran and we let them, but then they grew spines and followed us, probably because of Moran and one more. They'd both been injured, and we were trying to save them. We had to get them back to the doc, but Danny Johns saw them following and reengaged. We killed three of the four. Raftal was the only one to surrender. He's the only one who seemed able to think for himself. Moran has been a jerk from the start, but he's also missing an arm and bitter about that."

"They weren't volunteers," Deena said. "They were ordered to join that patrol. It seems the local soldiers don't like the Fristen soldiers. I haven't seen any so I don't know if there are more or not."

"No matter. They die just as readily at the end of a pulse

rifle as a regular Malibor soldier. Speaking of death, do you have any ideas on what we can do with this body?"

"That is a good question. I really don't want it in the apartment with us. On the roof, there are vents that we might be able to stuff him into. We'll wait until the middle of the night when the residents are sleeping."

Max kissed his wife. "Thank you for coming to Malipride and being our eyes and ears. I am getting a taste of what you had to go through."

"It hasn't been all bad. The boss has been kind, and a retired general who isn't enamored of the new Malibor leadership works at the restaurant. We might be able to use him to help sue for peace. He doesn't think the Malibor are fighting for the right reasons or for the right people."

"A Malibor general? That is interesting, but if he served, he's probably as bad as the rest of them, just a different bad. We need to think about what it would look like to bring him into the fold. Do you know any more about the planned strike on the gunship? Because we moved it. There's nothing for them to attack."

"No. I couldn't find out anything. Lanni's husband was my source and then the general has sway, but he's not up on current operations, at least he's not forthcoming. He's old and walks with a cane."

"I feel old and like I should walk with a cane," Max replied. "Time to clean up."

"Time to eat." Deena collected the groceries that had been tossed aside, stepped around the dead body, and made her way to the small kitchen.

Max went to the bathroom, but he had no idea how

anything worked. Deena showed him by climbing in the shower with him. The food could wait.

"Countdown to active systems. Ten, nine..." Slade counted while his fingers hovered over his panel. Everyone else's eyes were focused on the main screen that would populate automatically with information from the scans.

"Three minutes of full-power radiation," Jaq confirmed during the count,

"One. Systems are active," Slade confirmed. "Seven seconds to data receipt."

They were roughly a million kilometers away, traveling at a million klicks per hour. Light traveled that distance in three-point-three seconds. The radars would receive the reflections starting after another three-point-three seconds.

The six-point-six seconds came and went. The board slowly populated as reflections and data parsed into recognizable forms.

Slade made the announcement with the digital confirmations. "Two gunships at station airlocks. Four weapons platforms. Two cruisers in the shipyard with one unidentified large ship."

Unlike everyone else on the bridge, Jaq was standing. She crossed her arms and studied the screen. The initial data didn't change over time.

"I recommend we stay on course, Captain," Alby said.

"Confirmed. Stay on course, Mary. Maintain acceleration of one gee."

"Powering down active systems," Slade grumbled after three minutes.

"Look to power up again fifteen minutes out. One or more of those ships are going to move. If not, then radiating at that point won't change anything. Targeting. We need to knock out those weapons platforms with the longest shots we can manage. I don't want to encounter any fire from them."

"Donal, check my targeting solutions," Taurus asked.

"Time to target, three-point-zero seconds. That's a million KPH plus one-half c. Calculating for drift, gravitic interference, and deflection. Fire when ready," Donal advised.

"Targets one and two, four batteries each, firing," Taurus announced.

"Adjustments?" Jaq asked.

"Need active systems to track the rounds," Slade replied.

The weapons platforms may or may not have been destroyed. Optical systems were inconclusive at this distance.

"Radiate. Short, directional bursts for targeting purposes. Try not to paint the station or shipyard again."

"It'll be intimidating to not only know that we're bearing down on them but that we're going to hammer them into non-existence. We can use their terror against them," Brad suggested.

Jaq wanted the data, but she also wanted the element of surprise. She couldn't have both, and the Malibor had probably seen them coming much earlier. "You're right. Active systems as needed, Slade. Paint them until they glow."

"Roger that." Chief Ping tapped his screen. Alby and Slade dug into the data. Donal and Dolly tapped furiously to adjust the targeting solution based on where the E-mag rounds were going.

"Fire!" Taurus shouted with the new input. Seven seconds later, the first two weapons platforms had been destroyed. They adjusted and after twenty seconds more, the hum and vibration of the E-mags at their maximum rate of fire stopped. "Four platforms destroyed. Targeting the cruisers."

"Wait until we're a little closer and have high confidence that we won't destroy the shipyard," Jaq advised.

"Standing by. Donal and Dolly, give me the word when we're at ninety-eight percent of rounds on target." Taurus cracked her knuckles and flexed her shoulders before leaning into her screen to prepare for the next round.

"I like how this is shaping up," Brad said.

"That's what we thought last time, and they were hiding a small armada on the other side of the planet along with the ambush along our trajectory." Jaq pointed to areas around the planet and along their course. "Since you're burning up the waves, Slade, give us a view of neighboring regions. Look for smaller objects, too. Although we've run out of missiles, I doubt the Malibor have. They might employ them like we did, lying in wait to activate when we get close. Or mines. I'm not keen on running into any more mines. The front of this ship looks like we battered our way through an asteroid field."

"And those patches won't hold if we get hit again," Brad replied.

Jaq knew that would be a problem, but the risk was acceptable. "Mary, find an optimal location to rotate the ship so the power plants aren't exposed to enemy fire, assuming we'll get shot at from everything you see."

"Roger." Mary and Ferd collaborated to study the angles. The ship was already providing a minimal profile as it approached, but when they passed, that's when the ship's flanks would be most vulnerable.

"I hope *Matador* got our message. They should have already attacked the spaceport. I wonder how that turned out?"

CHAPTER 30

Only those who will risk going too far can possibly find out how far one can go.

"T plus nine minutes," Kelvis shouted from the engineering section.

"I know! We're late. There wasn't jack we could do about that," Tram groused while running through an abbreviated preflight checklist.

The power systems were online, but they weren't cleared to fly. There were too many people around the base of the ship who'd get blasted with radiation if Tram took off.

The council hadn't approved their take-off because Tram hadn't asked for permission. There was a tour gawking at the ship. They'd wanted to come on board, but Tram told them it wouldn't be possible.

"Screw this. We have to go." Tram opened the outer hatch and screamed with vocal-cord-ripping fanaticism. "Radiation leak! Run for your lives!"

He slammed the hatch shut as soon as he saw the visitors turn and head for the woods.

"Hold on!" he yelled up to where Evelyn and Sophia were supposed to be strapped in. "Taking off."

The ship accelerated off the pad. Tram immediately adjusted course to fly farther into the mountains and loop around to come at Malipride from the south, hitting the spaceport using a course that took the ship over the eastern part of the city. Would the Malibor fire anti-aircraft weapons over their own city?

He was hoping they wouldn't or that the weapons wouldn't be trained on that part of the sky. Or that they wouldn't see them at all. Tram was going to come in low, barely above the windswept grain.

He accelerated while making a wide turn but then had to slow down. He needed control more than he needed to hit the time. Crashing the ship would accomplish nothing. Hitting the city late was better than not at all.

Tram hoped the gunships were still at the spaceport. The time it took them to cover the forest took seconds compared to the hours and days they'd spent hiking from one place to another—or worse, riding the horses.

"Railgun is charged and ready to fire. Comm system is online," Kelvis called.

"Taking us in," Tram confirmed. The ship raced over the highest trees, a speck in the sky for anyone watching from beneath the foliage. Tram dipped it cautiously toward the rolling terrain of the fields, skimming the hilltops as they passed. "Prepare to pop. Hold on and pray," Tram said conversationally. The ship turned nose up and headed for three thousand meters before it would come over the top and angle the gun toward the ships on the ground, pulling out after firing and before they hit the ground.

Definitely before they hit the ground, so they could make a second pass.

"Over the top," Tram said to himself and rolled the ship. No anti-aircraft fire met them. As he angled in to target the gunships, he saw only two on the ground. The first pass was to take out two ships and the second pass to eliminate the communications center and the last ship. A third pass, if possible, was to hammer the headquarters building.

Tram brought the one gunship into his sights because that was the flight path they were on. He tickled the thrusters until the ship's nose was on target. He pressed the firing button, and the ship's forward velocity slowed with the rapid fire from the railgun.

The target gunship split and shattered. Tram brought the nose up early. He didn't need to stay on target because the third gunship was gone. It would shorten his turnaround time for the second pass.

"Missiles!" Kelvis shouted.

"Deploying decoys," Tram said while pressing the button.

Nothing happened.

"Evasive. Hang on!" He ran through a random series of maneuvers which took him off his planned return route, but once again, surviving to fight was more important than following a rigid plan. The mission objective was to destroy three gunships and the communications center, and drop some munitions on the headquarters building if possible.

One gunship was dead. They had a lot of work remaining.

Tram's lip curled. He'd been on Septimus for nearly three months. These precious few seconds were the entire reason for it all. He wouldn't be denied. Since they'd received the information about the spaceport and military compound, he'd run through it in his head.

"Coming around," he shouted. The ship jerked back and forth as Tram avoided a predictable course. The ship spun about and nearly stopped mid-air. The main engines were firewalled, running at one hundred percent. The refueling had given him all he needed and then some.

"Firing." Once turned about, he saw the target down the gunsight. He had no need to wait. The comm station exploded in a shower of sparks. Tram brought the nose up to race across the spaceport's open area. He hit the second gunship as the nose was lifting. The railgun fire sprayed through the ship and up, slamming into city buildings beyond.

Tram let off the trigger. He kept the ship low on this pass, not popping up to make himself a target again. He flew *Matador* over the city for ten seconds, then fifteen before banking wide to pass around the city center. He took the ship high enough to get a better angle on the headquarters building in the middle of the compound.

"More missiles," Kelvis noted.

"That answers the question of whether they'd shoot over their own city," Tram said while sending the ship back and forth, up and down, in an effort to stymy the inbound missiles.

They showed on the forward cameras, leaving a dirty smoke trail behind them. One fell off and dropped. The second held its course.

Old weapons, Tram thought. He took the ship down and then popped back up. The second missile didn't rise with him. "Clear," he reported, then continued to five thousand meters, which would give them more time pouring fire into the headquarters building.

The gunship rolled over the top. For a moment, they were weightless. The nose came down, and Tram hurriedly adjusted their course as they accelerated toward the ground. "Fire!" he yelled in triumph, holding the nose on the target below. The railgun vibrated the whole ship as Tram kept firing, burning through their ammunition, but it was for the right cause. Take out the command center and anyone who would issue orders from within it.

He waited as long as he could before pulling the nose up and teasing the engines for more thrust.

"Running for the hills," Tram informed the crew.

The gunship skimmed the spaceport and headed away from the city.

The sound of impacts was too familiar The gunship was getting peppered from somewhere.

Tram checked the screens but didn't locate the source. The impacts stopped, but the damage had been done. Tram tried to add altitude, but the ship wouldn't cooperate. The nose wouldn't come up, but it wasn't going down. The ship flew fast, too fast to land.

Indecision gripped him but only for a couple seconds. He

flipped the ship over and let the thrust slow it down. The ground was coming at them.

He added thrusters to the main engines, but the mains cut off. The ship had limited aerodynamics.

"We're going in. Brace yourselves!"

Tram would have loved to call *Chrysalis* and report their success, but he didn't get the chance.

"What was that?" Max wondered, checking out the window at the crack of an aircraft breaking the sound barrier. "Was that our gunship? Is the attack underway?"

Deena looked over his shoulder. "I don't know." She turned on the entertainment system looking for news, but there wasn't anything. There hadn't been enough time for the authorities to sanitize the message.

"We need to get out of here," Max advised. "Out of the city."

"What's happening, Max?" Deena asked. "Is it *Chrysalis*? Are they here?"

"I don't think so, but I'm not sure. I left before our last comm with the ship. I'm afraid I don't know who's doing what."

Deena raised her eyebrows at her husband. "You're not here with Crip's blessing?"

He shook his head.

"I ran out on them because you were at risk."

Deena hung her head. "This is bigger than you and me," she counseled, "but I'm glad you're here. That's a gunship doing what gunships do. I'm glad that body is upstairs, but when we leave today, we can't come back here. I have to stop by the restaurant, and you're coming with me."

Max stuffed his mouth with the last of a sandwich and chewed quickly while assuming his 'beggar under a blanket' look.

The officer had been carrying a great amount of cash, probably extorted from someone. It was now theirs to buy their way through the city. "We'll get a cab for a quick trip to the restaurant."

"That's the opposite way from leaving the city."

"But it's closer to seeing what's going on. It will give us a chance to talk with the general."

"What about your radio? We're going to need it."

The radio was hidden in an air vent. Deena climbed on a chair to get to it.

"If we get caught with this, we're toast."

Max waved his pulse rifle. "There are worse things to get caught with, not the least of whom is a Borwyn soldier, armed and dangerous."

They left the apartment and locked it on the way out. Deena carried her backpack with the radio, the rest of the bread, meat, and a bottle of water.

Max carried his rifle under the blanket he used to cover his head and most of his body.

The good news was that it was still early. Most of the city wasn't up yet, although with the sonic boom, it was doubtful anyone was still asleep.

Deena waved down a taxi and they climbed in, moving slowly to avoid exposing the pulse rifle concealed in the blanket's folds or Max's face, which would show him as different. Maybe he wasn't different enough, but they weren't going to risk it. Borwyn raised in space didn't look like Malibor raised on Septimus.

She directed the driver where to go. "You know what's going on?"

The driver shrugged. It took less than ten minutes to get to the restaurant. Deena tipped the driver and wished him well. They were the first ones to the restaurant, and Deena had to unlock it.

Inside, Max moved into the shadows before looking around. "This is where you've been working?"

"This is where I work." Deena checked the kitchen to make sure no one was there. "The main gate to the military compound is about a hundred meters that way." She pointed.

Max lifted his chin to her. He'd seen the gate the previous evening when he was scouting the restaurant. "I didn't see if it was closed right now or not."

"I'll take a look." Deena went outside and looked down the road. Smoke trails rose from the compound and the spaceport. They had attacked the targets she'd identified.

That meant the Borwyn were coming.

Deena returned inside and locked the door behind her. "The gate is secured. We might not have any customers today."

Max laughed. "Is that what you're worried about?"

"It's been my life for a while now. No, not worried about it but making small talk about the restaurant. It kept me off everyone's radar until the officer decided to harass us."

"What's next?" Max asked. "Are you here to save the

people you work with?"

"Is that so bad?" Deena asked.

Max nodded. "They could turn you in as a Borwyn spy. How many soldiers lost their lives because of that attack? We know ten did when they tried to infiltrate the forest. They might be your friends until they find out you're not one of them."

"The general called me half-breed. The boss didn't seem to care. Lanni hadn't noticed. But no one treated me less for it."

"That doesn't mean they'll accept you being married to me and who I am."

The door rattled as the boss used his keys.

Max put the blanket over his head and sat on the far side of the bar.

The boss entered and smiled at Deena. He immediately noticed Max.

"You brought your vagrant friend with you?"

"Kind of. Let me introduce you to my husband, Max."

Max recoiled in shock. This was the man who turned an enemy into sausage and then fed him to soldiers. What else was he capable of? Then again, his crimes would get him killed in any justice system. Max threw off the blanket.

"Max Tremayne, at your service."

"You brought your rifle, too," the boss observed.

"Standard equipment," Max replied.

"It's not Malibor standard equipment."

"No." Max stayed on the far side. The boss walked behind the bar.

"I've removed the blaster from under there. We can't

have any accidents, now, can we?" Deena said.

The boss stopped. "You're Borwyn, too?" he said with a hint of accusation.

"I'm half-Borwyn. You knew that. I was born here, and my stepfather was a right bastard. But he's not looking for me because I was lost in space when *Hornet* was destroyed by the Borwyn flagship. I was the only survivor. The Borwyn rescued me and saved me. They're nothing like what we were taught. They want peace more than anything. Your restaurant here? If the Borwyn win this fight, whose do you think it will be? Whose was it before a Malibor picked it up? A Borwyn who did not have the chance to keep it. I guarantee you'll still own and run this restaurant if the Borwyn win the fight that's ongoing up there right now."

Deena and Max both pointed straight up.

"I'm disappointed that I couldn't see it," the boss said.

"Why would you even try? We did good things in this restaurant. We turned it into a first-class establishment. *We* did that, Boss man."

"The general is going to be pretty angry," the boss said. He came back around and sat next to Max. "I guess you're the new boss. Call me Dintle."

"Dintle, nice to meet you. I thank you for taking good care of my wife, keeping her safe, even when those officers demanded money."

"Those *officers*." The boss looked sideways at Max while Deena leaned down to access the locked case and pulled the blaster out of it.

"Sorry. I didn't want any misunderstandings, but I'll hang onto this for now. Things could get ugly."

The boss turned away from her. "Did something happen to that second officer?"

"He showed up at my apartment last night. It was most inopportune. He won't be bothering you anymore."

The boss chuckled. "I don't feel bad about that. Welcome aboard, Max. Can I get you something to eat?"

"No thanks. We'll be fine."

"I don't think we'll need to prep anything for today. I don't see anyone coming," Deena said.

Two people showed up together at the front door. Lanni and the general.

Max threw his blanket over his head.

Lanni and the general opened the door when they found it unlocked.

"Pap," Deena said from behind the bar.

"I fear that I will be recalled to duty," he started. "We are under attack by unidentified Malibor. Probably the upstarts from Sairvor. They've been a thorn in our sides for the past two decades." He hauled himself to the bar and grabbed a stool. He finally noticed the cloaked figure. "You brought a leper in here?"

"No. He's my friend but was in an accident and keeps his face covered so you don't puke uncontrollably. Nuclear puking from your very toes. It would be ugly, and we can't have that in a restaurant."

The general looked down his nose at her. "Let's see it." He gestured toward Max. Lanni stood behind him, torn between looking and looking away.

Max flipped the blanket off while holding tightly to his pulse rifle. He looked sternly at Deena. "I didn't want this."

"Interesting. He's more than a friend. Your husband, perhaps?" the general pressed.

Deena nodded.

Lanni huffed. "You've been lying to me. Such a handsome man! Were you having problems?" She hurried around the bar to give Max a hug. She pushed him when she was done. "You treat her well!"

"I do, lovely lady. You must be Lanni."

She looked skeptically at him.

"Lanni, dear," the general started, "he's Borwyn. He's the enemy."

Lanni's mouth fell open and she stared.

"Doesn't have to be the enemy. If the Malibor would stop thinking of us that way, we'd be a lot closer to ending this war. As it is, your ships in space have been destroyed. They can rally the soldiers, but there's nowhere for them to go."

"Borwyn are in Malipride?" Lanni finally managed to squeak. "You're Borwyn and you stayed in my house!"

Deena shook her head. "You were safer with me than your own police."

It finally dawned on the young woman. "You knew about my husband because you were in touch with your people in the forest. Was that the truth?" She was nearly spitting with anger like a light switch had been thrown.

Max answered, "Raftal and Moran are our prisoners. They were members of an ill-fated reconnaissance mission to the woods. We caught them in a crossfire before they were able to find cover. Moran was injured, but thanks to Raftal donating blood, we were able to save Moran's life. He is getting better with each new day. I'm sorry to tell you that he lost his left arm, but he's right-handed. He's learning to do without."

"Did you shoot him?" Lanni asked.

Deena ushered her into a seat. She feared the young woman might run screaming for the police. They didn't need the authorities descending on the restaurant.

"I might have," Max admitted. "But when the fight was over, we took care of the wounded and we buried the dead."

Lanni started crying. "I thought you were my friend."

"I was a lieutenant in the Malibor fleet. I was on board *Hornet* when it encountered *Chrysalis*. *Hornet* was destroyed, but a few of us survived. The captain and senior staff attempted to bomb the Borwyn flagship. They were found out before they did any damage and they subsequently died in the battle that followed. I was spared because I wasn't able to fight back from lack of food, water, and being nearly frozen to death. I woke up on *Chrysalis*. The Borwyn saved me just like they saved Moran. I've seen both sides in this war, and there's no doubt in my mind that the Borwyn need to win so that decency returns and people like those police officers no longer prey on the innocent."

The general sucked on his teeth. "Are we your prisoners?" he asked.

Max wasn't sure how to answer. "What do you think you are?"

"I think I'm a prisoner of the Borwyn. Can I leave?"

"Do you promise not to bring the wrath of the Malibor authorities down on us if you do?" Max kept his hand on his rifle, but a shot from inside the restaurant would summon the authorities just as quickly.

"I'm not sure I can promise that," the general replied.

"Then I'm sorry to inform you that you are a prisoner, but it won't be for long. We're in the end phase of this war. We attacked your spaceport to prevent reinforcements from going to space, to cut off your leadership from those who might surrender. It's easy to order people to fight to the death when you're deep inside a bunker." Max stood and moved beside the staircase to remain out of sight of the front windows.

"Do you think our leadership would do that?"

"Your leadership ordered your troops to fight other Malibor, five times in the past fifty years. Tell me they won't."

The general looked less confident than before. "I can't tell you that. I'm not on the leadership council anymore. I think they're unhinged."

"You could talk to them on our behalf."

"I'm not a stinking traitor!" the general blurted.

"No, you're not," Deena interjected. "I see you as someone who doesn't want good Malibor to die unnecessarily."

"Why would it be unnecessary if they're fighting to save our city?"

"Save it from what? The Borwyn living here with you? There aren't very many Borwyn left. The Malibor genocide saw to that. The fact that you're going to lose the war to a military that is a pale shade of the Malibor's when it comes to numbers should be embarrassing," Max replied.

"We aren't what we used to be. Maybe we don't deserve to beat back the Borwyn. How many of you are in the city?"

"Can't give you military intelligence." Max snorted.

"Nice try, though, Pap."

"You don't get to call me that. Only Deena. But my name is Max, too, which is disconcerting, so you can call me General Yepsin."

"Sure thing, Max," Max said, shaking his head. "You're right. It is annoying. The question is, who are the good guys? Who will do right by the people of the city?"

"That is a good question." The general shifted uncomfortably in his seat.

"I better check our food delivery," the boss said.

"I'll go with you," Deena volunteered.

That left Max with Lanni and the general. "What do you think of today's weather?" Max asked.

They looked at him without answering.

The boss and Deena moved boxes into the kitchen from the stoop. The boss called through the service window. "Come on in. We can all do prep, in case someone shows up to eat."

Max followed them in and leaned close to Deena. "You'll want to lock the front door. No surprises."

She hurried away.

Max looked at the boss, who glared back and asked, "What are you looking at?"

"Did you actually feed an officer to the soldiers?"

"You make it sound like it was my first time. You'd be surprised what soldiers will eat."

"And I'm surprised at your rations. We've been eating them for the past six months and they are really good. If you had anything to do with that, General, you have my compliments."

The general laughed. He ended with a smile. "That's a soldier talking if I ever heard one. No, I won't take credit, but it did happen on my watch. Good food keeps morale higher."

"Wait a minute," Lanni interrupted. "We fed a person to the customers? That has to violate some food regulation, doesn't it?"

"Not as long as its prepared properly with extra tenderizer and cooked to a proper temperature," the boss replied with a straight face.

"Really?" Lanni was confused.

"No," the general added. "You can't feed people to people."

"That's disgusting." She sat down and held her head.

Deena returned and leaned against the wall while the boss and the general prepared vegetables and turned the meat into bite-sized cubes. Deena looked at Max with big eyes.

He made a face and tried to shrug. Their plans had gone astray starting with the boss's arrival, but the city was under attack, or so they thought. The restaurant was a place of comfort and consistency.

"Let me tell you a story of a captain by the name of Jaqueline Hunter," Max started to help pass the time and to give the Malibor something to think about. Winning the war without firing a shot. That was Max's new strategy. He was outmanned and outgunned should the military or police learn that he and Deena were in the restaurant. They would die that very day if they couldn't influence the prisoners' minds.

CHAPTER 31

Ever tried. Ever failed. No matter. Try Again. Fail again. Fail better.

"Ninety-nine percent, Captain," Taurus called. "Ready to fire on the cruisers."

"Light them up," Jaq said. They were less than two minutes out. It had taken that long to acquire the optimal firing solution.

"Fire!" Taurus beamed with the order. The E-mag batteries barked in a low rumble as they delivered a series of programmed volleys. The active sensors tracked the rounds to the bays in the shipyard, where the two cruisers were being repaired.

A bright light shone and flashed with the impact.

"What was that?" Jaq wondered.

A second volley accomplished the same thing as the first.

Two cannons each delivered minimum fire on the two

gunships, blasting them off their airlocks. The debris of the shattered frames drifted away from the station

Jaq didn't care about them. Gunships attached to the station were no threat, but the cruisers were. "Hit them with everything we have!" Jaq ordered before the ship passed them completely.

"Adjusting." Taurus frantically tapped her keys. The other barrels slewed around to join the firing batteries. They cycled at the maximum rate of fire.

Out of habit, Jaq glanced at the energy gauge to find they were still at ninety percent. A grim smile crossed her face as the E-mags shook *Chrysalis* like never before. Too much damage upset the ship's balance. Too many batteries firing at once on a single target.

The light flashed and sparked.

The E-mags hammered away, creating a whine instead of a steady vibration.

"Overheating cannons, twelve, fourteen, and fifteen."

A gunship appeared from behind the station and fired into the space that *Chrysalis* would soon occupy. There was nothing they could do. There wasn't enough time to slew the batteries back to engage.

The E-mag fire penetrated the light and pounded the defenseless cruisers. One split in half and broke free from its mooring. The other ship exploded with the fury of a breached power plant.

The impacts screamed and ripped at the very fabric of the Borwyn flagship.

Red indicators appeared on the main board from breaches and system failures, electrical relays exploded from overloads, but the engines continued to drive the ship forward. The Malibor power plants had been ninety degrees to the incoming attack and were safe. Energy and drive. The air handlers processed air and pumped it throughout the ship.

Emergency bulkheads slammed shut and separated the breached sections to retain as much atmosphere as possible.

A line of E-mag rounds trailed *Chrysalis* and slammed into the gunship.

"Got you!" Taurus cried out.

The overfire hit the space station, but it was inevitable that would happen when the Malibor used the station to hide their ships.

"Invert and slow us down for a return trip to the station. Was anyone else shooting at us?" Jaq asked.

"No other shooters observed," Slade said.

"Brad?" Jaq wanted his input. Did they follow their plan?

"Stay the course," Brad replied. "I'll get the damage control teams out."

"Not yet, Brad. High-gee decel incoming. Ferd, you have your orders. Seven gees."

The ship inverted, and the engines accelerated it to seven gees. The slowdown process began.

Alby, Slade, and Taurus worked to identify new targets. Alby slewed the cannons to cover all directions in case they needed to engage quickly, but no target presented itself.

"Review," Jaq grunted. "Was that an energy shield over the shipyard?"

Brad replied, "It had to be, but we beat through it. Ineffective if we can hold rounds on target for five to ten seconds. It's probably experimental, using the limitless power provided by the shipyard as opposed to the extra power available on board a ship, which isn't much."

"So, don't worry about it," Jaq said. "Concur. Too little, too late. Alby, order of battle review. Do they have any damn ships left?"

"They may have one cruiser and a few gunships, as their order of battle has changed from our expectations. I calculate one cruiser and five gunships, but we aren't sure about the three on Septimus. I feel in my gut that they have no ships to throw against us. They have expended the last of their combat power. Think about the one gunship that was flying. All the rest were moored, even though they saw us coming from at least an hour away."

The energy gauge showed eight-six percent. It would drop a few more percentage points by the time they turned around, followed by a few more in the return trip to the station. Red lights dotted the status board, but none of the major systems had been impacted. Damage reports had not yet been submitted.

"Ship-wide, please," Jaq requested.

"Go," Amie called out.

"All hands, we took some damage, and to the affected crew, we'll get to you as soon as possible. Until then, help yourselves as best you can and help each other. We're going to pull seven gees for sixty-four minutes. Your bodies will be under a great deal of stress. We'll slow to zero-gee. We'll do a quick damage assessment and then get back underway to return to the space station located at the zero point between Septimus and Allarrees. We're going to take control of the space station and from there, we're going to order the Malibor to surrender. It seems that they are out of ships to fight us. After fifty years, the Borwyn have returned to claim what is ours. All we have to do is clean up their mess and crush with finality any hopes they had of standing up to the Borwyn fleet. Captain Jaq Hunter out."

"Nicely said, Jaq," Brad offered. "They might have some ships in hiding, but they are better off staying that way. How long are you going to give us when we hit zero KPH?"

"Five minutes? I don't want to give the Malibor too much time to regroup and get ready to fight us. They'll get frantic when they realize we're returning and will be stopping. They'll know for sure when we start to slow down."

"Until then, they're cut off from the planet, I hope. Amie, can you raise *Matador*?" Brad wondered.

"I have been trying," Amie confirmed. "No joy. And not the ground station, either, but it's twelve hours from our normal contact window. It's early morning in Pridal."

"We don't know anything that's happening on the ground. I don't want to assume they've been successful." Jaq sighed. "Keep trying, Amie. We need to make contact with the combat team."

Sirens sounded in the city. People ran until the streets were deserted.

"Looks like the Borwyn are winning," Max said.

The others stared out the front windows. "Is this the end?" Lanni asked.

"The beginning," Deena said. She moved close, but

Lanni shied away, avoiding her touch. Deena knew what they wanted for the city and for the planet but not how they were going to accomplish it without the cooperation of the Malibor.

She could have been right that the real war had only just begun. To the citizens of Malipride, they'd been insulated from the battles that had been fought in space. They could no longer revel in their ignorance. The attack on the spaceport had put the war front and center in the civilians' lives.

"What are you going to do with us?" the general asked.

"It's too late to send you into the street. It's probably shoot-first out there right now. They'll think everyone they see is a Borwyn infiltrator. Maybe we can have an honest conversation about how to make Pridal a better place, welcoming to all."

"BOGSAT," the general tossed out. "It's just a BOGSAT. Bunch of guys sitting around talking."

"Like I said," Max began, "there aren't very many Borwyn. We're the first ones into the city, but Deena is the person who bridges both cultures. She's been less than welcome in yours and she's had her problems with ours. Who better than her to lead this city to a better place for both our people?"

"Don't you have a ship's captain and a fleet commander?" the general asked.

"We don't work how you're thinking. The right person in charge in the right place. To me, and probably everyone else, that's Deena."

"I don't want to be in charge. Pap could do it. He's never fought the Borwyn."

The general smiled. "But I have. We attacked the forests with some regularity when I could order troops around. We didn't want the Borwyn to gain a foothold too close to the city. But eventually, they took control over the entire forest on the western flank. I have fought the Borwyn but not successfully."

"I've fought Malibor, successfully, but I'm okay not killing more of you," Max shared.

"You're going to have to. They are not going to relinquish their authority easily. Turn on the radio. I guarantee the nationalist fervor is being spread across all the channels. They're coming for your children! The propaganda machine is running at flank speed. That was always the plan to whip up the population to fight an invasion."

Max looked at Deena and laughed. "An invasion. A couple hundred Borwyn soldiers. An invasion. No, General Yepsin. It's a removal of combat power followed by suing for peace. If the Malibor wanted to make problems, there wouldn't be anything we could do about it, but know that your ability to tell others what to do has come to an end. You can't order the Malibor around who are on Sairvor. Farslor is all but abandoned. There are some good people on that planet."

"You've been on Farslor?"

"Yes, and we lost two of our soldiers there. The survivors aren't happy about their plight. They've been reduced to wearing furs and carrying bows and arrows. My friend Crip traded them a pulse rifle for a fur. That thing is ridiculous. It stunk up the whole the ship. Jaq threatened to send it out the airlock." Max chuckled at the memory.

The general and the boss looked at each other. "You don't strike me as baby eaters."

Deena laughed. "You've been lied to your entire lives. This is who the Borwyn are. They don't want to get into your lives. The Malibor leaders have accused the Borwyn of doing everything that they do themselves. The Borwyn aren't your enemy."

"That's a hard pill to swallow," the general replied. "But you're not what I expected. Is that why you're a good fighter?"

Deena nodded toward Max. "He and Crip taught me how to fight and fight well."

"You two are married?" Lanni asked, coming out of her shell for a moment.

"Newlyweds," Deena replied. "We got married on the mess deck of the Borwyn flagship with as much of the crew as would fit sharing the moment with us, although they were there for Max. They didn't know who I was. We were at zero-gee, so more people stuffed themselves into the space."

"I can't imagine what that would be like," Lanni said softly while staring at the floor. "People who don't know you accepting you."

"But you do know what that's like. Moran asked me to watch over you, and I have."

"The Borwyn are evil!" Lanni blurted and threw her hands up. "I don't know what to believe."

"If we can get out of the city, we can take you to him," Max offered. "You have a baby, don't you?"

She nodded. "I need to get home to her."

Deena pressed her face against the front window to look

outside. A group of four soldiers marched down the center of the street. Deena opened the door. "We have a woman in here who needs to get home to her baby," Deena called.

"Get back in the building unless you want to get yourself shot!" one of the soldiers snapped.

Deena backed inside, closing and locking the door. "Not now," Deena told her. "If anyone goes outside, they're going to have a real bad day."

The general moved behind the bar and poured himself a stiff drink. "Before you talk about how early it is, I don't care." He drank it in one gulp, then poured another. "What's for lunch, Boss man?"

The boss shook his head. "Is this it? My restaurant is ground zero for the uprising? I'm not good with that."

The general snorted. "Makes no difference if you're good with it or not. This could be the safest place to be or the most dangerous. I, for one, was thinking about how I could escape, but I think I'll settle for keeping my head down. If the Malibor fleet is destroyed, then we have no options. The Malibor takeover of Septimus was based on having the strongest fleet. And yes, I know that we wrested Septimus from the Borwyn, although the history books teach it differently. Winners write the history, don't they?"

The general sipped from the second drink.

The boss joined him by pulling beer into a pitcher. He took a drink straight from it, claiming it as his glass.

"Are you okay?" Max asked Lanni.

"I'm not," she replied honestly. "In the course of an hour, my entire world has been turned upside-down, and here I sit with the man who killed members of my husband's squad."

Max frowned. "I haven't lied to you, and that has to be worth something. The Borwyn didn't start this war, but we are going to end it. If *Chrysalis* has done what it planned, then the end is going to come sooner rather than later."

"Yes, Madame President's husband." The general toasted Max and Deena by raising his glass and taking another drink.

"A politician through and through," the boss said with a snort. "I'm not taking the Borwyn's side, you traitors!"

"Then take my side," Deena said.

"You're making this too hard," he grumbled. "I'm not a traitor."

"Traitor to whom?" Max said. "If it's the Malibor people, then the leadership, the same ones who ordered you to fight other Malibor five times in the past fifty years? Is that who you're loyal to? You've fought only civil wars. Maybe the traitors are the ones who are in charge. We don't want any fighting at all. Killing your enemies isn't all it's cracked up to be, and I'm tired of it."

"How many people have you killed?" Lanni asked.

"Too many. I don't have a number because keeping track would be like looking into a black hole and wondering if there was a bottom. It's the part of life we can't dwell on. We fight battles and move on. It sucks, but my wife is incredible. I'd like to spend time with her hiking and looking at nature. Dining on the incredible food she says is served here. Is that too much to ask? Is it too much to ask that the Malibor have the same opportunity?"

Lanni ducked her head and stared at the floor again.

"What do we do now?" Max asked. "I'm not going to

shoot any of you." He slung his rifle over his back. "I'm hungry and am going to get something to eat."

He strolled into the kitchen. Deena walked in after him, leaving the three Malibor behind.

Lanni took one step toward the door, but another patrol was coming, so she thought better of it. "I could use some ranji juice." She headed for the kitchen.

The general and the boss looked at each other.

"If I had known it was going to be like this, I would have demanded the Borwyn invade and take over decades ago. I'm not a traitor, but I want more for my people. I think we've been holding them back. That revelation is sitting in my gut like a ten-kilo boulder. I was in a position to make a difference and didn't."

"Were you really? If you had made waves, they would have launched you out an airlock," the boss said. "Come on. I have to keep them from messing up my kitchen. Deena doesn't know the first thing about cooking, and I don't think space-boy does either."

They joined the others, and the boss started howling for everyone to stop touching his equipment. He belted out orders for a steak and egg meal with a side of cinnamon rolls. He let everyone know in no uncertain terms how incompetent they were.

Halfway through preparing their meals, gunfire sounded nearby. An explosion followed, and the lights went out.

"That wasn't us," Max said. "The Borwyn aren't in the city, and we're definitely not blowing up power plants." He was almost certain the Borwyn hadn't entered the city.

"Keep your heads down," the general advised. He

crawled out of the kitchen and to the front window. He cried out in anguish before crawling back.

"The war has started, but it's the one we know best. The soldiers are shooting their fellow Malibor."

A trail of smoke rose from the distant city. Crip stared at it. He thought he'd seen the dart of a gunship racing back and forth, but they were too far away to get a good look. The western Borwyn had the binoculars, not the combat team.

"What do you think?" he asked.

Larson was the closest. "I think we're attacking the city with the gunship, or Max is a one-man army. I prefer the former explanation."

"I do, too. The battle is joined," Crip said. "We're hanging out here blowing in the wind. We don't have the radio. We don't have any information. Dammit, Max!"

"Incoming," Danzig interrupted. "Commander Owain is here with his people."

Crip stood. "Make sure we don't get overrun by the Malibor army," he told Larson, using the running joke they'd had since setting up along the edge of the forest. In three days, they'd seen four total workers in the farthest fields and no soldiers.

Glen approached, looking ragged from a hard hike.

"Max has gone to the city," Crip reported as the two shook hands.

"I expected. We heard from *Chrysalis*. They attacked the

station and shipyard less than an hour ago. We were held up when we misplaced our prisoners."

"You brought the Malibor?"

"I thought it was a good idea, but the second we took our eyes off them, they bolted. We caught them, dragged them back to camp, and dug a hole in the ground to throw them inside. That was the deal if they tried to escape. It was the stupidest thing I've ever seen, but there's no accounting for Malibor intelligence. In any case, we're here."

"Did *Chrysalis* request anything? Give direction on how we can help?"

"Take out the three gunships, the comm relay, and the headquarters. It looks like Tram and Kelvis have done that. Begs the question: now what?"

Crip shook his head. "I honestly don't know, but I expect the people in the city are a little spun up."

"Just a little." The two looked at the tallest buildings that stood out over the horizon. The city was distant, even though it felt closer. With the smoke rising over the spaceport, it reinforced the fact that the war had come home.

The Borwyn were attacking Septimus.

"We brought your radio," Eleanor said as she approached.

Crip nodded in appreciation. "Larson, get it set up. I have to talk with *Chrysalis*."

To be continued in the final book of the series, Starship Lost Book #6 – Engagement. I apologize profusely for the quadruple cliffhanger at the end

of this book. I'm sure I'll get hammered in the reviews, but I think we have about 70,000 words of story left and it'll flow directly from this through to the end. There wasn't going to be a reasonable place to stop since all of Book #5 was a setup for the final engagements in Book #6. Bear with me. Book #6 is coming in a month, if not published already.

Please leave a review on this book, because all those stars look great and help others decide if they'll enjoy this book as much as you have. I appreciate the feedback and support. Reviews buoy my spirits and stoke the fires of creativity.

Don't stop now! Keep turning the pages as I talk about my thoughts on this book and the overall project called *Starship Lost*.

You can always join my newsletter at https://craigmartelle.com or follow me on Amazon https://www.amazon.com/Craig-Martelle/e/B01AQVF3ZY/ so you get notified when the next book comes out.

AUTHOR NOTES - CRAIG MARTELLE

Written Christmas Day, 2023

Here we are again, another book, another crisis resolved, yet more remain. The Borwyn have returned, but we have a four-way cliffhanger.

1. *Chrysalis* is attempting to seize the space station.
2. Max & Deena are trapped in the restaurant with three Malibor.
3. Tram, Kelvis, Sophia, and Evelyn were on a crashing gunship.
4. Crip and Glen and their soldiers don't know what they have to do.

By the way, things get worse in the next volume. You'll have to dive in to see what happens.

The engineering and technical aspects within these books remain sound. This is hard science fiction, space opera, and space adventure wrapped into one neat series. I planned it that way from the outset. I wanted the math to work. I wanted the relationships to be profound. I wanted the adventure to be gripping. And the military aspects? Those are my go-to. Nothing like a good space battle or land battle to keep the action genes thrumming.

For the chapter quotes, I usually use something from Lao Tzu or Buddha or something I made up. The Brainy Quote website (https://www.brainyquote.com/) has been immensely helpful in finding the right fodder to put up there, but since it's supposed to be in the distant future, they are not attributed within the text itself.

You'll see that I also borrowed the names G'Kar and Londo as a hat-tip to Babylon 5, a great sci-fi series. Look deeper at some of the dialogue and interactions and you'll find what is best about great SF.

During the winter, we hit the solstice where we have less than four hours of daylight, and it is grim daylight. The sun rises in the south, stays on the southern horizon, and then sets in the south. In the summer, the sun stays in the northern sky. It's odd and difficult for those not used to it to accept it as the norm. Everything depends on the time of year for little things like daylight. We are considered high desert here, and that means we don't necessarily get a lot of snow. Temperatures can get down to -50F in the winter, and we get a handful of days in the 80s during the summer. Nobody has air conditioning up here, but everyone has multiple sources of heat. I have four: electric, fuel oil, kerosene, and pellets. The fuel oil boiler does the heavy lifting. The pellet stove saves some money when we run it.

We traveled back to Pittsburgh, where my wife is from, to spend Christmas. I finished writing this book there. The last thirty thousand words were generated on the airplane as well as at my mother-in-law's dining room table. I am happy with how the words flowed. I hope you feel the story blossomed with more about the main characters.

I return to Alaska tomorrow, the day after Christmas (2023). Temperatures rose to unseasonably warm while we were gone but have taken a big nosedive, so it'll be chilly again. No surprise. It's Alaska at the end of December. It'll stay cold until March. The good news is that our ground maintenance crew have kept our trails open in the woods. That is way cool. We can continue to do what we do away from any cars or other dogs. We run across fox and moose in there, but no other dogs and no people.

We've been rewarded with some great auroras this year. I have a new phone—the iPhone 15—and that captures decent pictures of the night sky. You should follow me on Facebook where I share them.

How many planets can populate a solar system?

https://www.iflscience.com/this-is-the-maximum-number-of-planets-you-can-have-in-a-solar-system-like-ours-41537

This nifty article discusses those parameters and limitations. The part I didn't articulate properly is the counter-rotational aspects. I'll clarify that in the final book and who/how this system was created.

As a reminder, https://www.omnicalculator.com/physics/acceleration —need to keep that acceleration calculator close at hand.

Regarding structural materials, I quoted *Structural Materials for Fusion Reactors* by M. Victoria, N. Baluc and P. Spätig from the EPFL-CRPP Fusion Technology Materials, CH-5232 Villigen PSI, Switzerland.

That's it, a bunch of rambling thoughts and a finished book, but far from a finished story. More, coming very soon.

Peace, fellow humans.

If you liked this story, you might like some of my other books. You can join my mailing list by dropping by my website at craigmartelle.com, or if you have any comments, shoot me a note at craig@craigmartelle.com. I am always happy to hear from people who've read my work. I try to answer every email I receive.

If you liked the story, please write a short review for me on Amazon. I greatly appreciate any kind words; even one or two sentences go a long way. The number of reviews an ebook receives greatly improves how well it does on Amazon.

Amazon—www.amazon.com/author/craigmartelle

Facebook—www.facebook.com/authorcraigmartelle

BookBub—https://www.bookbub.com/authors/craig-martelle

My web page—https://craigmartelle.com

Thank you for joining me on this incredible journey.

THANK YOU FOR READING FALLACY

We hope you enjoyed it as much as we enjoyed bringing it to you. We just wanted to take a moment to encourage you to review the book. Follow this link: **Fallacy** to be directed to the book's Amazon product page to leave your review.

Every review helps further the author's reach and, ultimately, helps them continue writing fantastic books for us all to enjoy.

Also in series:
Starship Lost
The Return
Primacy
Confrontation
Fallacy
Engagement

Check out the entire series here! (Tap or scan)

Want to discuss our books with other readers and even the authors? Join our Discord server today and be a part of the Aethon community.

Facebook | Instagram | Twitter | Website

You can also join our non-spam mailing list by visiting www.subscribepage.com/AethonReadersGroup and never miss out on future releases. You'll also receive three full books completely Free as our thanks to you.

Looking for more great books?

ROGUE STARS
PURGATORY
BOOK ONE OF THE ROGUE STARS SERIES
JAIME CASTLE

Abandon ship, or go down in a blaze of glory. Commander Predaxes, former Marine in the Lazaab military, has been recommissioned to Prison Station 12, known colloquially as Purgatory. On the outskirts of the Centridium, PS12 relies solely on a wormhole for contact with the government -- not to mention supplies. His newest inmate, Samea Malik, is more than a bit of trouble. Son to the Minister of Justice, Malik is the target of both assassination and recovery. When the station is attacked and chaos rains down upon them all, those onboard must abandon their posts for the closest habitable planet, Faebos. With what little planning they could do, Predaxes and crew discover an old, defunct mining colony and quickly discover why the project was deserted. Faebos is home to violent and nasty creatures, but also great beauty. Survival will mean cooperation between PS12's captives and captors. But will it be enough? Faced with hardship no one expected, needing to tap into old skills and new, Predaxes and Malik find themselves in their own form of Purgatory.

Rogue Stars **is a brand new Military Space Opera series by #1 Audible and Washington Post bestseller Jaime Castle, creator of the** *Black Badge* **series. Perfect for fans of David Weber, Larry Correia, JN Chaney, and Rick Partlow.**

Get Purgatory Now!

FALLACY 359

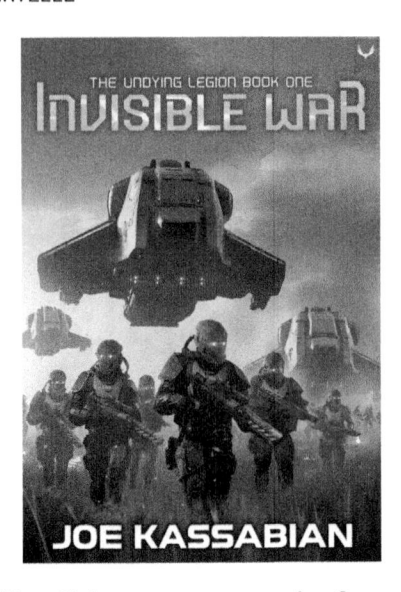

What if there was a war raging for one million years, but it was kept secret? Sargis is an upper middle class man living in Prime City, basking in the glow of the Techno King's so-called "Millenia of Peace." As far as he, or anyone else knows, humanity has no army, no weapons, and no wars. The people of Earth have been expanding into the stars for as long as anyone remembers, free of conflict while the Techno King and his Royal Cabal enrich themselves on the backs of their labor. All was as it always has been. Then, Sargis dies. Unbeknownst to him, an app he used every single day of his life hijacks his consciousness and uploads it into a synthetic engine of war known as a *sleeve*. Along with countless others, he has been conscripted into the Undying Legion, charged with fighting a secret, unending war in the name of humanity. **Experience the start of the next explosive Military Sci-Fi series from Joe Kassabian, author of the** *Liberty of Death* **Series. This boots-on-the-ground twist on being a soldier is perfect for fans of** *Rick Partlow, Galaxy's Edge: Legionnaire,* **and** *Starship Troopers.*

Get Invisible War Now!

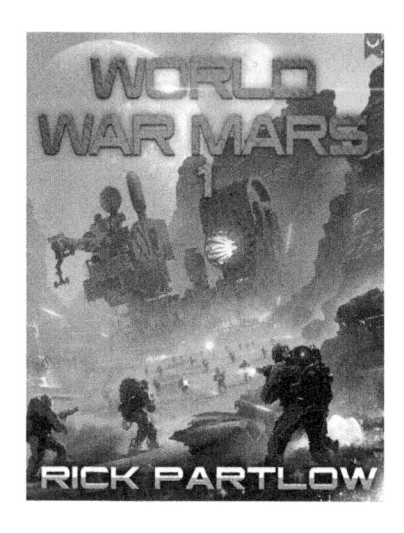

Alien tech discovered. The race to claim it could spark a new kind of War. When a derelict alien starship appears in the solar system and crash-lands on Mars, it ignites a desperate race to be the first to reach the Red Planet to claim the mysterious technological treasures of the Visitor. Space Force General Tom Bradstreet, ace Air Force fighter pilot and the only active-duty officer with actual space combat experience, is given control of the *Morrigan*, the first manned mission to Mars—and the first space warship. He and his elite team know their mission. In fact, it should be simple. The US is the only nation with a spaceship capable of making it to Mars. Or so they think... Maverick Russian General Mikhail Antonov has been handed the insane, desperate gamble of building an Orion-style spaceship powered by nuclear warheads. Launching it from the heart of Russia could be the spark that touches off a nuclear war but it's the only way the Russians and Chinese can hope to reach Mars before the Americans. The scene is set for a devastating world war, and the first shots may be fired on another world... **Don't miss the next action-packed, gritty military sci-fi series from Rick Partlow, the bestselling author of the *Drop Trooper* Series and *Taken to the Stars*.**

Get World War Mars Now!

For all of our science fiction titles, check out
www.aethonbooks.com/science-fiction

OTHER SERIES BY CRAIG MARTELLE

 # - available in audio, too

Battleship Leviathan (#)– a military sci-fi spectacle published by Aethon Books

Terry Henry Walton Chronicles (#) (co-written with Michael Anderle)—a post-apocalyptic paranormal adventure

Gateway to the Universe (#) (co-written with Justin Sloan & Michael Anderle)—this book transitions the characters from the Terry Henry Walton Chronicles to The Bad Company

The Bad Company (#) (co-written with Michael Anderle)—a military science fiction space opera

OTHER SERIES BY CRAIG MARTELLE

Judge, Jury, & Executioner (#)—a space opera adventure legal thriller

Shadow Vanguard—a Tom Dublin space adventure series

Superdreadnought (#)—an AI military space opera

Metal Legion (#)—a military space opera

The Free Trader (#)—a young adult science fiction action-adventure

Cygnus Space Opera (#)—a young adult space opera (set in the Free Trader universe)

Darklanding (#) (co-written with Scott Moon)—a space western

Mystically Engineered (co-written with Valerie Emerson)—mystics, dragons, & spaceships

Metamorphosis Alpha—stories from the world's first science fiction RPG
The Expanding Universe—science fiction anthologies

Krimson Empire (co-written with Julia Huni)—a galactic race for justice

Zenophobia (#) (co-written with Brad Torgersen)—a space archaeological adventure

Glory (co-written with Ira Heinichen)—hard-hitting military sci-fi

Black Heart of the Dragon God (co-written with Jean Rabe)—a sword & sorcery novel

End Times Alaska (#)—a post-apocalyptic survivalist adventure published by Permuted Press

Nightwalker (a Frank Roderus series)—A post-apocalyptic western adventure

End Days (#) (co-written with E.E. Isherwood)—a post-apocalyptic adventure

Successful Indie Author (#)—a non-fiction series to help self-published authors

Monster Case Files (co-written with Kathryn Hearst)—A Warner twins mystery adventure

Rick Banik (#)—Spy & terrorism action-adventure

Ian Bragg Thrillers (#)—a hitman with a conscience

Not Enough (co-written with Eden Wolfe)—A coming-of-age contemporary fantasy

<u>Published exclusively by Craig Martelle, Inc</u>
The Dragon's Call by Angelique Anderson & Craig A. Price, Jr.—an epic fantasy quest

A Couples Travels—a non-fiction travel series

Love-Haight Case Files by Jean Rabe & Donald J. Bingle—the dead/undead have rights, too, a supernatural legal thriller

Mischief Maker by Bruce Nesmith—the creator of Elder Scrolls V: Skyrim brings you Loki in the modern day, staying true to Norse Mythology (not a superhero version)

Mark of the Assassins by Landri Johnson—a coming-of-age fantasy.
For a complete list of Craig's books, stop by his website—
https://craigmartelle.com

Printed in Great Britain
by Amazon